THE NARROW DOOR AT

COLDITZ

THE NARROW DOOR AT COLDITZ

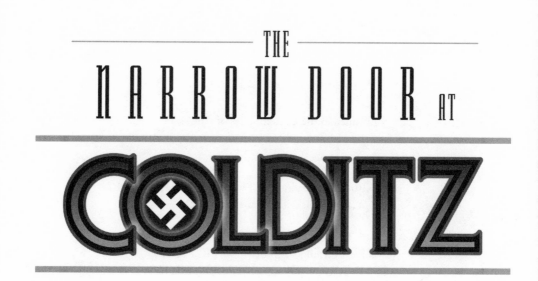

ROBERT L. WISE

B&H
BROADMAN & HOLMAN PUBLISHERS

NASHVILLE, TENNESSEE

0-8054-3072-5

Published by Broadman & Holman Publishers,
Nashville, Tennessee

Dewey Decimal Classification: F
Subject Heading: ESCAPES—FICTION
WORLD WAR, 1939–45—CAUSES—FICTION
HOLOCAUST, 1933–45—FICTION

1 2 3 4 5 6 7 8 9 10 08 07 06 05 04

TO THE ALLIED SOLDIERS OF WORLD WAR II
who considered political imprisonment an affront
to their human dignity.
No confinement could kill the hunger for
freedom.

CONTENTS

PREFACE

T his story of Colditz Castle and the attempted escape of World War II prisoners is fiction, but . . .

Behind the scenes of this story are real people and situations that existed in the mid-1940s. Located south of Leipzig, Germany, and north of Dresden, Colditz Castle rises into the sky as a remnant of the medieval world where knights in shining armor sallied forth to fight with sword and lance. Imposing and foreboding, Colditz Castle became the *Wehrmacht's* chosen prison for the "bad boys" who had escaped from other concentration camps as the war progressed. Soldiers of many nationalities, from armies fighting against Hitler's Third Reich, were imprisoned in the castle. In 1965, a group of French former prisoners at Colditz returned to the castle and found many of their hidden items, which were to assist them in an escape, still waiting to be used by inmates who had vanished decades earlier. Quietly concealed in the secret crevices and crannies of the castle walls lay homemade radios, portions of German uniforms, packets of dye, pencils, papers—all resting in place while the years slipped past.

No record reveals how many escape attempts were made between 1940 and 1945, and no one will ever know all the plans developed behind the massive walls of stone, but this story arises from the facts of what unfolded in 1942 and 1943. Elements are added from other attempted escapes at Colditz and a few characters dropped in that never appeared on any roster of prisoners. Oozing up from under the cobblestone streets and out from between the cracks in the massive timbers is this story of a search for freedom, a tale of the relentless search to escape oppression.

The story is fiction, but the account is in its own way uniquely true.

PART ONE
The Castle

CHAPTER

ONE

May 25, 1940

The spring sky shone a brilliant blue, the color of the cool waters of the English Channel lapping upon the sandy beaches just beyond Colais, Belgium, but the scene was far from peaceful. Nazi Ju-87 Stuka dive-bombers swirled out of the clouds like deadly fire-spitting gnats. The fixed undercarriages of the "Shrieking Vultures" airplanes resembled the talons of hawks, swooping out of the sky to devour prey. Along with striking the beaches, the small airplanes kept strafing the country lanes leading out of the small French town of Calais toward Boulogne and up the opposite road north toward Belgium's Nieuport and Ostend, forcing the retreating British soldiers to fight back from behind the meandering stone fences lining both sides of the road.

Tony Irving hurried down a narrow trench behind a winding section of the wall with a couple of British soldiers trailing behind him. Tony was a tall, broad-shouldered youth with a thick back and strong arms. Although he was a twenty-year-old American, several months earlier Sergeant Irving had been secretly assigned to the Forty-eighth Division of the British Royal Army Service Corps for advisory purposes. As if a bona fide Englishman, Tony's assignment was to teach the British how to use the long, metal tube that was now a new innovative instrument of war so they could stop the German's twenty-ton Panzer IV tanks. The maneuverable yet formidable medium tanks had been the cutting edge of the German sword, slicing with terrifying speed through the Low Countries. The 75 mm guns and agile maneuverability of the Panzers easily stopped the British Matilda tanks, but the strange black gun Tony called a "bazooka" could instantly wreck the arduous Panzers.

Tony listened to bombs exploding up and down the road. If he'd had a choice, he certainly would rather have been listening to Benny Goodman or, better yet, Bob Wills and His Texas Playboys, but the bombs didn't intimidate him. He felt almost invincible. After all, not only was he an American, but Tony was certain God was on his side. He, the Brits, and God would stop those Krauts no matter what happened.

"Come on, Lord," Tony prayed under his breath. "Help me put an end to these advancing bums. We can do it. Let's hit 'em hard! Amen."

Balancing the narrow missile launcher on his shoulder, Tony slowly raised out of the trench. "Hang on, boys. We're about to have one of those tasty little Panzers for supper." Irving leveled the bazooka quickly and took a deep breath. For a moment the scent of smoke and gunpowder filled his nose and irritated his eyes.

"Watch out!" the British Expeditionary Forces soldier behind Tony screamed. "The Germans are breaking through again!" With his overcoat flapping in the spring breeze, the soldier pointed toward a Panzer tank suddenly turning into the road.

Dropping to one knee, Tony aimed the bazooka at the Panzer only several hundred feet in front of him. He could see the 7.92 mm machine guns sticking out of the hull. "Steady," Irving mumbled to himself. "Easy does it, boys."

Tony squeezed the trigger. A moment later a blast of fire roared across the road and a ball of crimson flames rolled up into the blue sky. Irving instantly dropped into the trench and ducked his head. Pieces of metal whizzed by, and the rumbling clank of the approaching tank instantly stopped. Irving knew the iron beast was dead.

"Great shot, mate!" the Brit screamed in his ear. "But we've got to get out of here! 'Em bloody Panzers ain't stoppin' for nothin'. Run!" The Royal soldier trotted back in the opposite direction.

Irving picked up the bazooka and retreated behind the Brit, hustling down the fence line. Thirty feet ahead, the remainder of the platoon huddled together against the rock wall. Not many of the original squad had survived the *blitzkrieg* attack that was sweeping across the Belgium countryside like a summer storm.

A second Stuka dive-bomber strafed the lane, sending the British into the ditches. Irving's helmet tumbled into the dirt, and the American grabbed his head. His closely cropped crew cut felt like a boar-bristled hairbrush. His narrow spot in the ditch cramped him, leaving his back exposed. When the Stuka returned, Tony knew he was vulnerable.

"We can't stay here," the lieutenant insisted. He tightened the leather strap on his metal helmet. "Stoppin' one of 'em tanks won't slow down these monsters rolling all over us. More's a-comin'!"

"He's right," the sergeant agreed. "The Nazis are eating at us like a swarm of locusts."

Abruptly, the frightening rumble of another Stuka dive-bomber filled the air, sending the British platoon into the dirt again and pushing them even closer to the stone wall. The terrifying roar deafened. Suddenly a bomb exploded, sending dirt and rocks showering over the soldiers. The Stuka zoomed back into the sky out of sight, and for a few moments relative quiet filled the country lane. The biting smell of burning sulphur kept stinging Tony's nose, and smoke made his eyes water.

"Can't hardly hear anything," Tony mumbled.

"They'll be back," the sergeant insisted. "Don't worry. They intend to annihilate us until the last man is dead."

"Exactly where are we?" Tony asked, shaking his head to unstop his ears.

"We're probably a dozen miles or so from some town called Dunkirk, and directly behind us is the ocean," the lieutenant explained. "The Germans swept up from the south, crossed the Somme River, and have overrun Boulogne. They are squeezing us from the north as well. The Nazis got us in their grips like the teeth of a shark tearing off a hunk of meat."

"We need to get out of here!" the sergeant begged desperately.

Tony Irving cussed passionately. "Listen! I didn't sail over here from America to be overrun by these stinking Krauts. I'm not retreating anywhere until I knock out another one of those tanks! Come on, boys. We can do it!"

"Listen to me, mate!" the lieutenant's shaking voice gave away his fear. "We're in an impossible position. The platoon has learned what you can do with that long-fanged gadget, but now we must retreat quickly or they've got us. 'Em Germans are coming on with armor and motorized infantry in addition to the Panzers." The lieutenant wiped his brow. "We simply can't stop 'em."

"Maybe not," Irving said, picking up his bazooka. "But I'm from Texas, and I didn't land in Europe to be run into the English Channel by those green-shirted clones of Hitler. These lunatics don't frighten me." He wiped his brow and took off his metal helmet. "I've bulldogged bulls out behind the barn worse than chasing these pussycats. I'm going to get one more tank and *then* we'll leave."

The lieutenant shook his head. "Make it fast. I don't like this delay. We're in danger."

"We're *always* in danger!" Tony inched up the side of the wall. "Watch me, boys. I'll show you exactly how to use this little tunnel of fire. When the next one comes down the road . . ." He raised his head and shoulders above the stone fence and stopped, frozen in place.

"What's happening?" the sergeant called from beneath Irving.

Tony didn't move.

"Come on. What are you waiting for?" the lieutenant asked. "Shoot!"

Tony dropped the bazooka and raised his hands. In front of him inching their way out of the trees and across the road were at least twenty German soldiers. The Nazis' knee-length boots, green helmets hanging down over their ears, and bayoneted rifles made the men of the *Wehrmacht* appear ominous, horrifying. Their guns were aimed straight at Tony. "Don't move," he said quietly. "The Nazis have us trapped."

The lieutenant slowly peered over the wall. "Good Lord, the Huns are everywhere! We don't have a chance to run." He stood up slowly and extended his hands upward. "Stand up very carefully men, and leave your guns on the ground. The Krauts have got us."

One by one the remnant of the depleted platoon stood up with their hands over their heads. Artillery fell to the grass with dull thuds. The German soldiers kept walking forward cautiously, their bayoneted Gewehr 98 rifles pointing at the Allied soldiers.

"I messed up," Tony said quietly. "You were right. We should have run."

"The Huns would have caught us anyway," the lieutenant said. "They might have shot us fleeing down the road. We did our best."

Tony shook his head. "Our best wasn't good enough." Tony cursed again. "They got us."

"*Sich beruhigen!*" a German soldier shouted over the stone fence. "*Sei still!*"

Irving watched the man's face. As the German came closer, he looked almost like a boy, like Tony himself. The soldier appeared more nervous than murderous. He was only a kid doing his job. Tony took a deep breath. That's about all any of them were doing on that godforsaken road, but he had intended to do far more than simply fulfill his job. He had come to stop the advance of the Nazis across Europe . . . but now the Germans *had captured him.*

CHAPTER

TWO

September 20, 1942

The narrow-gauge German train puffed along the Mulde River, winding its way through the rich farmlands of central Saxony toward Colditz Castle. Chugging past the little villages of Wechselberg and Rochlitz, the train and its small load of POWs steamed toward Colditz, the site of concentration camp Oflag 4C.

"You are completely replacing Colonel Schmidt?" Major Reinhold Eggers asked. Eggers sounded too much like a gentle soul to be second in command of a concentration camp. "Taking control of the camp when we arrive?" He tried to sound more forceful.

"*Ya!*" Colonel Edgar Glaesche answered with the stern abruptness that the military had drummed into the naturally austere man. Edgar Glaesche maintained a harsh, distant look, sitting stiffly erect in his highly polished black military boots and well-pressed green uniform. "Schmidt is gone. Retired. He turned seventy this summer, and the high command has now sent him home to die." Glaesche's eyes narrowed. "He may have started Oflag 4C, but I will finish the task." He pointed his small leather riding crop at Eggers. "Count on it!"

Eggers nodded politely. "I assume we will continue to observe the rules of the Geneva convention?" he asked cautiously.

Glaesche twisted his officer's cap, the high flat front adorned by an eagle. "Technically," he said slowly, "we are bound to those disruptive rules Germany agreed to in 1929, but the Gestapo has grown tired of these constant escape attempts in all our concentration camps. The fools we are to oversee are slowly cutting their own throats."

"Our officers have no successful serious resistance," Eggers added quickly. "No violence. Only attempts to elude us." He coughed nervously. "Of course, all the prisoners pledged to attempt escape when they joined their armies."

"I mean to put a stop to it!" Glaesche snapped. "I will order any inmate escaping beyond the boundaries of the concentration camp to be shot on sight. I mean to drill fear into their collective hard heads."

Reinhold Eggers nodded. "I understand."

"And understand I can cut their rations. A few weeks of no food will snap these cabbage heads into line." Glaesche pounded the cushion with the riding crop he always carried with him. "Our special prison camp is not a vacation for these riffraff escapees the *Wehrmacht* sends us. I can be quite difficult, Eggers."

"I understand," the major repeated and looked out the train window. Silence fell between the two men as it had been for most of the trip.

The unusually cool fall weather signaled an approaching cold winter for the area around Colditz Castle. Leaves fell early from the trees, and the nights stayed crisp across the east German countryside. Although most German citizens knew little of the details of the actual battles between the Axis and the Allied powers, the aura stretching over the country remained one of victory and triumph. The *Wehrmacht*, the army of Hitler's Third Reich, was reported to strike with invincibility, continuing to hurl the Reich's foes back. The times appeared prosperous enough, but dealing with captured prisoners of war remained an infected boil on the German neck.

The train slowed, pulling into the small village of Colditz nestled along the Mulde River. Poplar trees soared into the sky, and the shallow river babbled over smooth rocks along the winding creek bed. The quiet German village lined the river with its quaint little houses of odd shapes and various sizes. In the center of the town square, a large church with an onion-shaped bronze cupola stood out over the rolling landscape. Stores and businesses crowded around the downtown central plaza, but even the large stone church cowered beneath the massive castle, silhouetted against the dark sky. Five tall stories of windows with tall turrets were surrounded by waving flags that rose from the slate roofs of the fortress. The huge castle leered down at the village, reminding the people of its violent and menacing past.

"Rather frightening, isn't it?" Major Reinhold Eggers observed.

Glaesche shielded his eyes with his hand and looked up, following the sweeping, massive lines of the walls protecting the narrow road that wound up to the inner courtyard of the castle. "Ought to be!" he snapped. "Few fortresses have a history as bloody as Colditz Castle," he said as the train slowed to a halt.

"This medieval relic has been used for everything from a castle to a lunatic asylum," Eggers said. "Its history of bloodshed and oppression tends to drive an icicle through one's heart."

"Indeed!" Glaesche beat his leather riding crop against the palm of his hand. "Take those prisoners out of this train, and we will get them on their way to their new home."

Eggers pointed beyond the station house. "A car is waiting for you. Our soldiers will march the men up the hill after us."

"What sort of prisoners came with us today?" Colonel Glaesche asked.

"I believe we have a contingent from the Queen's Royal Regiment. These three men escaped from the Rotenburg Camp in West Germany and were recaptured near Saarbrücken."

Colonel Glaesche continued thumping his palm with the riding crop. "I want to see them checked into our camp," he mused. "Yes, I want to begin my tour of duty with a clear sense of how everything happens here. Have my car follow our prisoners. I will watch."

Major Eggers nodded and immediately hurried through the station house to make the arrangements.

"*Aus!*" the German guard shouted at Tony Irving and the two men sitting beside him in the back of the train. The small man motioned with his Gewehr 98 rifle toward the train's exit door. "*Aus!*" he barked again. "Colditz."

Tony stood up slowly. His dirty clothes had been on his back for two weeks, and the smell wasn't pleasant. "Looks like the party is about to start—we're getting the engraved invitation right now," he said to the other men. "I do believe we have found our home away from home." He rubbed his closely clipped brown hair and grinned impishly. "Ready to boogie?"

"Indeed," British Lieutenant Bill Fowler answered. "Time for the dance." Wearing round horn-rimmed glasses, Fowler had thick, dark eyebrows and black hair. His handsome face didn't obscure an intense, intelligent stare. "I'm ready for the show."

"*Nun!*" The guard's voice raised a notch. "Now."

"Our little man appears to be ready," Royal Air Force Captain "Lulu" Lawton said, nodding toward the German. Tall and distinguished, Lawton carried himself with an aristocratic bearing. He wore a thin mustache with his hair combed straight back. "Can't keep the big boss waiting."

The guard looked under twenty, and his job of marching three prisoner-of-war escapees out of the train obviously seemed to make him nervous. He eyed his charges with suspicion and a menacing scowl that didn't quite mask his fear. "*Aus*," he repeated for the third time and kept nodding his head toward the train station. A second guard stood at the back of the coach.

"We're deep inside Germany," Tony said, picking up his cap. "Won't be easy getting clear back across this entire country. Probably shouldn't start upsetting these local boys yet."

"Right," Lawton said with his thick British accent. "I don't think we will be taking any casual jaunts out of this prison camp."

"*Sei still!*" the German demanded.

Irving shrugged as he trudged toward the door. "I think he wants us to quit talking. Big deal."

The three prisoners walked down the train's steps onto the platform leading into the station house and formed a single line, standing at ease. Their guard walked twenty feet away as if trying to get upwind, but he kept his rifle aimed at them. Three other German soldiers stood around the platform with weapons trained on the prisoners.

"Wow!" Tony gazed up at the castle towering over the village. "Look at that fortress. Frightening-looking."

"That's your new home away from home you were speaking of a moment ago," Fowler said wryly.

The German guard kept away from the prisoners, but he kept his finger on the trigger.

"Looks like Adolf wants to guard us from a distance," Lawton said. "The guy's a boy."

"Such boys can kill you," Tony said dryly.

"Indeed," Fowler answered. He turned and looked at Tony critically. "I say, old man, but you're not much older than that German kid."

"Yeah," Tony grinned. "But I'm from Texas and meaner than a junkyard bulldog. Makes a difference, you know."

"How come you're in one of our uniforms anyway?" Lawton asked quietly. "You're a Yank."

"It's a long story, but the Nazis thinking I'm British might help me escape this Colditz coffin they're nailing us in."

"And you're only a sergeant?" Lawton added. "A young one. Certainly not an officer like us."

"What the Krauts don't know *will* hurt them," Tony said quietly out of the corner of his mouth. "They think I'm an officer, and that's all that counts today or tomorrow."

"*Sei still!*" the young guard shouted abruptly.

A *Wehrmacht* colonel stepped out of a train car in front of them, carrying a riding crop under his arm. His spit-polished black leather military boots and a smartly pressed uniform created a dignified appearance, but the colonel had an arrogant look on his face, staring at the escapees with disdain and disgust in his eyes. The officer actually looked like a caricature of a bad Nazi from the funny papers.

Tony caught the man's eye for a moment. In their exchange he read the German's cold indifference and made an instant decision. He wouldn't accept the nonsense this jerk was putting out. The German might have the upper hand at this moment, but Tony Irving wasn't buying the haughtiness. He grinned back indifferently.

The colonel immediately stiffened but kept walking. Irving could hear the swish of the riding crop behind him and knew the man had every intention of intimidating them. The clicking of the heels of his leather boots echoed down the platform. Obviously, the officer didn't like his captives.

Tony and his two comrades stared straight ahead, attempting to exude their own form of arrogance to counter the German's. The contest proved to be a standoff.

Another officer walked quickly out of the station house, and the major spoke to the colonel. The senior officer nodded and motioned for the guard to bring Irving and the other two men with him.

"*Marsch!*" the guard demanded and motioned for the men to follow the colonel. The other sentries fell in behind them.

"For a few moments I was afraid we were only going to stare each other down," Lawton said under his breath. "Looks like the party's ready to start."

"Can't wait," Tony quipped.

Major Eggers walked quickly to the soldier in charge of the four German infantrymen surrounding the Englishmen. He relayed Colonel Glaesche's order, and the German soldiers started marching the Brits up the street. Villagers stopped and stared, watching the procession file past.

The sun was beginning to set, and evening was starting to settle over the village. Citizens paused from selling and buying groceries to gawk at the strange sight of their troops with rifles cocked and ready to fire, forcing the bedraggled prisoners up the road. Others stopped to watch the poorly kept foreigners marching while the black Mercedes leisurely lolled along behind the three men. Colonel Glaesche periodically waved his riding crop as if he were the honorary chairman of a holiday parade. Some people waved back; others only stared.

In the fading afternoon sunlight, the soldiers and their prisoners marched down the cobblestone road until they crossed the Mulde River over a narrow bridge and entered the town proper. From the village square the dark castle with its battlements appeared even more ominous than it had at the train station. The high, mud-colored towers rising up from behind the fortress walls had a brutal appearance, making the entire complex appear to be an institution for lunatics.

Without hesitation the soldiers forged on up the abrupt hill, and the Mercedes had to shift gears. The little parade marched round the bend of the road in front of the castle's first layer of protective walls until coming to the entry gatehouse with a bold, black-lettered sign over the top: "Oflag 4C." A German soldier immediately came out of the gatehouse with a clipboard in hand. Behind him a large clock towered over the castle entrance. Guards sat with machine guns aimed at the POWs. The soldier opened the narrow door cautiously.

The gatekeeper saluted. "You've only got three today?"

"Yeah, but they're a bad lot." The German soldier returned the salute. "Escaped from Rotenburg. Better watch 'em carefully."

The gatekeeper nodded and started walking among the men, taking their names and identifying each of them.

Glaesche watched the guard check in the new inmates for several minutes before turning to the major.

"How long have you been here?" the colonel asked Reinhold Eggers.

"From the first," Major Eggers replied. "I came on November 7, 1940, when the Reich first opened Camp Oflag 4C for prisoners from this war."

"You've watched these attempted escapes?"

"Yes." Eggers smiled politely. "So far, we've caught most of the prisoners who tried to escape. We are the toughest camp in Germany."

Colonel Glaesche nodded his head. "Are you tough enough for this job, Eggers?"

The major's mouth dropped slightly. "Most certainly."

Glaesche eyed him critically and then slowly turned his gaze toward the soldiers who were still giving their names. "We have some officers at headquarters who aren't sure about you. I will expect you to demonstrate your capacity to do whatever must be done."

Reinhold Eggers blinked several times and didn't seem to be sure of what he should say. He felt the colonel's piercing eyes turning back on him like cannons on a battleship. "As I said . . . *most certainly.*"

The colonel abruptly thumped the palm of his glove again. "We shall see."

The parade started moving again. The three Allied soldiers were marched forward from the bridge, which spanned a dry moat. Beneath the trestle a deteriorating coat of arms had been painted on the side of the moat, but Eggers could see that the Brits did not have time to sight-see.

Their procession tramped under the clock tower and into a large outer courtyard inside the castle walls. A gray army truck was parked in one corner of the odd-shaped area. The German soldiers continued marching their captives, leading them through a flat, open area and under another archway before turning up a cobblestoned alley. The men disappeared behind the castle's forbidding inner walls.

For a moment Major Eggers pointed around the expansive outer courtyard. "You will notice that all of the lower outside windows are barred," he began. "The castle is at the center of concentric circles of rock-and-stucco walls, which protect the inner area," he explained to the colonel. "Behind the center is a tight circle of ninety-foot-high buildings, standing on the original foundations, which go back to medieval times. The first builders chose this unusually isolated hunk of rock to build a most secure fortress."

"Humph!" Glaesche looked up at the roofline far above him. "A long way to fall. What can prisoners see from up there?" The colonel pointed upward with his riding crop.

"Clear out to the forest. The bridge. The railroad station. The town square." Eggers smiled. "Through the trees they can see the village."

"Let them look," Glaesche growled, "for that is all they will do."

Reinhold Eggers smiled.

"*You are smiling?*" Glaesche's voice was low and menacing. "Something amusing in what I said?"

"Ahem." The major couched and tried to sound harmless. "No. I only meant that it . . . will be . . . pleasant for us to have such ah . . . success in containing our prisoners."

The colonel shook his riding crop in Eggers's face. "Failure in this task will serve as the call for your immediate reassignment." He leaned closer. "Probably to the front in Russia."

Reinhold Eggers stiffened almost to the point of standing at attention. "I understand," he said in a quiet voice.

"Don't forget it!" Colonel Glaesche turned on his heels and marched back to his car. "Take me back to town," he demanded of the driver.

"Yes, sir!" the German soldier barked. The Mercedes immediately roared back down the same road they had taken up to the castle.

Eggers watched the car disappear. He stood stiffly until the sound of the car's engine vanished, and then he slumped. He hoped Colonel Glaesche wouldn't be inside the prison often. In fact, the despot probably would keep his distance from the castle, but he would still be a difficult man to please. Eggers took a deep breath and rubbed his face. He shuddered and looked thoughtfully toward the senior officers' quarters.

"I must succeed," he said to himself, "or I will surely die out there in that Soviet wasteland." He looked up at the imposing dwelling. "Far better here than in Russia."

CHAPTER

THREE

German guards marched the three new prisoners under the castle's stone archway and along the high wall, pushing them as fast as possible until they stood inside the enclosed area the Germans called the ramparts.

"Make a line!" the German soldier demanded in good English. "Line up. Immediately."

The three men stood shoulder to shoulder, looking straight ahead. Sergeant Tony Irving glanced out of the corner of his eyes to the right. The high-walled area looked like an oblong stone box with two sentries posted at each side and the end. One miscalculated move and they could all be dead men.

Got to be careful, Irving thought. *This fat guard looks unpredictable—has a mean look in his eye and he's no boy. It will take time to figure this place out.*

"Velcome to Germany's maximum prison camp," the heavy, round-faced sentry said. The man looked like a prototype of a Nazi in his metal-rimmed glasses. "You have come to an escape-proof camp because you have failed to take advantage of our accommodations elsevhere. Your insolence has now delivered you into our hands. Ve vill not fail this time."

The three soldiers kept looking straight ahead, but Irving glanced to his left and saw a heavy wooden door in the wall, leading out of the holding tank. He reasoned they would go through that door after the little "velcome to camp" lecture had concluded.

"Ve have a saying in German," the sentry continued speaking excellent English. "*Fur Sie der Krieg ist vorbei.* The cliché means, 'For you the var is over.' That is now true." He stuck his finger straight toward Irving's face. "Unless, of course, you try to escape! Then, ve vill shoot you dead."

Irving could feel the prisoners around him stiffen. The German's hardened voice sounded like he could kill any one of them at the snap of a finger.

"Some of you subhumans think escaping is a sport." The sentry crossed his arms over his large belly. "Ve do not play such foolish games here. Our new commandant has ordered ve treat all violators in the harshest terms. Do ve understand each other?"

The usual tough-boy talk, Irving thought. *Trying to jerk us around. I bet they think we are all from the Queen's Regiment because we wore these old uniforms for warmth.* He looked to his left where the muscular, heavyset soldier stood. *My identification I took off the dead Englishman fooled them. They think I am a Brit instead of an American.*

"Colditz Castle is escape proof." The sentry continued lecturing. "Augustus the Strong started the transformation of these walls in 1694." He strolled back and forth in front of the prisoners. "You English boys will appreciate the fact that Thomas Carlyle called him the 'Saxon Man of Sin.'" The sentry stopped, lit a cigarette, and blew the warm smoke into the faces of the men. "He is said to have sired 354 children and needed to enlarge *the Schloss* for this small army he was procreating. Of course, in the first great world war, *the Schloss* became a prison camp as it is today. Follow our rules and you will survive. Break them and we will break you."

Irving looked to his right again and made eye contact with Captain "Lulu" Lawton. Even before Rotenburg prison camp, Lawton had come to be affectionately called "Lulu." Both men had known each other before they had been carted into Oflag 4C Concentration Camp. Lawton winked as if to say, "Pure crap." Fowler fought to keep from smiling. Irving knew this officer of the Duke of Wellington Regiment was too clever to stay long in this ancient dungeon. Tony watched his thin mustache quiver when Lawton flashed a smile.

I can depend on Lawton, Tony thought. *He will have more than an idea or two about how we can crawl out of here. Give him time.*

The sentry gestured with his thumb. "On the other side of these walls are the inner courtyard and a delousing shed. You will not like a bath in the cool air, but you won't mind getting rid of your fleas." The sentry gestured to the guard at the door. "Go wash the prisoners down. Take them away!"

Irving, Fowler, and Lawton walked into the inner courtyard, which was surrounded by the towering edifices of the castle complex. Some of the walls looked crude and austere, while other areas had been built from stone with an elegant appearance. Most of the entrances were nothing more than old wooden doors, but one entry was surrounded by marble columns with ornate carvings above the lintel. Heavy masses of ivy vines covered several of the walls and hung down over the windows. Other prisoners milled around the yard.

"Take off da clothes!" a new guard ordered. "All of dem." Around the yard the other guards clicked their rifles into ready-to-fire position.

"*Nun!*" the sentry demanded. "Now!"

A cold breeze whipped over the wall and swept across the courtyard. The sun was about to set, and the entire area was filled with shadows.

"I don't think they are joking with us," Bill Fowler said out of the corner of his mouth.

Lulu Lawton had started unbuttoning his jacket. "Yeah, the faster we get this done the better."

"Stop de talking!" the guard demanded.

Irving raised an eyebrow and Lawton shrugged.

"At once!" the guard demanded and started clapping his hands. "Into de shed. Now!"

"*Now* seems to be his favorite word," Fowler half-whispered. "Here we go, boys."

The cold spray shocked Irving. His skin tingled and shriveled like water contracting into ice. Tony squeezed his eyes shut to keep the spray from burning them. The cold liquid sent waves of spiked pain through his body.

"Got to get out of here!" Tony wailed and ran toward the end of the shed.

The rest of the men piled their clothes on the ground and walked barefoot into the ice-cold spray. The foul-smelling disinfectant saturated their hair and ran down their bodies like rivers of ice.

"Hurry!" the sentry ordered. "Lose no time."

Irving rushed out the other end, shaking, shivering, and clutching his arms around his bare chest.

"Put de clothes back on."

Tony stared at the guard. Irving was dripping wet and needed to dry off.

"Got a towel?" Tony asked.

"Clothes on *now!*" The guard pointed at him.

"*Now* again," Tony grumbled.

"*Ya!*" the guard barked.

"Hey, I can dance for you." Tony wiggled his hips. The two other prisoners started clapping.

"No trouble or ve shoots!" the guard screamed.

Without saying another word, Irving started putting the dry clothes over his freezing, naked body. "Nutcases!" he muttered under his breath. "A bunch of jerks!"

"Take dem up to the permanent quarters of all da English in the

Furstenhaus, the Princes' House in da east wing," the sentry said. "All British soldiers are kept in dat area."

The German guard saluted smartly and turned back to the three men. Blotches of moisture appeared on the back of their shirts and pants. "*Marsch!*" the German commanded.

The Allied soldiers turned about-face and marched toward the high, mud-covered five-story walk-up. No one spoke, but the men tramped inside, following the narrow stairs winding up to the floors above.

The three soldiers stopped at a door on the second floor. "En dere," the guard insisted. "Go en." The Germans turned and went back down the stairs, leaving the soldiers staring into a large open room.

Irving looked carefully around the large bed area. The expansive room was better than he had expected. Each man had his own bunk, a mattress stuffed with straw, and in one corner was a large stove to provide heat. Cupboards and cabinets stood around the walls. The place looked surprisingly on the comfortable side. This camp certainly looked to be a notch up from Rotenburg. Even though Tony was only a sergeant, his escape with the British had indirectly elevated him to a higher status.

"Welcome to your vacation in Deutschland, gentlemen." A tall, thin Englishman stood in the back of the room. "Permit me to introduce myself. I am Donald Wardle, or as the rest of the boys call me, 'Stooge' Wardle. May I welcome you to our little abode where every man's home is quite literally his castle."

Another man stood next to Wardle. He was also tall and thin but with red hair parted in the middle and combed tightly to his head. His eyes glowered from behind a protruding brow, and he had a long thick mustache twirled to pointed ends. His deep-set eyes added an austere, foreboding appearance. The man stared at the new prisoners as critically as the German sentries had done.

"Please meet my Dutch colleague," Stooge said and patted the tall man on the shoulder. "His name is Captain Damiaem Van Doorninck. You'll find him to be an excellent friend to have around here."

Van Doorninck said nothing but nodded his head and strolled out of the room. The three new prisoners watched him disappear like a whiff of smoke curling up the chimney.

"Our pleasure." Bill Fowler extended his hand to Wardle. "Glad to meet you."

"Stooge?" Tony Irving asked. "How'd you get that moniker?"

"I am the master of looking as dumb as a country ox when the Krauts are up here nosing around. My mates started calling me Stooge because I was so good at faking the Nazis out."

"Excellent!" Lulu Lawton shook Wardle's hand. "I like that angle."

"You'll find this place to be rather decent," Stooge continued. "Several of us already bunk here. Usually there's hot water except when someone tries to escape or is a bad boy, then they turn off the heat."

"Looks like cold winter showers ahead," Irving joked. "We'll keep that hot valve turned off all the time with our escape attempts." Two of the men laughed and applauded.

"The mess hall is in another part of the building. Unfortunately, the food isn't much. In fact, without the Red Cross parcels we'd probably all have starved by today. Every now and then someone drags through a horse head or some tidbit of that order, but most of the time we don't see anything that's fresh or in wide enough supply to keep you running far."

"Nothing like a good horse-head steak," one of the regular prisoners quipped.

"Not exactly on the posh side," Fowler said, "but we weren't expecting steak every night."

"We don't see many German *Reichsmarks* inside the camp," Wardle continued. "Occasionally they pay us in *lagergeld*, camp money that isn't worth a plug nickel except at their canteen. If you want any of the real money when you escape, you're going to have to be rather resourceful."

"We'll try," Irving answered. The men nodded and started finding beds.

"I know it is not as cold outside as it will be in another month," Irving said, "but we just came through the delousing shed, and they didn't give us anything to dry off with. We could use some heat."

"Certainly," Stooge said. "Let me see if I can get a fire going in our quaint little fireplace." Wardle walked to the window and pushed it open. "Hey, Sas! Jacob Sas! Can you bring me a few pieces of wood? I've got some cold men up here."

"Certainly!" a voice answered from down on the inner courtyard.

A few minutes later a tall blond-haired man walked through the door, carrying several pieces of wood. "Here you are," he said. "Your special order delivered with the compliments of the Queen of Holland."

"Gentlemen," Stooge called to the men around the room. "I want you to meet Colonel Jacob Sas, another Dutchman, a gentleman of the highest order and a scholar to boot. This good man was standing with one foot in Hitler's backyard and one in the Netherlands the moment the war started. He knows our captors like the palm of his well-worn hand."

Sas bowed slightly. "Welcome to Colditz. The home of all the naughty boys in World War II," he said in excellent English.

Lulu Lawton extended his hand. "Good to be part of this unique gathering of naughty boys. You were there when the war started, huh?"

Sas smiled slightly. "The exact moment."

"I'd like to hear that story," Fowler said.

"Yeah," Tony Irving added. "The Nazis may have started it, but we'll finish the story." He thumped on his chest confidently.

"We will have plenty of time," Sas said. "Yes, ample opportunity to do nothing but tell stories. Life can get extremely dull at Colditz."

"Unless . . ." Stooge Wardle held his finger up in the air like a teacher making a point. "*Unless* you are working on an escape plan. *That* can take more time than you ever had."

"No problem," Tony Irving said. "We're ready to go to work first thing in the morning."

"Good." Sas nodded. "Yes, gentlemen, our daily task is to discover how to get out of this glorious German castle generally called a god-forsaken hole."

FOUR

The sunlight of a new day poured through the barred windows of the *Furstenhaus* while the roomful of men climbed out of bed and started preparing for the unavoidable day at hand. One night in Colditz Castle had done little to improve Tony Irving and his compatriots' opinion of the fortress. Their beds had been a vast improvement over sleeping in open fields trying to evade the Germans, but they were still in prison and nothing softened their loss of freedom.

After making their beds and straightening the room, the British soldiers marched down the hall toward the mess hall. The Dutch had already filed in and men were sitting around the room.

"We eat breakfast in this mess hall?" Tony Irving asked Stooge Wardle.

Wardle nodded. "Yeah," he said. "You'll love the place. The elegance overwhelms you."

"That's what I thought. A true ptomaine palace."

"We never get much, and the coffee tastes like the other side of awful." Stooge grinned. "You'll learn to love it."

Irving shivered. "I can't wait."

"After your stomach growls for hours on end, you won't even notice the taste of anything in this hangout," Stooge said.

"Hey, look. There's that guy we met last night. Jacob Sas." Tony pointed across the room. "I think I'll go sit across from him and get to know him a little."

Wardle nodded in the direction of some other inmates. "That's fine. I've still got rounds to make." He ambled off toward a table full of fellow Brits.

Irving slipped into an open space at the table across from Sas. "Hey, ole buddy. Remember me?"

Sas blinked several times. "Let's see . . ."

"I came in last night. You brought us wood to warm us after we survived the delousing shower."

"Ah, yes." Sas smiled. "You are a Brit."

"Close enough." Irving looked around. "Where's the food?"

"You got it. If you don't have a Red Cross parcel yet, a piece of black bread and this ersatz coffee is it."

"Ersatz coffee?" Tony grimaced. "This stuff stinks."

"It's made from acorns," Sas said. "You'd better drink it because that's all you're going to get."

Tony took a sip but had to force himself to swallow. "Never tasted anything worse! The stuff is like medicine."

Sas laughed. "Welcome to breakfast at Colditz Castle. Did you like those blue-and-white mattresses last night?"

"Beat the night before sleeping on the floor of a train."

"And a vast improvement over the flat wooden boards at most of the other concentration camps. I was imprisoned near the Baltic Sea where winter turns men into icebergs. These straw-filled mattresses are certainly a notch up from what we had up there in that icebox."

A long-legged Dutchman scooted in next to Sas and pushed his tin cup of coffee in front of him. The man's long, twisted mustache and his red hair were unforgettable.

"Hey, you're the other guy we met last night. You're Van . . . Van der . . ."

"Van Doorninck," the man said sternly. His eyes showed no emotion, only a constant, intense stare. "Damiaem Van Doorninck."

"I came in with the Brits, remember? You were standing with Stooge Wardle when . . ."

"Of course!" the Dutchman snapped. "I observed you and you *are not* English."

Tony stiffened. "Where'd you get that idea?"

"I pay attention," Van Doorninck said. "You have the accent of an American."

Tony glanced around quickly and leaned forward. "Keep that under your hat. The Germans haven't figured it out yet. It's my secret."

Damiaem Van Doorninck's eyes narrowed. "In fact, you have a western sound. You are certainly not from around New York or the East Coast."

Tony grinned. "I'm a Texan."

"Ah, yes." Van Doorninck maintained his sober, emotionless stare. "You must be a cowboy."

Irving rubbed his chin. "How did you put all this together?"

"As I said, *I pay attention.*"

"Captain Van Doorninck is a man of many talents," Sas said. "You'll learn to appreciate his skills."

"Yeah, I guess so." Tony took a small bite of the black bread. "Got to make this stuff last as long as I can. Not much here." The bread proved tough and not easy to chew. Irving had to take a hard bite. "By the way, Sas, how'd you get in here?"

Sas glanced at his friend, but Damiaem's face kept the same flat, emotionless gaze. "I was in the Settin concentration camp. Five of us tunneled out of that northern ice hole. We made a run for the forest, but the Nazi machine guns opened up like they were shooting a swarm of rats. If I hadn't stumbled and fallen, they would have killed me."

Tony nodded. "The others?"

"Killed them."

"I see," Irving said slowly. "Not a pretty story."

"Most aren't." Sas shrugged. "We didn't get in here by being compliant. My little attempt to run put me in here with the Poles, the French, Canadians . . . even a few New Zealanders and South Africans." Jacob looked silently at the top of the table for a moment. "You married?" He seemed to be changing the subject.

Tony shook his head. "Got a girlfriend. Best-looking woman in Texas. Her name is Rikki. Rikki Beck. You?"

"Yes."

"Tell me about her."

Sas shifted uncomfortably on the bench. "Her name is Anika. Anika from Gravenhage."

"Where is she?" Tony asked.

"I don't know," Sas said. "Hopefully she escaped to the north. But—" He stopped. "But I don't know."

The Dutchman suddenly turned cold and quiet. Tony sensed he'd heard everything Sas was going to say. Van Doorninck kept looking at the table and not saying anything either. A moment's reflection on Rikki Beck reminded him how sensitive the subject of women could become. Nothing more needed to be said. He knew the two Dutchmen sitting across from him had walked down a far more difficult path than he had yet traveled.

———

Jacob didn't want to think about what had happened to his Anika. If she hadn't escaped, God help her. Maybe the Nazis would have been kind to her; maybe they wouldn't. He could not let himself think about what they might have done.

Sas took a slow drink from his tin cup and stared at the table. He didn't want to talk with anyone. Damiaem understood and wouldn't say anything, but this American had a big mouth. Sure, he had wit and a sense of humor the man would need to survive life in the castle, but he asked too many questions. Jacob didn't want anymore of them.

One more time, for perhaps the hundredth time, he started remembering how this war had begun—from all of that mess left by World War I: the inflationary struggle in Germany, citizens nearly starving, political chaos that would inevitably produce Adolf Hitler, the war machine. The Allies should have had more sense than to have allowed Germany to drift toward a political promise that would turn out to be an incarnation of the devil.

His reflections inevitably led to one memory that always eventually floated through Sas's mind. If there was anyone who knew *exactly* how the Nazi invasion started in the Low Countries, he was the man. Sas had been standing there the instant it began. All Jacob needed to do was recall the situation, and the scene unfolded with such intensity that he felt it was happening again at that exact moment.

A pleasant evening breeze had floated across Berlin with only a hint of the fierce winter still lingering in the air. May 9, 1940, carried the hope of a spring filled with promise for Germany and the Third Reich, while disaster and devastation waited for the rest of Europe.

Colonel Jacob Sas had slipped his Luger 9 mm pistol beneath his simple, brown wool jacket and looked in the mirror one more time to make sure the gun didn't show. "I've got to be prepared for everything," the Dutch colonel had mumbled to himself.

Jacob could pass for a German any day of the week—he spoke the language like a native, but he didn't have much time left to stay in Berlin.

Sas shut the door behind him and hurried down the stairs. He knew the night would not be easy.

On a side street not far from the Brandenburg Gate, Sas had already made arrangements to dine with his old friend *Oberst* Hans Oster, a high-ranking officer in the *Abwehr*, the German military intelligence service. Over the years their friendship had given Sas a pipeline to some of the most sensitive information the German military had gathered on Holland. Both men wore civilian clothes with every intention of concealing their military offices.

Oster walked into the restaurant at precisely eight o'clock, carrying himself with the regal and disciplined bearing of the German aristocracy. In excellent physical condition, Hans did not look fifty years old except for his receding hairline. Because of his noble birth as well as cleverness, Oster had worked his way to a high level within military intelligence. The two men shook hands and immediately began their conversation. In short order, the waiters brought the evening meal.

Nodding now and then, *Oberst* Oster had eaten slowly and listened carefully to Sas's phrased and coded questions. Their friendship had developed into an unusually frank relationship because Hans Oster carried the unexpected political disposition of being a staunch anti-Nazi.

"Hans, you have been more than gracious," Jacob finally said. "You have given me important details of Hitler's war strategy and what Holland can expect."

Oster shook his head. "I have only done what was moral under these difficult circumstances. The truth is that I fear for both of our countries."

"Then nothing has changed?"

Oster nodded. "Nothing. As it now stands the German offensive against the Low Countries and France is set to commence at five o'clock tomorrow morning."

"*Tomorrow morning?*" Jacob's voice uncharacteristically squeaked. Sas pushed the remaining hunk of steak aside, his appetite instantly disappearing. "No question about the day?"

"Earlier plans called for the final order to be given at nine-thirty tonight." Oster glanced at his pocket watch. "I fear nothing will stop the attack."

Sas looked at his own wristwatch. "We don't have much time left."

"I will return to our offices and check. If everything is in place, I will come outside and tell you."

Colonel Sas gulped a last drink of wine, finishing half of the glass in a single swallow. "God help us!"

Hans Oster stiffened. "Exactly! Europe will never be the same again." He folded his napkin carefully. "Look as casual as possible when we leave. One never knows who is watching these days." He stood up and beckoned Sas to follow. "Stay close to me, my friend."

The two men had strolled up the street, talking casually as Berliners often did. People nodded. A few people spoke.

By nine o'clock the streets had become empty and blacked-out, offering Sas even more concealment when he took his place next to a darkened light pole on *Bendlerstrasse*. Jacob kept looking at his pocket watch, but nine-thirty came and went without the German returning. The hands of the clock had almost reached ten o'clock when Hans Oster abruptly hurried down the stairs of the massive building.

"There have been no cancellations," Oster said. "The invasion is to begin at five o'clock tomorrow morning."

Colonel Sas shook his hand. "Thank you, Hans, dear old friend. God protect us both."

The two men quickly parted, and Sas sprinted back to his hotel to find a telephone. He immediately called the Ministry of War in the Hague.

"Yes," Albert VanderBeek, his superior, answered the special number.

"This is Colonel Jacob Sas. I have the final word. Can you hear me?"

"Yes, yes," VanderBeek barked. "Tell me immediately!"

"I have only one thing to tell you: *Tomorrow at dawn. Hold firm.* Have you understood me? Please repeat."

In cold, precise words VanderBeek recited the message exactly as Sas had given it. "Correct?" The phone line suddenly went dead.

Colonel Sas hung up and hurriedly hailed a taxi. His only hope was to catch a flight out of Germany before the invasion began.

Jacob blinked several times and realized he was still sitting in the prisoners' mess hall in the east wing, staring at the top of the table. Irving and most of the other prisoners had already left. As he often did, Sas had become so completely lost in his memories he had nearly forgotten where he was.

"Tonight?" Damiaem Van Doorninck said, nudging Sas gently with his elbow. "Are you ready?"

Jacob nodded his head slowly. "Yeah. *Tonight.*"

CHAPTER

FIVE

Major Reinhold Eggers was working at his desk when the gentle knock came at his office door. *"Ya?"*

The door opened and a man came in. Wearing his military cap, Corporal Otto Schadlich, with his blond hair and large nose, looked more like a German farm boy than a guard in a concentration camp.

"Otto!" Eggers beckoned for the corporal to sit down opposite him. "Good to see you this afternoon."

"Seig Heil." Schadlich saluted unenthusiastically.

Eggers responded with a perfunctory salute. "How's my old friend?" He pointed to the chair.

"Been an interesting day. I've been making my rounds and see on the entry report that we picked up three new prisoners last night."

"Yes. Englishmen."

"Same types as usual?"

"I think so." While he could be stern, the major had a kindly face. With his graying hair combed straight back, he appeared to be more of a schoolmaster than the whip cracker in Oflag 4C. "I didn't interrogate them. Of course, the prisoners will immediately start looking for an escape route out of here, and the inmates will test us."

Corporal Schadlich grinned. "And we will stop them. The usual game we play." He reached in his jacket for a pack of cigarettes. "May I?"

"Of course."

Schadlich lit the cigarette. "Dare I ask about our new colonel?"

Eggers's smile disappeared. "We are going to have a problem with Glaesche. I believe he is here to make a point."

Schadlich frowned. "A point?"

"The man's going to push us in his attempts to promote himself. You can expect him to be demanding and difficult."

"I see," Otto said slowly. "That is not good news. Colonel Schmidt was old and didn't demand much out of us, but he was fair. Honest. Certainly he was not a problem for the staff."

"Don't expect the same from Glaesche." Eggers raised an eyebrow. "And be sure you stand at rigid attention when he is in the castle. The man will be trying to catch us in some mistake."

Otto took a deep drag off of his cigarette and blew a big puff of smoke into the air. "I am sorry to hear of this situation."

"You'll be even sorrier if good old Edgar catches you in some miscue. Spread the word. Tell the men to be particularly wary when the commandant is around."

"I will." Schadlich stood up and put his cigarette out in an ashtray on Major Eggers's desk. "Anything you want me to watch out for with these new prisoners that came in last night?"

"No." Major Eggers turned back to his desk. "Just the usual. Late this afternoon we have a load of ten prisoners coming in from the east. We caught them trying to cross the Rhein River. The POWs will require your inspection."

"I will watch them carefully." Corporal Schadlich saluted and walked toward the door. "I believe everything in the castle is under control. I don't pick up hints of any prisoners trying to escape."

Shortly after the ten new prisoners were checked through the entry gate, night descended on the castle. Corporal Schadlich processed each man, and by nine o'clock the day was finished. Once the electricity in the prisoners' portion of the castle had been turned off, blackness settled over the fortress and its multitude of concealed chambers. The Germans controlled the light switches, but the darkness of night still covered whatever any of the prisoners planned. Sleep had already descended on Sergeant Tony Irving, Lieutenant Bill Fowler, Captain Lulu Lawton, and the rest of the prisoners in the *Furstenhaus* section of Colditz Castle when the two Dutchmen made their move.

Earlier in the evening, Damiaem Van Doorninck and Jacob Sas had hidden in the prisoners' kitchen behind sacks of potatoes and waited for the early hours of morning. The Germans had not missed them yet, and the two inmates had taken turns napping and standing guard until the hands of the clock passed three o'clock in the morning.

"Think it's safe now?" Colonel Sas whispered.

Van Doorninck looked at his watch again. "It will take time to get out of here and over to the other roof. We will need every minute we can secure."

"I'm ready," Sas said. "Say the word."

"We must not make a sound going up the steps to the roof." Damiaem pointed to the door and glared at Sas from under his thick brows. "Not even a squeak!"

"Of course."

"Follow me." The lanky Dutchman beckoned with his thumb and Sas followed.

Van Doorninck bent low, creeping toward the door so there wouldn't be a chance of a German sighting them through one of the windows.

Out of his pocket he pulled a piece of metal notched and cut to pick most of the castle's door locks. After a few minutes the door lock clicked, and he slowly opened the heavy wooden door wide enough for Jacob Sas to slip through. Damiaem shut the door behind them and locked it again.

"Remember!" Van Doorninck held Sas by the shirt. "Not even a bump!"

Sas nodded and started up the narrow, winding spiral staircase in his bare feet, carrying his shoes in his hands. After several minutes they reached the roof and stealthily tiptoed across the flat surface until they reached the edge of the *Kellerhaus*.

"See any guards?" Van Doorninck whispered.

Sas sat motionlessly on the edge, studying the lay of the castle's courtyard stretching beneath him. He waited for a couple of minutes. "No," Jacob finally said. "We are safe."

Damiaem glanced at his watch again, leaned out over the edge, and started waving. A face appeared two stories above them. Donald Wardle hovered out a window, smiling with that stupid grin he used on the Nazis. A few seconds later a rope woven out of bed sheets and pieces of rope dropped out of Wardle's window and slowly inched down toward Sas and Van Doorninck. Even though the rope was made mostly from cloth, it had been so carefully and tightly woven the long strand could support a man's weight.

"Excellent." The Dutch captain smiled for the first time that night. "We are exactly on schedule. Stooge is performing perfectly! He will drop the packages."

The slowly lowering rope caught the wind and swayed in the breeze, but it finally dropped into Van Doorninck's hands. Clutching the rope tightly, he pulled it toward himself. "Grab the bundles," he whispered to Sas.

Two sacks dropped from above them. Damiaem pulled the rope as quickly as he could, and Sas reached out to grab the packages.

"Got 'em!" Jacob gasped, pulling the knapsacks back onto the roof. Wardle waved from above and disappeared back inside the window.

The Dutchmen quickly opened the two bags and started laying out their escape equipment. Each bundle had a makeshift German officer's jacket and pants dyed to match the colors worn by the guards. They slipped on the suits with small, handmade compasses in their pockets. Each man adjusted a cap made to look like the ones worn by the *Wehrmacht*.

"We are ready!" Van Doorninck said confidently. "Now the real job begins." He pointed to a narrow strip of cement running along the side of the building in front of them. "You ready for the long walk?"

Sas held his finger up in the air. "No wind tonight." The colonel swallowed hard. "But we've got to walk that four-inch-wide rim for at least ten yards. No easy task."

Van Doorninck nodded. "It's forty feet down if we slip." He took a deep breath. "This is not child's play. That's a cobblestone pavement underneath us."

Sas nodded. "But it's better than rotting in this lousy jail. I'm ready to face whatever comes."

"Okay." Damiaem stood up. "This is the hard part, the long walk. Here we go."

The captain slowly maneuvered his way out to the narrow ledge. Sliding his feet carefully, he maneuvered inch by inch along the thin cement strip. Damiaem tried to relax, but every muscle in his body stayed tense. Pushing all thought of time out of his mind, he crept forward hesitantly. Finally, he came to the end. With one final burst of energy, Damiaem leaped across, landing on top of the German guardhouse with a gentle thud.

Lying on the roof and gulping in large breaths of air, Damiaem waited patiently and quietly, desperately hoping no one heard him and that Sas would not slip. Five minutes later Sas landed next to him. Neither man moved.

For several minutes, they lay side-by-side in the cold night air, hoping against hope no Germans sleeping beneath them in the guard-house had heard a sound. No sounds of running feet floated up. Apparently, they were safe.

"Let's go," Van Doorninck said. "We must slip over to that attic window to secure our rope tightly. That's where we will slide down."

Both men slid along the tile roof until the captain pushed the narrow attic window open. Van Doorninck reached inside and found an exposed two-by-four wall stud.

"Got to be secure," Damiaem mumbled. "Remember it's fifty feet to the ground from here." Pulling as tightly as possible, he secured the rope.

Sas nodded. "Don't make any mistakes."

Van Doorninck slung the rope over the side. It swirled around, bouncing silently against the wall until it hit the cobblestone street far below.

"Okay," Damiaem said resolutely. "I'll try it first. Then, it's your turn. All we've got to do is hit the ground, and we'll be out of here." He stuck his foot over the edge and made the sign of the cross. "God protect me." Van Doorninck dropped over the edge.

Damiaem's rubber-soled shoes allowed him to silently bounce on the rocks. He carefully descended the building until he dropped noiselessly on the pavement. He looked up and saw Sas peering down at him. The Dutchman waved and motioned for his friend to start down.

Van Doorninck watched Sas shimmying down and quickly realized Jacob's shoes were not rubber-soled. A high-pitched squeal and bumping noises echoed across the outer courtyard. Damiaem covered his head and leaned against the guardhouse wall. "God help us," he moaned. Sas was doing his best, but the noise was far, far too loud. The captain pressed his hands against his ears, praying the racket wasn't as obvious as he knew it was.

A window on the third floor flew open only a couple of feet from Sas. "*Stoppen!*" a German yelled out the window.

Sas paused momentarily as if trying to decide what to do, then abruptly spun down the rope so fast he nearly burned the skin on his hands—but it was too late. The man in the window kept screaming at the top of his voice.

"*Stoppen! Entgehen!*"

Van Doorninck stood up slowly. He could hear the hobnail boots of a German soldier running toward them from the sentry gate. They could not go to the left because a sentry always guarded the store shed. An element of surprise was all they ever had on their side, and now it was gone.

"*Entgehen! Entgehen!*" the German in the window hollered.

Sas dropped next to the captain. "We've got to run."

"No!" Van Doorninck grabbed his arm. "They'd kill us on the spot. Our luck just ran out."

"No move!" a sentry from the gate screamed at them. "I shoot!"

"Don't do anything dumb or we're both dead." Damiaem stood up slowly, raising his arms above his head. "We tried but just didn't make it this time."

Sas hesitated for a moment and then followed suit. Sounds of men running seemed to be coming from every direction. It didn't take the Germans long to respond once the alarm was sounded. Two approaching sentries pointed their rifles directly at the Dutchmen's chests and edged forward cautiously.

The door to the guardhouse flew open, and Major Reinhold Eggers came running out, tucking his shirt into his unzipped pants. "What is going on out here?" He grabbed at his belt that was flapping behind him.

Van Doorninck smiled and nodded politely. "Oh, nothing."

"So, you decided to take a night walk?" Eggers barked, walking back and forth in front of the two prisoners. "You didn't think we would notice?" He zipped his pants and pulled his belt tight. "Maybe you thought it wouldn't make us any difference."

Van Doorninck smiled pleasantly. "Seemed like a nice night for a walk."

"Listen, you pighead!" Major Eggers growled in his face. "Listen carefully to what I tell you. We have a new commandant, and he is not going to tolerate this nonsense!" His voice dropped so low the German soldiers standing around would have a difficult time hearing everything Eggers said. "I would suggest that you spread the word that this is a good way to get killed. If you'd gotten beyond the walls, we would have shot you. Do you understand? This isn't a game anymore."

Sas and Van Doorninck kept looking straight ahead without speaking.

"Okay," Major Eggers said. "Take them to the solitary confinement cells in the inner courtyard and lock them up." He turned to the sentry next to him. "Call an *Appell*, a roll call, for the entire castle. We want to make sure no one got away. Stand them all out there in the inner courtyard until we know the exact head count." He pointed to the two Dutchmen. "Make them an example. Help these fools remember that escaping is *now* dangerous business."

Van Doorninck watched Major Eggers stomp back into the guardhouse. He couldn't decide exactly what the camp overseer meant, but Eggers seemed to be unusually serious this time. "*Marsch!*" the German sentry demanded. "*Nun.*"

Van Doorninck and Sas turned and walked through the gate into the ramparts area. By the time they had crossed the entrance gate into the inner courtyard and walked beyond the solitary confinement cells, prisoners had begun to pour out of the dormitories and fall into formation.

"Think they'll beat us?" Sas asked from behind.

"I don't know," the captain answered. "They might, but I imagine we'll be more than a little cold before they lock us up."

"Yeah," Sas said.

"*Stille!*" the guard demanded. "Quiet."

The Germans marched the two Dutchmen up against the inner wall under the corner light and stripped off their handmade, German "look-alike" uniforms as well as their shirts. The men were chained to the wall.

Captain Van Doorninck looked out over the more than two hundred men lining up for the *Appell*. Abruptly, a few inmates started clapping, then the entire assembly of prisoners broke into applause.

"At least our team appreciates us," Jacob said to Damiaem. "We may not have scored, but we haven't lost the game yet."

"Yes," Van Doorninck said. "Some other day we'll break out of this castle."

CHAPTER

SIX

*A*us!" the German guard screamed at the top of his voice. "*Nun! Hinaus!*"

Sergeant Tony Irving shot straight up in bed. "There's a fire?"

"*Aus!*" the German yelled in his face. "*Nun!*"

"Okay. Okay." Tony jumped out of bed. "Don't have a cat." He looked around the *Furstenhaus* at the other men rolling out.

The guard grabbed the sleeve on the shirt Tony was sleeping in and jerked him forward. "*Nun!*" he repeated.

"Good Lord," Irving griped. "You'd think we'd done something."

"Someone did," Bill Fowler said, lining up next to him. "Must have been an escape attempt."

Tony glanced at his watch. "My gosh, it's four o'clock in the morning!"

"Well, they're running everybody downstairs for some ridiculous reason."

Along with the rest of the prisoners in the *Furstenhaus*, Tony Irving walked out on the cobblestone plaza of the inner courtyard. Irving quickly identified Frenchmen, Poles, and Czechs. Belgians were somewhere in the mix. A few Americans had gathered at one side. He was surprised to discover so many prisoners locked up in the castle. Sergeant Irving lined up with the English because the Germans had not yet discovered his American nationality.

"Hey!" Lawton said. "Over there on that wall—the guy in chains looks like the same man who was with Stooge Wardle yesterday afternoon when they hauled us into this castle. What was his name? Dornock or something like that."

Irving looked hard. The sun hadn't come up yet, and it was still dark. "Yeah, the red hair does look like that Dutchman—his name is Van Doorninck."

German NCOs trotted back and forth in front of the prisoners, yelling at the men and demanding silence. Lawton studied the guards carefully. Most were older men with wrinkled faces, looking more like farmers pressed into military service. Some of the guards were only boys. Undoubtedly, they'd shoot a resistant prisoner, but these Germans didn't really appear to be people with a will to kill.

Irving scrutinized the two men chained to the wall beneath the barred windows. "The other guy's name is Sas."

"Guess they got caught before they broke out," Lawton said.

A German officer in black military boots walked briskly from a side door into the center of the prisoner roll call and stepped up on a small platform. The gray-haired man wore the professional uniform of an officer of the *Wehrmacht* with a black collar and iron cross over the lapel pocket along with the usual straight, stiff military hat.

"He looks like one of the officers riding on the train when we were hauled in," Lawton said to Irving. "The man rode in that Mercedes that followed us up the hill."

Standing at rigid attention in the middle of the platform, the major began speaking. "Once again you have tried to escape and failed. May I remind you that Colditz Castle is an escape-proof prison. Each of these attempts fails because our capacities are resolute and indomitable." Major Eggers started pacing back and forth with a stiff military gait. "We now have a new commandant, Colonel Edgar Glaesche, who brings firm determination to this task. He will not tolerate your foolishness *any longer*." The major stiffened. "Anyone escaping from this camp will be shot on sight."

German NCOs hustled by the Englishmen, counting each man and comparing their numbers with what was listed on a clipboard they carried. "*Ein . . . zwei . . . drei . . . vier . . .*" The head count continued on and on.

"These two Dutchmen were caught virtually before they got out of the dormitories." The major turned and pointed to the men chained on the wall. "Following this *Appell*, they will be placed in the isolation cells directly behind them for a significant period of time. Any future attempts at escape will be dealt with in the same harsh manner."

Silence fell over the Allied soldiers. Time dragged by but the counting continued. The major stood resolutely with his arms crossed over his chest until finally one of the NCOs brought him the completed head count. They spoke for about thirty seconds, and then the major nodded to another soldier wearing a simple head cap. The counting started again.

Irving watched the two men chained to the wall. Van Doorninck had the same distant, indifferent stare Tony had seen at breakfast that morning. Nothing seemed to touch him, but Sas seemed more vulnerable and more aware of the danger they were in. Tony wondered if Damiaem was as tough as he appeared to be.

He glanced around the courtyard. Were all of these prisoners as indifferent as they seemed to be? Undoubtedly they weren't, but they all looked equally as durable as Van Doorninck. Of course, they had been thrown in this "bad boys" camp because they had already proven themselves to be difficult. But what was *bravery* anyway? Just the capacity to endure? To hang on when times were hard? Did it involve doing some frighteningly horrific act when everybody else was hiding to protect themselves? What was this supreme quality *really* all about?

Tony looked around at the Poles and Czechs. They had already paid a great price, having their homes and towns blown to pieces by the rampaging Nazis. He hadn't ever experienced any calamity of such an order. Life in Texas had been quiet, predictable, easygoing. The big excitement was a rodeo, a runaway bull—not a twenty-ton Panzer IV tank plowing through your backyard. The truth was he'd never known anything like what these men and their families had faced.

I came to Europe for the adventure, Tony thought. *The excitement! I wanted to be part of a great crusade to stop this abominable little tyrant Adolf Hitler. That was about it. Little more.*

For the first time an icy chill slid down Tony's back. He had been firing that bazooka at the Germans like he was playing a game . . . a game in which he was invincible, indomitable, indestructible. And the truth was, *he wasn't.*

"That's Corporal Schadlich," Stooge Wardle said from the row behind Fowler. "Not a bad guy and somewhat on the funny side. We don't have problems with him."

Schadlich blew a whistle, and the NCOs immediately began returning the soldiers to their quarters. The large assembly quickly broke up and vanished inside the five-story buildings.

Tony trudged along behind Stooge, but his mind was elsewhere. He glanced over his shoulder and looked again at the two Dutchmen standing there, bare-chested and chained to the wall. Men could easily die in this prison. *He* could die as easily as those two men standing next to the isolation cells. The realization was unnerving and disconcerting.

Wardle led the men back up to the second floor. The new prisoners gathered around Wardle, sitting down on the edge of one of the bunks. Stooge waited for a moment, listening carefully to make sure no one was eavesdropping outside the door.

"I knew about this escape long before last night," Wardle began. "Been planning it for some time."

The men crowded closer. "We had actually planned it for a couple of weeks from now, but the arrival of this new toad Glaesche concerned us. He's got a reputation for cruelty, and we wanted to get the escape underway before that Nazi swine tightened the screws."

"Where's Glaesche staying?" Tony Irving asked.

"I'm not sure," Stooge answered. "Schmidt, the first commandant, lived on the grounds in the *Kommandantur* with his wife. We didn't see him much as he rarely came around the prisoners. Soldiers like Eggers actually run the place. I've got an idea that this Glaesche may stay in town."

"How come you know so much about everything happening around here?" Irving asked, not hiding the suspicion in his voice.

Stooge laughed. "Think I'm one of the bad guys, huh? An informer?" He laughed again. "You'll have to do better than that, Irving!" The easygoing tone in his voice shifted and became hard. "Pay attention, you clowns. I wasn't up here by accident when you arrived." His eyes narrowed and his smile disappeared. "I'm on the escape committee. Understand that?"

The men stared with quizzical looks on their faces. "You've been checking us out?" Tony asked.

"Exactly. We pay close attention to everyone coming in here."

"We met those men who were captured tonight in this very room yesterday," Irving said. "Didn't we?"

Wardle nodded his head. "Captain Van Doorninck is probably one of the finest lock picks around. You ought to get to know him after he gets out of that godforsaken hellhole they've put him in. He's a fine man." Wardle looked straight into Irving's eyes. "The other man chained to that wall brought the wood up for your warmth after the little delousing experience. Got me?"

"So, you've been watching us," Captain Lawton said. "To see if we're trustworthy?"

"Among other things." Wardle stood up and walked to the door again and looked out. Satisfied, he sat down once more. "We have an International Escape Committee in this castle. No one tries to get out without our approval. We keep things lined up, sorted out, to make sure all attempts are equipped with any resources we can bring to bear on them. Understand?"

Bill Fowler shrugged. "Sure. We read you. The idea makes sense."

"Every nation has a representative on the committee, an escape officer. We make sure all lines of communication with other nations stay open."

Lawton rubbed his chin. "So, you're our local supersnooper kid on the block? Our Mr. Escape Officer?"

Stooge nodded. "You're getting the picture. We prefer to be called 'the toasting committee' for obvious reasons. You never know when one of these Krauts has his ear plugged in at the door."

"Good point," Tony Irving said.

"Look," Stooge kept talking in a hard voice. "This castle has a thousand nooks and crannies that the Germans don't even know about. Our job is to identify every one of them. We assume the men coming through the front door are 'good folks' or they wouldn't be here, but we have to get some sense of them, know who they are, and how they tick. You boys passed quickly because of your sense of humor. Obviously, you're part of us, but you've got to learn some rules if you hope to escape this place. Don't underestimate these Germans. Colditz is a most difficult castle to escape from."

Wardle eyed Tony with a hard stare. "You're obviously not British. How come you're staying with this unit?"

The American quickly glanced around the room. "Look, I merged with the Brits to break out of that last prison camp, and the Nazis never figured out I wasn't one of you. I concluded my confused identity might give me an advantage in an escape attempt. I never figured I'd have to line up and take a number before I could try to bust out of here."

"But you do!" Stooge insisted. "You have to be part of the same scheme every man in this castle is a part of. Don't dare try it on your own, or you'll probably end up dead rather than in solitary confinement."

"Hasn't anyone escaped from here?" Irving pushed.

"Not many hit a home run," Stooge said, "but despite the German claim that this place is escape-proof, a few have made it out. One of the first was Alain Le Ray back on Good Friday in 1941. He put on some civilian clothes under his uniform and found the right moment to break away during one of the camp football games. He got out of the castle and walked to the village of Rochlitz about five miles from Colditz. He caught a train, but about halfway out of the country Alain found that his German *lagergeld* money wouldn't work."

"Must have spoken good German," Tony said.

Wardle nodded his head. "Sure. After three days of traveling and without sleep, Le Ray was running out of gas. That's when he decided to make a break for Schaffhausen, Switzerland."

Irving edged closer. His eyes narrowed and he became more intense. "*He made it?*"

"A border patrol nearly got him just outside of the Swiss border, but Le Ray managed to get back to the train station and crawled on the front of a train that rocketed across the border. Yeah, Le Ray knocked the ball over the fence for a real home run."

Tony pounded his fist. "All right! Count me in that game. I'm ready to get out of this place."

"You just got here," Wardle snapped. "Get in the lineup. This isn't a party, you know."

"Okay, I'll wait *two days!*"

"Oh yes. Very good," Stooge said. "You have to keep your wits because this place can drive you batty. No one knows how long this war will last, and it could go on for years." Wardle looked long and carefully at each man. "Do you hear me? You could be sitting in this dormitory years from now."

"Not me!" Irving said defiantly. "I ain't planning to put any roots down in this soil."

"Really," Stooge shrugged. "I'm telling you right now there's not a clock in the world over which you have any ultimate control. You can't make time stand still or speed up. I've watched men sit here month after month with nothing to do. Before long they are standing in front of one of those cabinets 'locker puttering.' Know what that is?"

Irving shook his head.

"They stand in front of their cupboard taking whatever is in there and moving it around like pieces on a chessboard. They arrange and rearrange anything a hundred times like they were doing something important instead of simply wasting time with nonsense. They get goofy, compulsive, obsessive, just flat nutty." He shook his finger in Irving's face. "Don't kid yourself. No one escapes the harsh bite of boredom."

Tony nodded his head. "I hear you." He broke into a broad smile. "But I plan to do better! Lots better."

"Good luck." Wardle winked and slapped him on the shoulder. "Let's get back in bed. Maybe we can catch a few minutes of sleep before they roll us out for wake-up call."

Tony sat down on the edge of his straw mattress and watched the men returning to their bunks. They all looked resolute, ready to face the Germans. But were they? More importantly, was *he* really prepared? For the first time in his life, the question was troubling.

CHAPTER

SEVEN

Following the disruption of the unexpected early morning roll call, the prisoners in the *Furstenhaus* section of Colditz Castle marched down to the mess hall. At eight o'clock, they filed across the inner courtyard where they could see Van Doorninck and Sas waving at them from behind the bars of their isolation cells. The new prisoners whistled to applaud the two Dutchmen, but the guards kept the inmates marching toward the mess hall, making sure no one talked to the prisoners.

"One of the prisoners told me that the parcel post office is on the other side of the solitary confinement cells," Bill Fowler said. "That's where we pick up our Red Cross packages."

"I hope a package comes through today," Tony Irving said. "I need the food."

"Who doesn't?"

"The world I grew up in was certainly different from these premises," Tony said. "Why, living in Dallas, Texas, wasn't much different from growing up in any old cow town, except it was a bigger town than most of 'em. Nobody spoke anything but Southwestern American." He winked at Fowler. "Saying 'y'all' is just part of the twang of the Texas prairies. I didn't even know people talked differently until the army picked me up and dropped me in England."

"Why'd they send you to us?"

"Oh, I guess it was part of some secret deal that President Roosevelt came up with to help Churchill and company." Tony grinned. "I seem to have this uncanny ability to make a bazooka sing and dance."

"Bazooka?" Fowler squinted. "Yes, I've heard of it."

"It's a new American gun—a long, shoulder-positioned cannon that can knock out one of those Nazi PzKpfw III armored tanks as easy as snapping your fingers."

"I hear this bazooka is scaring the Germans to death. They seem to think the gun is a weapon of terror."

"Glad to hear it. I came over here to teach your people how to shoot those long tubes of steel, and your boys have proved to be right good students. We must be making progress."

"There's the guard looking at us. We'd better stop talking."

Tony glanced over his shoulder. Behind them stood the castle's chapel. Directly in back of the chapel and the castle walls, a steep cliff dropped off, ending at the edge of a little stream called the Hohnback. Breaking out of that portion of the castle was impossible.

"Move it," the German sentry shouted at the men. "You prisoners already made one mistake today. Don't make two." The men trudged forward.

The line into the mess hall abruptly stopped well outside the door. Immediately the inmates started grumbling and complaining.

"*Halt die Klappe!*" a guard at the door demanded.

"Sounds like 'shut up,'" Tony grumbled under his breath.

"Yeah," Fowler whispered.

Tony tried to remember something that would lighten his irritation at having to wait. Whenever he needed a diversion, Tony always thought about Rikki Beck. Tony could make Rikki come reeling up in his mind like a Saturday night movie. She'd be waving at him just as she had done the day he left on the train. Rikki hadn't wanted Tony to join the army, but in 1940 he had come to the conclusion that someone needed to stop

Adolf Hitler and had developed the conviction that the American government would eventually get in the European war. He graduated from high school and signed up with the army only months before the Pearl Harbor attack.

Rikki wasn't petite. In fact, she looked like a good Texas girl should: tall, strong, and ready to ride a horse. Underneath the magnificent dark brown hair that hung below her shoulders, Rikki's skin was as fair and smooth as the spring winds. Her mouth had a heart shape, giving her face the look of a true American pinup girl.

"Hurry up!" the German soldier at the door suddenly changed his demand. "Keep dis line moving."

Tony stomped out of his reverie and into the mess hall, finding a place across from Lawton and Fowler. Cups of steaming coffee were passed down the table, dipped out of a cauldron. Some of the prisoners had carried the large vats out of the inmates' kitchen into the mess hall and lined up the multitude of tin mugs.

"We all get our turn at passing out the coffee?" Tony asked.

"I expect so," Bill Fowler said. "These Germans don't intend to be our waiters. You can bet on that one."

"What do we eat?" Tony asked.

Captain Lulu Lawton looked around the room. "I think we're on the low end of the totem pole again this morning. These old-timers seem to be making up their breakfast out of what came to them in Red Cross parcels. It'll be awhile before we get one."

"Exactly what I was afraid of." Tony's voice sunk in disgust.

"Enjoy that coffee," Fowler said. "It's going to have to hold you until noon."

Stooge Wardle sat down next to Irving. "You boys won't have much to eat this morning, but you'll be getting a Red Cross box before long. Certainly makes a difference."

"I'd say so," Tony groused.

"Who was that guy standing out there on the platform making the big speech in the middle of the night?" Fowler asked. "Tell us something about him."

Stooge nodded. "That was Major Reinhold Eggers. He basically runs the place. There's also a senior camp officer named Priem who's not much more than an old drunk. Of course, Corporal Schadlich hangs around cracking jokes and trying to pump information out of us. The worst clown we try to avoid is Heinz Gephard. The sergeant-major is a pig and a mean man to get entangled with. The prisoners call him Mussolini." He shook his head. "No, ole Reinhold is the man we have to do business with when we get caught trying to escape.

"He's actually an old schoolmaster," Stooge said. "Best I can tell he'd prefer a baseball game to getting drunk. Not really a bad guy. I think he's stationed here because his experience in running a school probably makes him better qualified than the average soldier to deal with old bull-dogs like us."

"He's not such a difficult Kraut to deal with?" Tony asked.

"I didn't say that," Wardle corrected him. "Eggers is extremely efficient at his job. He doesn't miss a trick. Because he's so cautious and careful, the man can be a mean pain in the rear. He'll punish you hard just like he's done to Van Doorninck and Sas."

"You're saying he's a good news/bad news type to deal with?" Fowler asked.

"That's about it. Eggers wouldn't order a mass killing like the Gestapo's rumored to do, but he intends to run this place in a shipshape fashion, which means escaping will always be difficult."

"How about writing letters?" Tony scooted closer to the table. "I've got a girl at home, and I'm sure she's worried to death about me."

"There's no limit to how many letters you can receive," Stooge said.

"But you can only write one a week. The Germans will give you a *Kriegsgfangenenlager* form on glossy paper."

"*A what?*" Tony's voice rose.

"You'll get adjusted to these German tongue twisters," Wardle advised. "You'll certainly hear enough of them." Stooge lowered his volume. "The Germans check letters carefully, so you have to be cautious because they'll toss out anything that looks funny. The mail is sent to Switzerland or Sweden, and it can take better than two months to get home. Often letters just disappear."

"Thank you," Bill Fowler said professionally. "We appreciate the information."

Wardle picked up his Red Cross box. "I need to check with several other men. Keep your eyes open and get a good feel of the castle. It's an extremely big place."

"Thank you," Lawton said and tipped his head politely.

Stooge Wardle got up and made his way to another table. He and the men huddled together, speaking in low voices so no one could hear them.

"Looks like our local escape committee officer is going full tilt this morning," Tony said.

"I'm sure he's still sizing us up," Fowler said. "Probably watching every movement your eyebrows make."

Tony swallowed the last of his coffee. "It won't be easy to get out of here. I'm sure of that fact." He set the tin cup down. "Well, I think I'm going back outside to take a look at the chapel across the way."

The two Englishmen nodded and Irving stood up, knowing he'd be hungry before long. Outside several sentries stood with rifles resting against their shoulders, and a guard sat on the flat roof with a machine gun aimed into the courtyard. No one seemed to be paying much attention to him. Tony walked slowly toward the entrance to the chapel.

Like most of the rest of the castle, the outside wall of the chapel had a dull coating of brown stucco, but the inside of the old sanctuary proved to be ornate and elegant. In the front of the chancel, a stone altar stood majestically with two candlesticks poised on the ends of the altar. Hanging on the walls, plaques written in German commemorated deaths. Tony sat down in one of the ancient wooden pews. For the first time in weeks, he found himself in an atmosphere of quiet sanity.

Irving drank in the atmosphere, letting the serenity settle around him. The quiet made him realize how his world had been filled with nothing but noise, disruption, bizarre craziness, and fear. Now he had come into a holy room where the subdued calm restored a sanity he didn't even realize he had lost.

Fifteen minutes passed without Irving moving. The quiet reprieve and the solitude settled his mind, and he felt an inner refreshment wrapping around his soul.

His first religious experience had occurred when he was sixteen. A friend of his had taken him to a church down the street from Tony's home. The building was a one-story wooden church painted white, sitting isolated on a very ordinary Dallas street corner. The pastor had talked with Tony several times before they prayed together. Without fanfare or trumpets blowing in the sky, he had simply stepped into the Christian faith. Not many kids talked about their faith, but Rikki had been thrilled about his decision and started attending the church with him. Tony quickly discovered this new faith did change his life. He became bolder and more self-confident. Although they were only teens, his relationship with Rikki deepened into what he believed was love . . . but it was good and pure because that's what his new faith demanded.

Tony reached in his shirt pocket and pulled out a black leather-covered New Testament. He'd gotten into the habit of reading the Bible often and found it gave him consolation during the times when everything was uncertain. Tony thumbed through the pages, looking for something to speak to his heart.

The New Testament fell open to the Gospel of Luke. Tony read down the page until he came to the twenty-fourth verse of chapter thirteen. "Make every effort to enter through the narrow door, because many, I tell you, will try to enter and will not be able to," he read aloud. "Once the owner of the house gets up and closes the door, you will stand outside knocking and pleading, 'Sir, open the door for us.'" He stopped.

What an odd passage, Tony thought. *Enter through the narrow door?* He shook his head, then used a piece of paper to mark the page, closed the little New Testament, and put the book back in his pocket.

For a long time Tony sat quietly. He finally slipped down on the kneeling pad below the pew. "O Lord," he prayed under his breath, "help me understand what I've just read. Please help us find our way out of this castle. Keep us safe and give us the strength to endure these difficult days . . . and please bless Rikki. Amen."

Tony took a deep breath and stood up. He was ready to go back outside and face the struggle once more.

CHAPTER

EIGHT

Sergeant Tony Irving glanced at his watch. Only two hours had passed since breakfast, and no one had told him to do anything. The German guards stood around and silently stared at him. Surely somebody would lay on him an order, an injunction, a command—something—telling him what to do next, but the Germans didn't appear to have any such inclination.

For several minutes, Tony watched the inner courtyard. Metal bars over the windows contrasted with the ornate columns and expensive carved rock work over the large doorways. Inmates stood around idly, not doing anything. The morning air was cool enough for puffs of steam to roll out of the prisoners' mouths when they spoke. Gathered together in small groups, the prisoners talked, smoked, and generally seemed to be apathetic. Most of the prisoners were complete strangers to him and didn't speak English. Tony didn't see anyone he felt comfortable to talk with.

Stooge Wardle abruptly came down the steps from the dormitory. The Brit stopped, lit a cigarette, and looked around the exercise area as if he owned the place. He appeared to be studying the courtyard for some inconsistency. Possibly Wardle was assessing the area for a weak link in the chain the Nazis had wound around all the prisoners. Wardle would have some insight about what Tony could expect next from the Germans. Tony started walking toward him.

"Well, here comes our cowboy," Wardle said. "A living, breathing Texan."

"Don't say that too loud," Tony cautioned.

Wardle grinned. "Sounds like you're on the conservative side this morning."

"Can't tell who is listening," Tony said. "Simply playing it prudent."

"Ah, you're learning! Colditz Castle will teach you many things, my son. Wisdom will eventually flow out of the rocks."

"Yeah, well, when do I start the graduate course?"

Wardle blinked several times. "What do you mean?"

"When does the drudgery commence? The pain? The forced labor?"

"You expecting the Germans to beat you with a whip every morning?" Wardle raised an eyebrow. "What'd you want them to do? Pound on you?"

"Don't want them to do anything," Irving said. "But I thought they'd drive us out into the fields and make us do heavy work. Scream at us. Do something more than not pay any attention to us."

"Oh, the Nazis are watching. The trouble with you, Irving, is you've been so busy being a cowboy that you never had anyone teach you how to be an officer. You may not deserve it, but you're now one of the elite, an Allied officer in this great world war. The Nazis are supposed to treat you like a gentleman."

Irving scratched his head nervously and looked puzzled. "I don't understand."

"Look, we may be the 'naughty boys,' but we're still officers. In the old European system they usually don't push us if we don't push them. If we sit around here and don't attempt to escape, the only thing we have to worry about is mind-crushing boredom. Like I told you when you came in, doing nothing will eventually drive you over the edge."

"So, the Krauts aren't going to make us do anything?"

"That's a gross overstatement, but it's close to the truth. Our job is to look innocent and compliant while we are secretly working like crazy to break out of this jailhouse."

"But the prisoners have to be doing *something*," Tony protested. "I mean we've got to spend our time involved in some sort of work to keep our minds and bodies active."

"We're big on football, or soccer as you Yanks call it. We play some rather rough and tough games, and the men even get hurt occasionally." Stooge put his hand up to his mouth and whispered. "Of course, most of the skirmishes are only a cover for a variety of schemes, investigations, and explorations to break out of here. Got me?"

Tony nodded his head.

"Periodically, we put on shows. Some of the men play guitars, others sing, and some even dance. A few dress up like women and parade around. The acts are little spoofs, farces, and are good for laughs . . . and maybe somebody will break out during the show. See how our system works?"

"Hmm. The real story is what's going on in the back room. I'm beginning to get the big picture, but I didn't realize we would have so much free time."

"There's a price for everything," Wardle said. "All that free time comes at a high price."

"I get you." Tony nodded and started walking away. "By the way," he said over his shoulder. "Are there any narrow doors around here?"

"Narrow doors?" Wardle laughed. "Don't think so. Most of the entrances are big enough to ride a horse through, and some are so ornate they would welcome a king in a royal carriage. But a narrow door? Sorry, none come to mind."

"Just wondered." Tony turned around and started to walk away.

"Ah, here ist our new man!" Corporal Schadlich caught Tony by the arm. "Wardle, you must introduce me to your new partner."

Tony stared at the blond German. Smaller than he was, Tony was surprised that the man seemed so friendly.

"The name is Irving," Tony said in a low, threatening voice. "Lieutenant Irving."

"You vill enjoy Oflag 4C," the corporal began. "Ve only keep the finest of gentlemen in our special camp."

"You shoot the rest?" Tony growled.

"I see your new friend is quite the comedian," Schadlich shot back. "You must include him in your next talent show."

"Why, Corporal!" Wardle answered. "You've again demonstrated your ability as a talent scout. You're always so quick to size up our men accurately."

Schadlich raised an eyebrow indifferently, ignoring the jab. "I vas vondering vhat you thought about the attempted escape last night."

"Escape?" Stooge looked at Tony as if he were mystified. "I didn't know someone escaped." He faked a horrified look. "Someone got away?"

"Of course not," Schadlich grinned. "Ve caught them."

"Oh, good! I'm so relieved to hear that, Corporal. For a moment I thought we'd lost one of our simple community of country folks."

"Van Doorninck doesn't look so happy this morning." Schadlich pointed over his shoulder. "I suppose you noticed."

"I'm sorry," Stooge continued. "I simply don't pay attention to talk about escape or causing trouble for our German protectors. Irving and I are too busy enjoying our accommodations and nutritious meals."

The corporal stiffened slightly. "You boys keep out of trouble." He saluted. "I vouldn't vant to have to put you in those confinement cells."

"Why, Corporal, we wouldn't think of it." Wardle saluted back.

The German walked on to the next group of men and started talking with them. Wardle waited until Schadlich had drifted on to a second group before he spoke again.

"Schadlich's a butt kisser. He's trying to pick up some reading from us about how we view the failed escape so the Germans can goad us because they caught our men so quickly. Typical Nazi harassment."

"I don't like that snake," Tony said.

"The corporal doesn't have any idea that we read him like a road map. Schadlich's harmless."

"No German soldier is harmless."

"Well, you've got a point there, Irving. I'll hand you that one."

"How do you think Van Doorninck and Sas will face their time in those confinement cells?"

Stooge shrugged. "They're tough men. Time will wear on them, but they'll come marching out. Well, maybe walking, not marching, but they'll be heroes."

"I guess the solitary part of confinement is rough on anyone. It must test their faith."

"Faith?" Wardle pursed his lips and shrugged. "I suppose it would affect some men that way, but Damiaem Van Doorninck isn't a man of faith."

"What do you mean?"

Stooge shook his head. "Damiaem doesn't believe in God or any of the divine stuff."

"Doesn't believe?" Tony frowned. "You mean like an agnostic? An atheist? Is he some kind of nut?"

"Well not something of that order. At the least, Damiaem has a God problem, but I certainly wouldn't call him crazy. Far from it."

"What else? How could anyone not believe in God? Why, everybody in Texas believes in God. Even our criminals have some sort of faith that God—"

"You ain't in Texas anymore, cowboy." Wardle feigned a western accent and grinned his stupid smile. "You're English, remember? And we have a number of intellectuals running around this camp who aren't so sure there's a God up there hiding behind one of those clouds. Just so happens Van Doorninck is a bright man who lives on the skeptic side."

Tony shook his head. "I see," he said slowly. "I've never met a man before like one of those sorts. When he gets out of confinement, I'll have to talk with him about his lack of beliefs."

"I'd be careful," Wardle warned. "You'll find that Van Doorninck has a sharp tongue. He might just slice you up like a cucumber if you make him angry."

Tony rubbed his chin. "I'll have to think about this problem for awhile. Thanks for warning me."

Wardle kept grinning. "You might find a rough and tough game of football easier than arguing with that long-legged Dutchman."

"Hmm." Tony started walking away. "How strange." He kept walking across the courtyard, staring at Van Doorninck's solitary cell and thinking about the unexpected things Stooge had told him.

CHAPTER

NINE

Two and a half weeks had passed since Major Eggers had thrown Damiaem Van Doorninck and Jacob Sas into the isolation cells. Damiaem stood on his tiptoes and looked out of his isolation cell, watching the soldiers march into the mess hall until the last man disappeared inside. Their applause and cheering encouraged him, but with nothing to do but stare at the bare, cracking black walls, time had turned into a heavy weight dangling around his neck.

Damiaem had on the same clothing he'd worn the night they caught him. The dirty makeshift uniform stunk, and the Dutchman felt rotten. Each night had gotten progressively colder, and all Van Doorninck could do was curl up in a ball and press himself against the frigid wall.

Damiaem coughed and struggled to stop the hacking. Though Damiaem had always been tough and able to stand a hard winter, this dismal, leaking sewer trap had nearly pushed him beyond his limits. On some days no food came in under the door. On other days, even the supply of drinking water had been meager. The Nazis obviously intended to break him.

"Got to keep my mind together," Damiaem said to himself. "Can't let the isolation get to me." He shivered.

Van Doorninck slowly pushed himself up to his feet and started shuffling around the small cell but immediately realized how depleted his energy was. His muscles ached and his skin itched. The stink of the room almost overwhelmed him, but he made himself walk, hoping in a few minutes his muscles would warm up and the pain would decrease.

Ten minutes dragged past, and Damiaem realized the endless monotony was starting to pry into his mind. He ground his fist in his palm, swearing to himself he wouldn't crack.

At that moment a draft whistled through the openings between the iron bars, filling the cell with another icy reminder that snow wouldn't be far behind. The sentries wouldn't give him a heavier coat, and a sudden cold snap might prove dangerous. Damiaem knew he had to do something to get his mind off his condition. If he didn't find a distraction, the nipping wind would eventually defeat him.

Damiaem slid down the sides of the wall, pulling his knees up against his body and pushing his chin down into his chest, trying to spread hot breath over his cold body. After a few minutes, he wondered if revisiting some incident from the past might encourage him and keep his hopes up. He decided to think about the day the war began . . .

Damiaem had been working unusually late in Rotterdam when the fateful phone call came. Though he had been in the Dutch army for a number of years, the small size of the country had allowed him to continue working part-time in the Van Doorninck's family watch shop located not far from the city's cathedral. Van Doorninck had once been a locksmith but eventually had gone back to repairing clocks because he missed the challenge of tinkering with the intricate mechanisms.

Within minutes after the phone call that ordered him to return to the military, he kissed his wife good-bye and told her to leave Rotterdam immediately and retreat to her parents' home in the north. Van Doorninck locked the shop behind him and hurried down the side streets to mobilize his men to prepare for the next day's war.

At dawn, hundreds of German airplanes swept over the country's borders along with surging waves of tanks and infantry that marched into Belgium, Luxembourg, and Holland. The German Eighteenth Army broke into the Netherlands, unleashing a cavalry division as well as six ordinary infantry divisions that were only the vanguard of an army of two million men marching across Europe toward the Atlantic Ocean. Four paratroop groups sailed down, landing on the big highway and the railroad bridges at Moerdijk, Dordrecht, the Dutch capital at the Hague, and Rotterdam.

On May 10 before dawn, Captain Van Doorninck marched his men toward the Dutch bridgeheads around Rotterdam, expecting they would encounter German troops, and he was not wrong. After four days of fierce fighting, Van Doorninck's troops had proven resolute in stopping the surprise Nazi advance at the outskirts of Rotterdam. Intelligence had already informed Van Doorninck that on May 13, Queen Wilhelmina and the government had fled the Hague for London. Their national cause was hopeless, but Van Doorninck's men were not ready to surrender. On the morning of May 14, Van Doorninck and his troops made one last determined assault on the Nazis.

A young lieutenant put down his binoculars and rolled over next to Captain Van Doorninck. "I believe those tanks are part of the German Ninth Panzer Division," he said. "No question, sir. They are preparing to attack the southern approaches to the bridges to Rotterdam. I don't think we can hold them back for long."

Damiaem nodded. "I understand. We have no alternative. Let us give the Germans something to remember even if they roll over us. We have the advantage of holding the bridge and firing from our side of the river."

"The tanks are Panzer IV twenty-ton *Wehrmacht* killers. We won't have an easy time even slowing them down."

"Yes," Van Doorninck said. "We can only give our best."

Lieutenant Leudens sat up on his knees and saluted. "For God and country. We will give it all we've got, sir." He turned and hurried down the road.

Van Doorninck heard a thundering roar off in the distance. Shielding his eyes, he watched the sky. From the east an endless formation of *Luftwaffe* bombers flew steadily toward Rotterdam. The awful sight carried a frightening display of power and strength.

Bombs began falling, and Van Doorninck started shooting again across the bridgeheads at the German soldiers and the tanks. The Nazis kept up a steady stream of return fire. The ground beneath Damiaem's feet quaked as the bombs destroyed Rotterdam and tore at his eardrums.

Van Doorninck tried to figure out why the tanks hadn't yet attacked. The Dutch defense had done an amazing job of containing them for two days, but the Germans should have been able to overrun their defenses immediately, particularly with the Panzer IV tanks waiting on the edge of the city. Why weren't they rolling onto the bridges?

Captain Van Doorninck kept edging forward on his stomach, shooting at everything that moved, but behind him he could hear buildings exploding, trucks disintegrating, people screaming. The roar intensified until the explosions forced Damiaem to roll into a ditch and cover his ears.

In the maddening thunder of endless destruction, Van Doorninck suddenly realized the truth. Rotterdam had held while the rest of Holland fell. The Nazi's response to their intransigence proved massive and to the point. *Hitler was bombing the town into oblivion.* The tanks had stayed on the outside, waiting until no one was left to resist their entry.

Smoke increasingly rolled over Captain Van Doorninck's position and made it impossible to see anything. He struggled to breathe.

Periodically, gusts of wind split the smoke and gave him some view of what was ahead. The Germans weren't trying to cross the bridge but only returning rifle fire.

After an hour the bombing decreased, leaving only flames and smoke. Eventually the bombers quit flying overhead, but then the tanks opened up their 75 mm guns, smashing everything in front of the bridge.

Damiaem crawled out of the ditch. Scattered around the edge of the bridge were the bodies of the Dutch soldiers who had gone out with Lieutenant Leudens. At the edge of the bridge he saw the still, bent shape of a man lying facedown. Lieutenant Leudens had, indeed, given all.

The sight of his dead comrade held Van Doorninck transfixed. Two bullets had smashed through Leudens's chest and killed the officer instantly. Damiaem reached out and gently touched the coat covering his back. Leudens had always been a faithful member of the Reformed Church of the Netherlands, attending church week after week with total fidelity to the faith, and then, in an instant, he was forever gone.

"Is this what believing in God got you?" Van Doorninck asked bitterly. "You were always a good man, Leudens, and then suddenly the world caved in and in a second you were gone forever."

Damiaem felt the tears welling up in his eyes, but they weren't for the loss of a colleague as much as from the anger that churned inside him. The injustice of a senseless death of a good man plunged the Dutchman into fury. He hated the Germans for killing a man who was only defending his home, and Damiaem despised God for allowing such hopeless inequity to occur.

For a moment the Dutchman was lost in his rage and a furious desire to kill someone, something—anything. Suddenly, a machine gun opened up, spraying the area just in front of him and only missing him by inches. Captain Van Doorninck started crawling backward as quickly as he could. The Panzer tanks would soon come crashing across the bridges, killing everything in sight. At this point, his only hope was to try to reach the other side of the city . . . if the Germans hadn't completely surrounded Rotterdam.

Damiaem got up on his knees for a moment and then started running. After a couple of blocks he realized that the entire city was nothing but burning buildings.

Taking a main street, Van Doorninck looked to his left and saw that a margarine factory had taken a direct hit, spewing burning fat over blocks of the old town. The stench of smoldering lard singed his nose. He had no place to go except into a sea of fire and destruction. After several more blocks of running, the captain realized that the Nazis had already surrounded the entire city and he had nowhere to hide. With no other alternative, he crouched down, leaning against a stone wall and hoping that his wife had arrived at her parents' home.

Damiaem didn't see another living person up and down the entire block. The downtown area of Rotterdam appeared entirely abandoned with only burning buildings crumpling to the ground. Any intelligent person would have disappeared quickly once the 2,200-pound delayed-action bombs started raining down on the city. The heat of the fires and the hot smoke burned Damiaem's eyes. He covered his head and waited, hoping the superheated air wouldn't kill him. For a long time he pounded the dirt and cursed. Finally, Damiaem collapsed in a heap on the ground.

Near the end of the day, a column of Nazi soldiers marched down the street through the debris and the ruins. Only then did Van Doorninck lay down his gun on the sidewalk and stand up. The bombs, the fires, the never-ending smoke left him dazed and no longer able to fight. At best, he could shoot only one or two of the enemy before they killed him anyway. He had no alternative but to surrender.

Van Doorninck slowly turned to face the approaching enemy with his hands in the air.

"Look," a German lieutenant-colonel called out, "one of the few remaining survivors."

Van Doorninck said nothing. In his heart, he felt lost and broken like the burned bricks scattered around his feet. If any God existed up in the sky, the Almighty had surely closed His eyes and ignored the plight of the people of Rotterdam. No, the sky must be a vast empty entity offering no solace, no comfort, no hope.

"You know," the lieutenant-colonel continued as he crept closer to Van Doorninck, "your futile resistance forced our Fuhrer to bomb your city into submission. This devastation is all *your fault*."

Van Doorninck only looked off at the charred horizon and said nothing.

"More than six hundred acres of buildings and houses destroyed because of your silly resistance!" the lieutenant-colonel lectured. "I hope you Dutchmen have learned a lesson today. Seventy-eight thousand of you will be homeless tonight simply because of hardheaded soldiers like yourself."

The captain maintained his silence. He turned around slowly, preparing to be shot in the back. They might kill him, but he would never be their captive.

"Oh, come on! You have an Aryan background. Fall in with us," the German soldier demanded. "We will not hurt you. Simply march along like a good boy. Today you have become a prisoner of war." The lieutenant-colonel grinned. "You are fortunate. The war is now over for you."

Captain Van Doorninck started walking. The war had only begun, and his military career was finished. He didn't feel lucky at all. Even if he was the only Dutch soldier left in Rotterdam, they had not broken him. No, the war *was not* over.

Another draft of cold fall air swept through the castle's isolation cell. Damiaem's memories of the battle of Rotterdam faded, but the realization of his own strength and determination lingered. No God had been there standing with him; he had endured only through his own strength. Holland had been overrun by a vastly outnumbering German horde, but Van Doorninck had given no ground. No matter how bad the isolation became, he could endure another day. The war was far from over. Neither the Nazis nor this castle with its towering battlements would stop him.

TEN

Major Reinhold Eggers sat hunched over his desk inside the officers' quarters at Colditz Castle, listening with the telephone pressed tightly against his ear. He glanced up when Corporal Otto Schadlich walked in. Rather than his usual pleasant smile, a grim, determined look stayed stretched across Eggers's face. Corporal Otto Schadlich stood at attention across the desk from Eggers.

"Yes, sir," Eggers snapped into the telephone receiver. "Of course." He motioned for the corporal to sit down.

"I warned you," Colonel Edgar Glaesche's voice boomed over the telephone. "There are important officers who question your ability."

"No one has escaped," the major said firmly. He could hear the colonel thumping on his desk with his riding crop.

"We had the regional command in Dresden as well as the *Wehrmacht* High Command in Berlin send special agents to Colditz to help your officers search for evidence of tunneling."

"And their experts found nothing," Eggers insisted.

"I am only reminding you that many eyes are focused on Oflag 4C camp, and you will do well to uncover any and all escape attempts *immediately*." The *thump, thump, thump* of the leather crop echoed menacingly in the background.

Eggers sucked in a deep mouthful of air and blew it out forcefully. "I understand, Colonel."

"No mercy!" Glaesche barked. "I want these dogs treated with the contempt they deserve."

"Yes, sir."

"Good," the colonel snapped. "Keep me informed." He hung up.

Eggers hesitantly dropped the telephone back into the holder and leaned back slowly in his desk chair.

Corporal Schadlich shook his head. "Not good?"

Eggers took a bottle of cognac out of the bottom drawer of his desk along with two small glasses. "Correct," he said. "They are after us, Otto." He poured the cognac in both glasses and pushed one toward Schadlich. "At least, they'd like to bring *me* down."

"To your health, sir."

Eggers clicked glasses. "Thank you, Otto. I am not sure what this Glaesche is pushing other than his own career, but he's making it difficult for me."

"Your oversight is excellent, sir."

"Although it's been awhile, we have had men escape," Eggers admitted, "and I'm sure it will happen again, but we must do everything in our power to stop any prisoners from getting away."

"You've also been quite humane."

Eggers shook his head. "That's part of the problem. We have some officers who would prefer that I drive pieces of glass under the prisoners' fingernails."

Schadlich shivered. "That's slightly on the savage side."

Eggers nodded. "Good Lord! I've been a schoolteacher all my life. I'm not some murderous villain. I'm a country teacher who worked with children."

"We've known each other for twenty years, Otto, and we have lived in the most civilized country in the world, but don't let those *former appearances* deceive you today."

"What are you suggesting, Reinhold?"

"We were raised on the usual strict discipline that makes good soldiers out of German farm boys, but there's a new element now. You won't read about the beast in the newspapers, but some horrible atrocities are happening."

"You're talking about the Gestapo?" Schadlich asked.

Eggers nodded his head. "And we've also got some vicious men in the government. Glaesche may turn out to be one of them."

Schadlich swallowed the last of his cognac and set the glass down on the table. "I've heard stories."

"Pay attention to what you pick up. I'm not sure our prisoners understand what could happen to them." He folded his arms over his chest. "We've heard the sounds of their tunneling somewhere in the castle."

Schadlich stood up. "You want me to leave those two Dutchmen in solitary confinement? They've been in there for more than three weeks."

Eggers shrugged. "No. Send them back to the dormitory. They probably haven't learned anything, but at least the high command's agents snooping around this castle saw them locked up and that was good. Go ahead and turn them loose."

Schadlich saluted. "It will be done immediately."

The door flew open and Sergeant-Major Heinz Gephard burst into the room, barking an impromptu, "*Heil* Hitler," with his arm in the air.

"*Heil* Hitler." Eggers made a weak perfunctory return salute.

"I think I've found it!" Gephard panted for air. "The tunnel!"

"The tunnel?" Eggers's mouth dropped.

"Come with me, Colonel. I will show you." He pointed out the door.

"Take us at once." Eggers motioned for Schadlich to join them.

Gephard led them into the outer courtyard where the prisoners first entered the castle. He pointed toward the clock tower above the first entry gate. On the other side lay the moat. Gephard continued at a near run. The sergeant-major rushed into the tower and up the stairs.

"I came to check out the area," Gephard puffed as he climbed the stairs. "Nothing else. I was no more than making sure every aspect of the clock was working when I opened the door to the long shaft that holds the weights for the clock." He stopped on the landing and pointed to a narrow door hanging open. "In there I noticed the deep drop, and I threw in a pebble." Gephard pointed down the shaft. "When the rock hit the board below, it made a hollow sound. That's when I started my full exploration."

Eggers looked over the edge. "Quite a ways down."

"You haven't seen anything yet!" Gephard started back down the stairs. "Let me show you exactly what I found." On the bottom floor he pointed to another open door. "I discovered the prisoners had constructed a false floor, and that's why the bouncing rock made a hollow sound." Gephard pointed into the darkness. "We lowered one of the electrician's helpers down into that hole and found that it goes down nearly to the bottom of the castle's foundation. We caught three prisoners in there working."

Eggers stiffened. "Three prisoners!"

"They grabbed a timber pole and started using it as a battering ram, sir. They broke through a wall into a bathroom in the prisoners' area. The prisoners got away, but we discovered their tunnel." For the first time a smile broke across Gephard's face. "See?" He pointed into the hole.

Eggers rubbed his chin and stared into the darkness. "I'll be darned." He suddenly laughed. "These men are more devious than mischievous schoolboys." He looked into the dark hole again and shook his head. "Gephard, you've saved our honor." He slapped the officer on the back. "Extremely well done!"

"Thank you, sir." The sergeant-major nodded stiffly as if he were about to receive a medal of honor.

"With a tunnel that deep they must have been on the verge of breaking out," Corporal Schadlich concluded. "I would assume they were within hours of escaping."

"Heinz, have our men repair the bathroom wall and then start getting this hole filled up." He turned to the corporal. "Otto," Major Eggers said, "I want you to go out and spend some time talking to the men. You're good at getting inside their confidence. See what you can sniff out." Eggers smiled. "I have a little phone call I need to make right now."

"To Colonel Glaesche, perhaps?" Schadlich asked.

Eggers winked. "I think a little chat might be in order."

The major watched his two staff men disappear. He kept chuckling to himself. "So, officers in the *Wehrmacht* High Command doubt my capacities? Ha! I will enjoy reminding them that we discovered what none of their soldiers could find!" He hurried back to his office.

———

Tony Irving watched Otto Schadlich walk out of the door from the ramparts section and into the inner courtyard. The corporal sauntered along at a slow, easy pace.

"Here comes the funny corporal," Wardle said. "He likes to be our good buddy."

"No kidding," Irving said.

"Schadlich will be Mr. Comic—either milking us or trying to drop a little tidbit down our chimneys."

"I'll fix him," Tony growled and clenched his fist.

"No, no." Stooge shook his head. "We play along with him and see what comes out."

"I don't like letting that jerk think he's one up on us, but I'll take your word for it."

The corporal picked up his pace. "Ah, gentlemen!" Corporal Schadlich waved at the two men as if greeting old friends. "Wardle, you're looking healthy this morning."

"You're eyes must be getting weak, Corporal." Stooge grinned his stupid smile. "You have to eat a good breakfast to look well, and I'm afraid mine was on the slight side."

"I believe I met your friend a couple of weeks ago." Schadlich clearly ignored the jab about the food.

"I say, old man," Irving answered with as good an English accent as he could muster, "top of the morning to you."

"And the best to you," Schadlich answered.

"How'd you ever get this job, Corporal?" Stooge asked. "You function like the doorman at the front door of an English hotel."

"Pure luck." Schadlich stopped and lit a cigarette. "We are most proud of our Prussian traditions." He pointed around the yard. "You've probably noticed some of our guards are grandfathers and some are adolescents. Actually, they may be from the same family . . . grandfather and grandson. Our strict heritage of discipline and following orders precisely without question has allowed us to maintain such splendid examples of military authority."

"*Military authority?*" Wardle squinted. "I think I'm missing something here."

Schadlich broke into a broad smile. "Perhaps, *you have*. Picked up the gossip yet? This morning we discovered the tunnel under the bell tower and even at this moment are pouring dirt into that little gem of a cave."

Wardle's jovial expression shifted instantly. His face became hard and tense. "What?"

"Oh, you haven't heard?" The corporal frowned and fringed a look of concern. "I supposed you would know all about the dig."

Wardle stiffened. "Wouldn't know anything about that sort of thing, remember? I avoid conversations about escapes."

"Really?" The corporal blew a long trail of smoke in the air. "I'm surprised."

"Don't be," Wardle snapped. "We're good boys."

"I like you, Wardle." Schadlich patted him on the shoulder. "You have such a marvelous sense of humor. Well, have a good day." Otto Schadlich wandered off to another group of prisoners. "And let your boys know the tunnel is permanently closed," he said over his shoulder.

Wardle cursed. "The French nearly had their tunnel dug! It would literally have allowed every Frenchman in the castle to escape."

"What are you talking about?" Tony asked.

"We approved the tunnel escape plan months ago," Wardle said. "The Germans have just disrupted one of the best plans anyone ever laid out." He started backing away. "I need to go find out what's actually happening. Keep walking around in the courtyard like there's no problem."

Tony nodded. "Sure." He watched Wardle disappear back inside the dormitory. Tony knew there was nothing good about this situation. He started walking.

Every inch of the castle reflected a grim, empty appearance. Tony looked across the massive battlements and down the long, bleak stucco fronts of the apartments.

"Big," he repeated, "but not big enough to allow those Nazi swine to keep me in here. I'll find my way out."

Tony walked on toward the parcels office to inquire about a letter from Rikki that he knew wouldn't be there. The search, the quest, the hope made all the difference in keeping him going.

"No sir-e-e," he said to himself. "I'm not going to be kept caged in this pen."

PART TWO
Searching for the Door Out

CHAPTER

ELEVEN

By the first of November snow had started falling, giving every indication the winter would be long and hard. Occasionally the days warmed, but each night brought a freeze, and the snow piled up against the castle walls in small drifts. Tony Irving and the two Brits had now been in Colditz Castle more than forty days.

Tony Irving sat in the mess hall sipping some of the black coffee, but his tastes still had not adjusted to the awful bitterness. The big castle had seemed to shrink as the days passed, but he had explored many of the chambers and realized how few good options the inmates had to break out of the fortress.

"Easy there," a prisoner suddenly said to some man walking briskly across the mess hall. "You've got no problem here. Slow down."

Tony looked up but didn't recognize the rather strange-looking man trotting through the hall. The Englishman walked briskly carrying a wooden spoon and an iron poker. The immaculately dressed prisoner appeared to be mumbling to himself.

"That's Edmund Hannay," Stooge Wardle said into Irving's ear. "Sad sight. I'm afraid the old boy has slipped over the edge."

Tony watched prisoners step out of Hannay's path. His eyes looked glazed, and he seemed to be lecturing some invisible man marching beside him.

"What happened to Hannay?"

"Nothing in particular," Stooge said. "He's simply been here too long. The contrast between boredom and the tediousness of camp life causes some of the prisoners to crack. I'm afraid poor Edmund snapped."

"It's no act?" Irving said.

"Some of the men are good at slipping into a crazy performance, but I'm certain the problem with Edmund is real. Be careful not to set him off."

Tony watched the Englishman stop at the end of the mess hall and continue talking to a nonexistent person in a corner of the room. Other prisoners watched Hannay with a weary look in their eyes. The Englishman turned on his heels and started marching back across the hall, walking in front of Irving's table.

"Got to find him!" Hannay clipped. "Must find the man today. I have no idea where Hamilton is right now, but I must wake him up from the dead. Got to get him back on his feet."

Tony watched Hannay come to the end of the hall and then turn on his heels again, disappearing into the kitchen. "What will become of him?" Irving asked Wardle.

"I don't know. The Germans aren't particularly sympathetic to mental illness. I don't think we have much choice but to let Edmund run his course. I hope the Nazis eventually send him back for repatriation, but it will take a long time." He stood up and walked outside.

Irving kept sipping his coffee. It was obvious that even ill-conceived attempts at escape were better than allowing oneself to deteriorate to the point where Hannay now was. Maybe this poor man would deteriorate so completely he wouldn't make it back to sanity.

Prisoners came and went from the mess hall, but Irving kept sipping the coffee slowly, making it last as long as he could. He had been getting Red Cross parcels that provided a breakfast of some meager sort or the other, but there wasn't enough to last long. He knew that stringing out the sparse supplies at least gave him a psychological edge on the feeling that he was starving. All that he could look forward to at noon or supper would be at best thin soup, more coffee, and a slice of black bread. If he allowed his feelings of hunger to dominate his thinking, he would end up like crazy old Edmund Hannay.

Suddenly Irving heard a crashing noise in the kitchen. Tony rushed to his feet and darted into the doorway. Other men followed, but they couldn't all get into the kitchen.

Edmund Hannay stood with one leg inside a large vat of potatoes, stomping up and down, shouting at the top of his voice. "Got to make hooch!" Fragments of potatoes flew in every direction. The man's uniform had gone from ultraclean to a smear of gooey white mush. "Got to get this hooch smashed down."

A large, heavyset German cooking woman kept trying to hit the Englishman with a ladle. "*Stoppen! Stoppen!*" she kept screaming.

"The brew must be ready by tonight!" Hannay kept insisting as his one foot stomped up and down inside the vat.

"Get him out!" another prisoner shouted. "Someone grab this man."

One of the prisoners preparing to carry a vat of coffee stopped and grabbed Edmund's hand.

"Let go of me, you fool." Hannay swung his iron poker at the man and barely missed him. "No time to lose."

"Help me, somebody!" The prisoner covered his face to avoid getting hit.

Two other inmates grabbed Hannay from behind and pulled him to the floor. Another glob of potatoes flew through the air as the Englishman's boots went over his head.

"Out of the vay!" A German soldier pushed Irving aside.

"Back!" Another sentry swung a rifle around at the men. "All prisoners back!"

The inmates started thinning out and crept away from Hannay, now lying on the floor.

The Germans trained their weapons on him, but Hannay seemed oblivious to the danger. "Got to get this hooch smashed down so we can prepare the fermentation process."

Irving slipped out of the doorway and returned to his place at the table. Other prisoners were clearing out in case the ruckus turned any nastier than it was. Tony stayed at his seat determined to see if the Germans would do anything to the poor Englishman.

After a few minutes of rattling and clamor, the two sentries came out of the door with Edmund walking between them. They had his arms firmly in tow.

"I tell you, the hooch will not be done at this rate," Hannay insisted as the guards marched him past. Mashed potatoes ran down the leg of his uniform and over the top of his boots. "These matters take time!"

Drumming on the table with the tips of his fingers, Irving watched the disheveled man disappear into the inner courtyard. Something needed to be done, and Tony was determined to do everything in his power to find his way out of this place. He intended to find Stooge Wardle. Tony got up quickly and rushed outside. Men were sauntering around the large walking area, but he didn't see Wardle.

"What's happening, mate?" Irving turned around and found Bill Fowler standing behind him.

"Some guy named Edmund Hannay just went nuts in the kitchen."

"I saw the two guards go in. What happened to Hannay?"

"I don't know. He came in acting strange, talking to himself, and went into the kitchen where he exploded."

Fowler shivered. "Don't like the sound of any of it."

"We've got to start working on an escape plan to get out of here. I tell you that's the only sure way to stay sane."

Fowler nodded. "You're right, but this guy has probably been here a long time."

"Sure, but we're going to be here for a long spell too if we don't get ourselves in gear."

Fowler rubbed his chin. "Indeed so! Got any suggestions?"

"I know the French got caught digging their tunnel, but I certainly liked that idea."

Fowler shrugged. "One tunnel is as good as another. I like the thought, but I don't know if the escape committee would buy it."

"Look. I'm not big on getting anybody's approval on any plan that would get us out of here."

Fowler shook his head. "No, we've got to play this game by the same rules everybody else does."

Irving frowned. "I suppose we've got to stick together, but I don't know . . ."

"We might need the help of other people, and we don't want to mess up what anybody else is doing. We've got to stay on the team."

"Let me think about it." Tony looked around to make sure no Germans were watching them. "You give an escape plan some hard thought."

"Sure." Fowler grinned. "I do every minute of the day."

Tony nodded and walked on. He needed some idea, some insight, some bright novel approach. There had to be a way out of this place no one had tried yet.

A few flakes of snow drifted down. Most of the men were walking briskly around the courtyard, trying to get as much exercise as possible. Some talked to each other; others tossed soccer balls back and forth. A lull of calm hung in the air. Tony turned around and glanced up at the top of the mess hall. A couple of Nazis sat there with machine guns aimed at the prisoners in the courtyard. Another boring day of the totally predictable had started.

Tony fell into the line of men, walking slowly around the yard. Workmen were carrying mattresses up the steps into the dormitories. He passed the chapel with prisoners coming and going through the large, ornate front door. The snow started drifting down more heavily. He strolled beyond the solitary confinement cells and waved to the men standing at the barred windows. Beyond the delousing shed the parade of men continued walking. Irving stopped and snapped his fingers. The plan was suddenly clear. He knew what he must do . . . instantly!

---- CHAPTER ----

TWELVE

Irving's notion had come in a flash. If he had thought about the idea very long, he might not have tried such an absurd attempt to escape, but the plan came together so quickly and completely he didn't lose any time reflecting. Without waiting for anyone's approval or permission, he dashed across the courtyard and bounded up the dormitory steps. In the room, he found several English soldiers standing around the sleeping area.

"Quick!" he whispered. "You've got to help me."

The men looked puzzled.

"What do you mean?" a prisoner asked.

"The Krauts are unloading some new mattresses. I think they'll bring some fresh ones into the dormitories. I want to escape inside one of the old ones."

Lulu Lawton walked into the room, rubbing the end of his thin mustache. "What's happening, gentlemen?"

"I've got to get inside one of these mattresses." Irving hustled around the room, grabbing some socks, shorts, and a jacket.

"Sure is easier to sleep on them," Lawton quipped.

Tony glanced out the window. "A couple of you men must carry me downstairs and put this mattress wherever the Germans are dumping the old ones. When they drive out, it will be my escape out of the castle."

Lawton scratched his head for a moment. "Well . . . this is an impromptu attempt for sure. I don't know if we've got enough time to pull it off."

"Then we've got to hurry," Tony insisted.

"You got any maps, supplies, anything?" Lawton asked.

"No." Irving shook his head. "I'm ready to face whatever I have to in order to get out of here."

Lawton instantly pointed to two of the prisoners. "You men haul him down there after we get Tony inside the mattress. Let's go!"

The men swung into gear, grabbing the mattress off the bed and starting to pull straw out.

"You got any money?" Lawton asked.

"No, but I'll make it."

The Royal Air Force captain rushed across the room and started digging behind his bed. In a few moments he hurried back. "Put this in your pocket," he said. "It's not much, but a twenty-*Reichsmarks* note will help."

Tony stared. "Gosh, Lulu, that's a lot of money to have disappear in this concentration camp."

"It's just cigarette money. If you get away, send it back in a letter."

Irving laughed. "You bet!" He crammed the money in his pocket.

"Got to get you packed in this mattress," one of the prisoners said, slinging a handful of straw behind him. "We don't have much time left."

Irving dropped to his knees and started wiggling inside the cloth covering. He twisted and squirmed, pushing his way through the mattress and making the straw settle around him. Abruptly, he realized the dust and the particles of straw were working overtime on his respiratory system. Tony caught his breath, struggling to keep from sneezing.

"You okay?" Lawton asked.

"Yeah," Tony said. "It's hard not to cough or wheeze."

"Don't make a sound," Lawton warned, "or the great escape is all over."

"Take me away, boys," Tony ordered.

"You've got to carry the mattress so it looks light," Lawton said. "They can't suspect anything but that you're hauling a sack of straw, or they'll grab Tony in a minute."

"We'll do our best," the man in front said.

Tony could feel the two men picking him up, and he heard Lawton talking, but all that was in front of his face was the straw. The dry old straw tickled him, making his nose twitch. Tony knew he had to take short, quick breaths lest he break into a fit of coughing. His nose started to run and his mouth turned dry. Tony had to bite the sides of his cheeks to keep from sneezing.

"Get him down there fast, boys." Lawton's voice drifted away behind him. "Be careful you don't bump his head."

Irving felt the jogging and shifting as the men climbed down the stairs. He tried to relax, but his muscles tensed. Tony kept swallowing hard to keep from sneezing.

"This guy weighs a ton," one of the men said. "It won't be easy to drag him across the courtyard."

"Yeah, but we've got to at least get him across the outer courtyard because we'll have to take him through the ramparts area."

The other man swore. "I'm going to have a hard time not dropping him."

"Hang on. We're going to have to stop talking."

Tony listened as voices echoed around him. They had to be going over the inner courtyard. He started praying they wouldn't trip or that the cloth covering would not split and dump him on the ground.

"We're taking the mattress to the truck," one of the prisoners said to someone . . . probably a sentry. The two men carrying the mattress kept walking.

Irving pushed his finger under his nose and tried to keep the dust out of his nostrils. He kept biting his lip, fearing he would start a hacking cough. In a few moments, he felt the men stop. German guards barked some sort of question at them.

"Taking it out," the Englishman answered. "Hauling the mattress away."

The guard ordered something or the other, then the men started walking again. Tony heard the hinges on a door squeak and then the door banged shut. He concluded they must have cleared the courtyard and were out in the ramparts area. The mattress was slowly lowered to the ground.

"Get a good grip," one prisoner said softly.

"Yeah," the other answered. "We need to get him completely across to the other gate without stopping."

The procession picked up and started moving again. Irving felt his two carriers trudging the length of the ramparts. They couldn't be too far from the gate that opened into the outer courtyard. Tony knew he couldn't be too far from the truck or cart or whatever they would use to haul the old mattresses away. He crossed his fingers, hoping against hope that nothing would slow them down.

"*Stoppen!*" a distant voice demanded.

"We're hauling the old mattresses out," one of the prisoners said.

"Humph!" The guard hit the edge of the mattress with his rifle. A soft thud resounded. "Go on," he ordered.

The rifle had hit the edge of the mattress and missed Tony's leg by only inches. Fortunately, the soft hay didn't betray a body lying closer to the center. The two prisoners shuffled on through the gate.

"Hey, over there!" one of the prisoners said. "It's a cart filling up with old mattresses. We can put this one in."

"En dere!" a German guard ordered. "Throw dis one en."

The prisoners shifted their weight, and the mattress shook. Tony felt another whiff of dust shoot up his nose. He tried to catch his breath. Every muscle in his body tensed, wanting him to sneeze.

"Throw it in!" the sentry demanded. "Now."

"Oh, boy," the prisoner groaned. "Make it easy."

Tony felt the mattress swing back and forth a couple of times and then glide through the air. It stopped on top of another mattress with a more gentle landing than he would have expected, but the fragments of hay and dust exploded. He could hold it no longer.

"Ah-choo!" Tony exploded. "A . . . a . . . choo!" He sneezed again.

"*Wachter!*" the German officer roared. "*Wachter!*"

Tony froze, knowing his ruse had come to an end. If the first sneeze hadn't betrayed him, the second certainly had. He could hear men running. Tony couldn't stop sniffing.

"Eggers!" the German yelled. "*Herr* Eggers!"

Tony thought of trying to crawl out, but realized it would be difficult so he settled for lying still. The sound of running soldiers came closer.

Tony could feel he was being lifted out of the cart and lowered to the ground. Hands began pulling at his feet and he felt himself being dragged out of the end of the mattress. Brushing the straw off of his shirt, he slowly stood up.

"You prisoners vill never learn," a major said.

Tony looked at the man in the *Wehrmacht* officer's uniform with the high black collar and an Iron Cross on the front pocket. Tony had seen that slicked gray hair too many times before. He knew Major Eggers.

"I was taking a nap," Tony explained. "Must have slipped inside the mattress by mistake."

A smile cracked across Eggers's face. "They are generally more comfortable when you simply lie on them."

"You're certainly right about that, Major. I think these men must have picked me up by mistake."

The major shook his head. "Maybe a little time in the isolation cells will help you remember how to use a mattress properly." He turned and beckoned to the man standing behind him. "Corporal Schadlich, please put this confused prisoner in solitary confinement for a week. A few cold nights will help him get himself back into perspective."

The corporal saluted. "Yes, sir."

Tony put his hands on top of his head and started marching forward.

"A week can turn out to be a long time during the winter," the corporal said. "You'll find that it gets rather cold at two o'clock in the morning."

"I suppose," Tony answered, "but maybe we'll have a warm spell this week."

THIRTEEN

Major Reinhold Eggers stood in his office, looking across the courtyard at the isolation cells. The snow had started falling again and piling up against the windowsills. He knew the entire day would be cold and blustery.

"How's our mattress escapee doing this morning?" He turned to Corporal Otto Schadlich.

"I imagine he's shivering. Last night was quite cold."

"Humph!" Eggers turned and looked out the window again. "Too bad, but we warned these prisoners about attempting to escape."

"Unfortunately, he'll still be in the cold cell through tomorrow morning." Eggers looked down at the papers on his desk. "Otto, you said you discovered something I should know?"

The corporal pulled off his soldier's cap and slipped his gloves from his hands. Although looking thoroughly German, Schadlich also had close-set eyes, making him appear deceptively on the simple side. "Yes, sir," he said.

"Well?" Eggers motioned for him to speak.

Schadlich edged closer to his desk. "Reinhold, I am afraid to say much."

Eggers frowned. "I don't understand?"

"You're sure this room isn't wired?"

Eggers shook his head to say no while saying the contrary. "Of course it isn't." He pointed to the window indicating they should talk over there. Eggers put his arm around his old friend's shoulders and pulled him close to the glass. His voice dropped to a murmur. "What's the problem?"

"Yesterday we had prisoners arrive from Warsaw, Poland. They were in terrible shape, and we put them in the sick bay," Otto explained in a whisper. "They looked so bad we knew they needed special attention."

"I understand," Eggers said.

"But I overheard these men talking later." Schadlich whispered directly into Eggers's ear. "They had barely escaped from German suppression for the uprising in the Warsaw ghetto. These men had stories of unspeakable atrocities they claimed were performed by our troops."

"Do you believe what they said?" Eggers asked.

"Why would they lie?" Otto threw up his hands. "They had no idea I was listening. I believe what I heard them say."

"And their stories detailed brutal behavior on the part of German soldiers?"

Otto nodded. "The Gestapo did it! They also had tales of Jews being assassinated and murdered for no other reason than that they were Jews."

Eggers nodded only slightly. "*I see.*" Eggers rubbed his chin thoughtfully. "Thank you for bringing this information to me. Make sure no one knows what you have seen and heard. I fear for the repercussions."

Schadlich shook his head. "Exactly. We must keep ourselves out of this sordid debacle, lest the Gestapo comes for us."

"As long as we are part of the *Wehrmacht* there is nothing the SS can do to us," Eggers said. "They have no jurisdiction over the army, but we must not tempt them. The Gestapo is a dangerous organization to offend."

Otto put his military cap back on his head. "These are dangerous times, Reinhold."

Eggers smiled. "Actually, some aspects of our work are better than you might think, Otto. We are doing well here in Camp Oflag 4. We've had eighty-eight men involved in forty-four escapes and caught thirty-nine of them before they even got out of the castle. Only sixteen actually escaped. Glaesche wouldn't ever admit it, but I think the high command is basically impressed with our record. We shouldn't have SS agents looking at people like you and me."

Schadlich took a deep breath. "I certainly hope so, but are you certain about . . . ," Otto whispered directly into Eggers's ear, "Colonel Glaesche."

"No!" Reinhold shook his head. "I am not positive about this man, but I do keep my eyes carefully on what is said and done by him."

Otto shrugged. "I hope so."

Reinhold glanced at his watch. "When the proper hour comes, send this prisoner in isolation back to the dormitory. I think we've made our point."

"Yes, sir!" The corporal saluted.

"And keep me up on anymore of these stories." The major returned the salute.

"Indeed!" The corporal turned on his heels and briskly marched out of the room.

For a long time Reinhold Eggers looked out the window. The weather had certainly taken a raw and bitter turn. This was not the world Eggers wanted to live in, but he had no other choice because the alternatives could be worse.

Tony Irving had awakened several times in the night feeling cold. With his clenched fist pushed into his stomach to stop the cramping, he finally slipped into a troubled sleep after doubling up and sticking his face inside the jacket he'd brought into the cell with him. The added warmth helped him rest.

Irving had quickly learned the only way to sleep was curled up in a ball. The rocks Tony had to sleep on showed no mercy, gouging him and shoving cold, hard edges into his side and back. The unforgiving hard surface of the stone floor made his muscles feel like he had been beaten with a club. No one could ever adjust to sleeping on the rock. Each day Tony's body ached, and he found himself hobbling around the cell, trying to exercise but not wanting to feel the pain in his muscles.

Because of interruptions during the night, Tony had slept longer than usual the next morning. When he awoke, his body was again stiff and sore. Cold wind drifted through the bars of the windows, and Tony knew the temperature was in the low thirties at best. He huddled against the wall, praying he wouldn't freeze. He now well understood why the isolation cells were such an effective punishment.

Sounds of men working or exercising on the other side of the stone wall echoed in through the windows but only reinforced his sense of loneliness. The incessant hours of boredom became worse than a beating. No faces appeared in the door, and no voices asked questions of a prisoner. The inmate had nothing to look at but the dirty, pitted walls. Only a hole in the corner served as a toilet, and the pungent fumes left the narrow, small cell immersed in the stench of filth.

For the thousandth time, Tony studied the ceiling, the walls, the floors, tracing lines and patterns in the rocks. Obviously the primitive builders of this rat hole knew how to make sure there was no way out except through the locked iron door. The "joint" was a dead-end street.

Tony had known the normal aches and pains of playing football in high school, and boot camp hadn't been a pleasure trip, but never had he been in a situation like the isolation cell. Hunger never left him, and the hole stayed cold. Sooner or later, Tony feared, he'd become sick. If nothing else, the sewer hole at the end of the room had to be spreading infection.

In the beginning, Tony had prayed periodically through the day, but the Germans had not allowed him to bring his New Testament. He was forced to sit in a corner and try recalling passages he'd memorized over a few years. Again and again, Tony brought back to mind Bible verses he'd learned at church until eventually he couldn't remember anymore.

I wonder how Damiaem Van Doorninck survived, he wondered. *I'd go crazy if I didn't know God was with me. Something must have gone terribly wrong in his life. He seems so distant, detached, and lonely. Van Doorninck appears to be a man with a wound through his heart. He can't have stumbled onto his doubts by accident.*

For a long time Tony thought about why this Dutchman had a problem with God. He had never met an agnostic although they were rumored to be around. If nothing else, Tony was determined to discover why this man couldn't believe in God as he did. Sooner or later he would have a straight talk with this strange man.

Eventually Tony's mind moved in another direction, and he began to think about Rikki Beck. He recalled their dates, school events, parties, and anything he could dig out of his memory and relive again. Eventually, Tony had gone back to the first minute he remembered meeting Rikki and had recalled every second he had ever spent with her. Conversations were savored like a delicious confection picked up in a candy shop.

Tony could see her dark, inviting eyes twinkling in the moonlight with Rikki's radiant dark brown hair swirling over her shoulders. He particularly loved the feel of her hands. The softness of her skin always allured him, and Tony could almost hear the sound of her voice . . . almost . . . but not quite. When he realized the exact intonations of her voice had slipped out of his memory, Tony nearly wept.

But even Tony's thoughts of Rikki were slowly pushed aside by the increasing, gnawing pain of hunger. The meager supply of rations was obviously part of the German plan to reduce a prisoner to compliance. He found himself continually thinking about food, fantasizing about eating, imagining pies, cakes, meat . . . the list went on and on. He even dreamed constantly about eating. Thoughts of steak nudged Rikki aside. Tony found himself startled by his persistent memories of food.

Tony ran his hands slowly down his side and realized more fully than he had before that his ribs had become much more pronounced. The lack of food was clearly wearing on his body, and he knew his attention had to be fastened in some other direction or the bleak deprivation of the cell would destroy his resolve.

The idea of breaking out kept returning. If he could put together an effective escape plan, when he got out of the cell he'd be ready to go into action. The single idea of gaining freedom again galvanized his energy and started Tony reflecting on a plan that would focus his imagination elsewhere.

The idea of a tunnel kept coming back to his mind. It had certainly been tried often enough, but the castle was set high on a hill. Digging under the foundations seemed like such a logical idea, and there certainly were an adequate number of prisoners working around the place to provide enough labor. Maybe it wouldn't work, but possibly the Germans wouldn't expect the prisoners to try a dig immediately after another tunneling attempt had been discovered. All of which made a passageway an even more attractive option.

The idea of a tunnel made Irving feel the first enthusiasm he had known in days. He could envision it, sense it, almost taste it. He simply needed to identify the right place to start.

Tony began to flex his fist and stretch his arms. For the first time since the Germans had thrown him in this hellhole, he felt a sense of purpose. He was still hungry, and Rikki's face remained the most beautiful sight in the world. But now a new purpose motivated him, and, if nothing else, Tony had a burning desire that made living in this grim pit endurable.

"I may be alone today, but I'm not singular," Irving said aloud. "The guys are out there, waiting for me to come back with a new vision, a new idea."

Suddenly the sound of keys turning in the lock on the large metal door stopped Tony's mumbling to himself. He looked in amazement at the door. Food had always been pushed under the bottom, but no one had come in since the first day they threw him in the slammer.

The metal door creaked as it slowly opened. On the other side stood Corporal Otto Schadlich with the sentry who guarded the place every night.

"Having a nice time?" the corporal asked. "You are looking well."

"Ha ha." Tony faked a cynical laugh. "Now you are the comedian."

"Have you enjoyed de nights in our special accommodations?" Schadlich asked with his own unique twist of irony. "Ve hope you found your stay comfortable."

"Nothing like it," Tony said.

"Vell, your time in solitary is up, and ve hope you've learned something about trying to escape from our castle."

"Oh, I have," Tony answered. "I certainly have some new thoughts."

FOURTEEN

The afternoon sun had started to set. From his office windows Major Eggers watched Corporal Schadlich lead the "mattress escapee" across the inner courtyard. The inmate looked dirty and bedraggled but far from beaten. His gait had a provocative, challenging quality. Eggers knew little could deter these defiant prisoners from trying to escape, and he actually admired their insolent attitudes.

Reinhold Eggers had grown up near Mannheim and spent much of his childhood on the banks of the Rhein, where tenacious fishermen sailed forth every day to brave the cold winds in search of a catch. He had known many laborers with the same persistent defiance of authority he saw in these Allied prisoners. Eggers had not been of this type and tended to buckle to the demands of powers that be. Good Germans weren't supposed to appreciate obstinacy, but a stiff backbone appealed to a carefully hidden part of Eggers's past.

As Schadlich led the prisoner back to the inmates' barracks, men were clapping, and the released inmate kept waving like a hero returning from battle.

Well, Eggers thought, *I suppose he is something of a hero today. He tried to escape and got caught, so that makes him significant in their sight. So be it!*

The phone rang and Reinhold picked it up. "Major Eggers," he said, then his voice shifted into the professional military tone he knew was always expected. "*Heil* Hitler."

"*Heil* Hitler," the all-too-familiar voice of Colonel Edgar Glaesche answered. "I have been reviewing a report on the investigation of our suspension of the prisoners' right to walk in the exercise area down in the valley on the eastern side of the castle."

"Yes, sir," Eggers said slowly. "I understand the British took this matter up with the Swiss government, protesting our actions." A long pause fell on the other side of the line. Eggers grinned, hoping he had at least pinched the colonel's sensitivities.

"Yes, the swine started the problem." Glaesche sounded irritated. "Unfortunately, the Geneva convention states the prisoners must have fresh air . . . it simply doesn't say how much."

"Yes."

"Well, it makes no difference. The matter was argued in Berlin before the *Oberkommando der Wehrmacht*, and they were reluctantly forced to reinstate the walk." Glaesche gave a short, embarrassed cough. "Personally, I believe that side of the castle should be considered a luxury and not available to the prisoners unless their behavior is exemplary. My predecessor completely agreed with me."

"Yes."

"One other matter. The high command noted your discovery of their tunneling attempt. They are awarding you and Sergeant-Major Heinz Gephard a two-week leave of absence to be taken at your leisure."

Reinhold broke into a broad grin, but he tried to keep his voice from sounding jubilant. "Thank you, sir."

"Don't thank me . . . thank them." Glaesche hung up.

Eggers exploded in laughter. "We've beaten that mongrel at his own game." The major laughed again and picked up the phone. "Send Sergeant-Major Gephard in."

Reinhold sat down at his desk, but his snickering quickly faded. He had been thinking about his last conversation with Otto Schadlich concerning the reported outrages. The stories of German atrocities in Poland only confirmed what he had heard at other times, and the stories troubled him deeply. He had grown up in the Roman Catholic church and had always been faithful. He expected others to do the same.

Sure, Reinhold thought. *Unbending and demanding military discipline is a normal part of German life. Everyone is expected to follow the superior officer's commands to the letter of the order. I've done so even when I didn't agree. I do so with Glaesche even though I deeply detest the man. Nothing about these situations fits my expectations of what German Christians should do in a war.*

The door opened and Gephard walked in. "You called, sir?"

Eggers smiled. "Sergeant-Major, your diligence in checking the clock tower has paid significant dividends. The high command is giving you a two-week leave of absence."

Heinz Gephard beamed. "Thank you very much."

Reinhold leaned back in his chair. "Every now and then, persistence has its own reward. I trust everything is going well with the prisoners." He opened a metal cigarette case. "Care for a smoke?"

"Thank you, Major." Heinz lit the cigarette. "We had one experience last night I think you'd find amusing. I believe the prisoners call the practice 'goon-baiting.'" Gephard kept smiling. "It's intended to annoy us."

"Yes, I'm well aware of their attempts to harass us with these non-sense vexations. Sit down and relax, Heinz."

Gephard stretched out his long legs in a completely relaxed posture. "We had a surprise nighttime roll call last night to make sure the men were not planning another escapade under the cover of darkness."

"Good!" Eggers said. "We have to surprise them more than occasionally."

Gephard tapped his cigarette on the ashtray and grinned. "Our raid turned into a mutual surprise."

"Oh?"

"We normally have the men stand by their beds in their pajamas until we have completed the head count, but this surprise *Appell* gave us a little something to remember." Gephard blew a puff of smoke into the air. "We rushed into the dormitory only to find all the prisoners standing by their beds stark naked."

"*Naked?*"

Gephard laughed. "The entire raid was so funny and unexpected our soldiers even started laughing. We made the head count as quick as we could and left snickering. Quite a show!"

"We have an interesting collection of eccentrics floating around this castle. I'm sure we haven't begun to see the end of what they will come up with!"

"We'll be on top of it," Gephard assured the major.

Really, Eggers thought to himself. *Don't you realize that the Allied soldiers knew you were coming or they couldn't have played their little joke on you.*

"We are truly an excellent crew," Gephard continued. "You can count on us."

"Yes," Eggers said with the same inflection he had used when talking to Colonel Glaesche.

Irving stumbled into the dormitory and fell on his straw mattress. Relief from lying on the rock floor felt so consoling he nearly passed out in sleep. Tony stretched out on the bed, letting his aching muscles shag.

"You okay?"

Tony opened his eyes. Stooge Wardle stood above him.

"Am I okay?" Tony blinked his eyes several times. "Let's simply say that I'm still alive, and that counts for something."

"We thought about you in that isolation cell last night," Wardle said. "Had to be rough in this cold weather."

"Certainly was." Tony sat up on the edge of the bed. "That hole smelled worse than any place I've ever been."

"I suppose you got approval from the toasting committee before you tried that escape?" Stooge asked.

Tony clenched his eyes shut. "You know that I didn't."

"I thought we had a little talk about the application process and approval before anyone tried a jailbreak."

"Yes." Tony sighed. "I broke the rules, but the opportunity came up so quickly that I wouldn't have had a chance to . . ."

"We understand," Wardle said, "but you got caught about as fast. I imagine the entire escape lasted less than ten minutes."

"I'm sorry."

"We're not here to impede any escape process," Wardle explained. "The fact is you didn't have any maps, direction, or even money beyond what Lawton gave you. We would have helped."

"I understand," Tony apologized. "Believe me. It won't happen like that one did again."

"You ready to settle down now and be a good boy?" Stooge asked.

"Not on your life!" Tony shook his fist. "In fact, I've got a proposal to take before your escape committee."

"That's called the *toasting committee*," Wardle corrected him.

"Whatever. I want to start a tunnel out of this place."

Stooge held up his hand. "Hang on. According to my count we've had more than two hundred prisoners attempt about a hundred such escapes, and most of their tunnels didn't even get close to the edge of the castle. You're talking a tough task."

"Look." Tony jabbed at the air with his finger. "I've been in that icebox over there and . . ."

"And next time they'll keep you in that freezer for a month," Stooge warned. "How'd you like another three weeks in there?"

"I'm not planning on getting caught the next time."

"I'll have to give you credit, Irving. Most of the time after prisoners have paid their dues in the slammer, they're not too interested in going back for awhile."

"Like I said, I'm not planning on anymore time behind those walls."

Stooge scooted closer. "Okay. We have a meeting planned for tonight after the last *Appell* of the day."

"Tonight?"

"When the roll call is over, we'll come back up here, and then I'll lead you to the place where the rest of the committee meets. Agreed?"

"Sure."

Wardle's countenance changed. "But you'll need to have a specific, concrete plan," he said sternly. "Understood?"

"Sure."

Tony watched Wardle walk away. The truth was he didn't have any plan. He had to come up with decisive directions quickly or look like a fool. He fell back on the pillow and stared at the ceiling. What felt like the gentleness of the bed proved even more seductive than he thought. Tony didn't even feel himself drop into deep sleep.

"Irving! Wake up!"

Tony bolted straight up in bed. For a moment he had no idea where he was.

"Hey." The prisoner shook his arm. "You're going to miss supper."

Even though the words sounded distant, *supper* threw all the "on" switches in his head. Mechanically, Tony's feet hit the floor, and he started walking before he was completely awake.

"You don't want to miss even the watery soup."

"No sirree," Tony answered. "Thanks for waking me up."

Falling in with the rest of the Englishmen, Irving plodded back across the courtyard and into the mess hall. As had been predicted, the supper wasn't of much substance but considerably more than the Nazis had put under the isolation cell door.

"Smells so good." Tony whiffed the weak vegetable soup. "I want it to go down slow and easy."

"It'll be easy enough," Lieutenant Bill Fowler said. "The stuff is just like swallowing water."

Tony started eating. Unfortunately, he devoured the entire bowl faster than he intended. "Didn't last long," he said more to himself and licked his lips.

Captain Lulu Lawton sat across the table, and Tony could feel the pilot watching him. "You don't look so good tonight." He pushed a piece of black bread toward Tony. "Eat some of mine. You need a little extra 'pick-me-up.'"

"Oh, Lawton, I can't." Tony started to push the bread back.

"Yeah, you can." The captain put his hand down on the table. "Eat it."

Tony stared at the bread for a minute. "Thank you," he finally said. "I can't tell you how much I appreciate this."

The Royal Air Force captain got up quickly and walked away as if he didn't want to watch Tony eat. In the clatter of the dining hall, Tony sat thinking about the generosity he'd just experienced and quietly nibbling on the bread. Tony was deeply moved by the depth of the kindness he had just seen. Although it was only one piece of bread, it was a significant amount of food in this concentration camp. He certainly owed Lawton a return gift of gratitude for the bread as well as the twenty *Reichsmarks* Lawton had given him earlier.

The food gave Tony more energy than he'd had since they threw him into isolation. His stomach felt warm, and the nap had taken the edge off of his fatigue. He walked out of the mess hall and strolled over to the prisoners' canteen. The Germans had taken the twenty *Reichsmarks* out of his pocket before they threw him in the tank, so he didn't have any money to pay Lawton back or to spend, but the stroll still felt good.

Inside the canteen Tony walked past an old German sergeant sitting opposite the counter and looked at some of the goods behind the glass counter. Candy, cigarettes, toothpaste, and personal items lined the shelves. At that moment, he noticed something that had not caught his eye before. Out in plain sight in the middle of the floor lay a manhole cover!

The possibility of a previously constructed hole down into the bowels of the castle almost took his breath away. This was exactly what he'd been looking for! Tony wandered nonchalantly over to the cover and confirmed it was slightly larger than the size of his body. All he had to do was get the lid off and drop inside. He turned back and looked again at the sergeant, who wasn't paying any attention to him.

Tony could see many places around the canteen where a prisoner could hide after the door was locked. All that he needed was a duplicate key to open the cover, and he'd be gone in a flash. Probably the locking mechanism was simple, and it wouldn't take much to unlock it. Tony remembered hearing that Damiaem Van Doorninck had been a master locksmith. He needed to talk to the obstinate Dutchman anyway. The pieces of a plan tumbled into place.

For several minutes Tony stood at the front of the canteen and thought about what he'd discovered. The manhole cover was so obvious it was a wonder no one had ever thought about it before. He now knew *exactly* what he would tell the escape committee that evening.

FIFTEEN

Stooge Wardle listened attentively. Tony Irving carefully laid out his plan for getting inside the manhole in the middle of the canteen. Wardle liked this ambitious young Texan with the daring the English always associated with the American Wild West. Tony sounded confident, but he lacked some of the maturity needed to turn his determination into a bona fide escape. Then, again, American ingenuity might pull off such an audacious plan. Who knew? At least the idea captivated the international group of prisoners.

"Gentlemen, I am prepared to begin at once." Irving finished, brimming with all the confidence in the world that he'd pulled off the presentation successfully.

"The International Escape Committee appreciates your careful thoughts," the French escape officer said slowly. "We want to encourage your efforts, but we must give the entire matter our most considered analysis."

Irving frowned. "Of course," he answered perfunctorily.

"In one week we will be back in touch with you through your escape officer, Donald Wardle," the Frenchman said.

"*One week?*" Irving's eyebrows raised.

"That is our normal custom," the French officer said firmly.

Wardle watched Irving's face fall. He hoped Tony wouldn't make some wild, defensive statement that could get him in trouble with the committee.

"One week . . . ," Irving mused with a fallen sound in his voice.

"Do you have any problem with Irving contacting Captain Van Doorninck about the possibility of making a key to unlock the manhole cover while we are contemplating his request?" Wardle asked. "Helps a prisoner save time if they check out the details."

"*Save time?*" The French officer laughed. "By all means. We have so little time around this camp." The other men laughed.

Tony brightened and saluted. "I'll have Van Doorninck take a look."

"Be sure you tell him that this matter is still under consideration and no positive answer has been given to the request yet."

"Of course." Tony smiled. "I *wouldn't think* of doing something on my own."

"Certainly nothing like being hauled out of the castle inside a mattress," Wardle said.

Irving's face turned slightly pink.

"Amusing," the Frenchman said. "I know you are ready to start work, but please appreciate the price we pay to be on this committee. You should know that any officer who sits on the Escape Committee will never try to escape." He looked at Wardle and nodded resolutely. "We'll all be here to the very end . . . including Donald Wardle."

"That's right, Tony," Stooge said. "We give up our right to escape when we sit here. Each of these men asks nothing of you that they aren't ready to pay for themselves."

"I see," Tony said slowly. He looked at the floor for a moment. "I appreciate the cost."

"Good!" The Frenchman looked around at the other committee members. "We will begin our deliberations at once. You may leave now."

Wardle watched Tony slip away with less enthusiasm than he had come in with. He needed to understand it wasn't some Halloween trick they were playing on the Germans. Escape had become a deadly serious business.

For a couple of days Tony said nothing to anyone about his proposed escape plan. Several times a day he walked through the canteen, surveying the manhole cover out of the corner of his eye. The drain had to lead somewhere inside the castle's sewer system and should then wind out of the facilities. The only issue was getting into the canteen unnoticed with a key to open the iron cover.

For the first time Tony stopped in his assessment of the plan and let himself think about the one issue he had steadfastly avoided facing: The hole was small and he was claustrophobic.

Tony could barely allow himself any reflection on the problem he had struggled with since childhood. The truth was that the reason he often appeared brave and was so erratic when facing danger was an attempt to force this singular fear out of his life. He didn't even want to think about the inevitable anxiety and apprehension that bubbled up within him when he felt narrowly confined. The truth was that he had no control over his problem.

"I'll overcome it this time," Tony mumbled to himself. He pushed the bleak thoughts away and went back to his ruminations over the escape plan. "I have to!" he said under his breath.

On the third day, Tony noticed Damiaem Van Doorninck standing out in the courtyard. His unusual height, red hair, and long, handlebar mustache gave him the distinguished air of a Dutch diplomat making a survey of the adequacy of the activities. Tony approached the man casually as if he only happened to be standing where Irving was walking.

"How's it going?"

Damiaem looked up with his deep-set eyes casting a foreboding shadow over the conversation. "Why?"

"I thought we might have a little religious discussion." Tony stopped, feeling like he had made an awkward start.

"Are you crazy?" Van Doorninck's voice was filled with disgust.

"No. I was watching you in that solitary confinement cell and thought about how important it was for God to be with you."

"God?" Van Doorninck's eyes narrowed and his faced reddened. "Listen, you American cowboy! God wasn't with me in that hole. I made it by myself. Do you understand me? I'm not interested in any discussions about God! Not today, tomorrow, or ever." He crossed his arms over his chest and stared defiantly at Irving.

"Okay, I won't pursue that topic," Tony said nervously.

"Don't!"

"Well, let me try something else. Maybe I can make your day better."

Damiaem blinked several times. "What?" he finally said.

"Want to get out of here?"

"You *are* crazy!" The Dutchman abruptly laughed with a coarse guffaw that resounded across the courtyard.

"No." Tony's countenance shifted into the same emotionless stare the Dutchman's formerly had. "Not at all."

"What do you have in mind?" Van Doorninck looked straight into Irving's eyes.

"If you can make a key to open a manhole cover, I think I have found a way out of this pen."

The Dutchman's expression didn't change. "*Really.*"

"Really. I also need you to unlock the front door of the canteen or at least show me how to do so at night."

"Going after a little extra candy?"

"No." Tony shook his head slowly. "There's a manhole cover right in the center of the store. It has to lead out of this castle."

Van Doorninck rubbed his chin slowly. "Interesting."

"You can see it for yourself." Tony gestured over his shoulder toward the canteen. "It's in the very center in front of the counters."

Damiaem nodded. "I'll be back." He walked straight toward the front door of the canteen.

Irving watched the Dutchman disappear inside. Tony stood motionless, waiting and watching the front of the shop. He fully realized he had made the wrong approach in talking about God. He'd have to think further about how to talk with Van Doorninck on this problem.

After a couple of minutes, Van Doorninck came out again. He stood outside for a few moments and then started walking the long way around the courtyard. After a complete turn around the area, he ended up in front of Tony.

"You are absolutely right, old boy." Van Doorninck sounded exactly like an Englishman. "No one's noticed the most obvious exit in this entire place."

"I'm ready to give it a try if I can unlock the cover."

"The toasting committee knows about this?"

Tony nodded. "Yes, but they haven't given me permission yet. I believe they will say yes quickly."

Van Doorninck twirled the end of his long mustache in his fingers. "Most interesting." For a moment, he dug at the corner of a brick paver with the toe of his shoe. "Yes, I can make a key to open that manhole cover. Actually, they are rather simple and don't take much. The front door lock will take longer."

"Good. Good. You're sure we can get inside?"

"*We?*" Van Doorninck smiled. "You've gone from a one-man show here to a full cast. I suppose '*we*' includes me?"

"Listen." Tony started jabbing with his finger. "I'd be delighted to spring you out of this hoosegow. You're more than welcome to take the ride with me."

Van Doorninck lowered his bushy eyebrows. "Aren't you the American who just got out of solitary confinement?"

"Yeah," Tony groused.

"Remember that winter is coming and you could end up in that icebox long enough to turn into a frozen hunk of meat."

Tony bristled. "I ain't afraid. We're tough where I come from."

Damiaem narrowed one eye and studied Tony's face. The long, silent probing look made Tony nervous.

"Something wrong?" Tony asked.

"No," Van Doorninck said slowly. "No, I don't think so. Just don't bring up anymore of that God talk with me. While you wait for the toasting committee to give you an answer, I'll do a little work on those locks. I think you're on to something that might make an important difference either now or later."

"Excellent!" Tony shoved his hand forward to shake hands with his new cohort.

Van Doorninck didn't move. "Put your hand down," he said unemotionally but with an unmistakable firmness. "They may be watching us from somewhere in one of those windows at this very moment."

Tony dropped his hand instantly.

"Got to be careful," the Dutchman said. "These walls may not have ears, but they certainly have eyes."

CHAPTER

SIXTEEN

Tony Irving sat on top of his bed's blue-and-white mattress cover, thinking about all he'd seen in the last few days and wondering how Van Doorninck's investigation of the lock problem might be going. It was difficult for him to wait and sit still while some strange committee of foreigners thought about an attempt that really put only him at risk. The delay made Tony all the more irritable.

"How's it going, mate?"

Tony looked up. Wearing his usual black-rimmed glasses, Bill Fowler stood in front of him.

"Just sitting here thinking," Tony said.

"You look a little on the down side."

"Let me ask you a question, Bill. We came in here together, and I know you faced great danger in trying to escape last time. You're what I would call a brave man."

"Brave man? Ah, come on, Tony. We all do only what we have to do."

"I don't think so. I watched other men who had the chance to escape not do one cryin' thing when the opportunity came to get out. It takes guts to run when the occasion comes. So, I want you to tell me what bravery is. Is it fearlessly running across a battlefield when bullets are flying everywhere? Is it not having fear when you have to fight? Is it pushing your fears aside when you think you can't?"

"Bravery?" Fowler shrugged. "I don't know. Listen, my knees were knocking like a simmering gong out there on the battlefield. Every time those cannons went off, it scared the bejabbers out of me. I wanted to run and disappear in a bottomless ditch. No, I'm not a brave man."

"Yes, you are!" Tony insisted. "Now tell me what you think bravery is. Give me your definition."

Fowler scratched his head and stared at the floor. "Look, Tony. I don't think about the problem in those terms. The truth is that I want to be a free man. Escaping from a concentration camp and having the freedom God gave me is what counts. I'm willing to do what it takes to obtain that goal. That objective's more important than being fearless. The truth is that I'm afraid all the time when I'm on the run."

"Very interesting," Tony said. "You've helped me. Helped me a lot."

"Okay, let's go back to where we started this conversation. Why are you looking on the down side?"

Tony shrugged. "I'm not good at doing nothing. I want to get my shoes running and move out of this place."

"So they tell me." Fowler sat down on the end of the bed. "Van Doorninck's been up here asking questions about you. He wants to make sure you're not a nut or a fanatic."

"Oh, *really!*"

"Yeah, he wanted to make sure you were on the up and up."

"Well, bless his little Dutch heart."

"Wardle verified you are trustworthy. The Dutchman seems to think that you and he might be on to a route out of here."

"Yeah, and it turns out *Damiaem's the one doing the talking,* huh?"

"Not really. I simply overheard his conversation with Wardle. It was more of an accident than anything else, but I got the entire escape idea. Count me in if you need another man to go down that manhole."

"That's the spirit, old man." Tony slapped him on the shoulder. "We'll probably need all the help we can get."

Fowler nodded. "Good. I'm going to let the Dutch captain know I'm in on this scheme."

"Let him know I checked *him* out."

Fowler grinned. "I will." He got up and walked out the door.

Irving sat against the end of the bed and stared out the window. Maybe Fowler had given him the encouragement he needed. Bravery wasn't being fearless, but having a strong enough desire to push one's natural fears aside in trying to obtain an important goal. He wanted out of this castle. In fact, Tony wanted out of any prison they tried to keep him in. Maybe that desire would be enough to push his claustrophobic fear aside.

Thanksgiving would soon be coming, but they certainly wouldn't celebrate the holiday in Germany or in this prison camp. No turkey this year. He looked out the window over the trees and down toward the village of Colditz. Somewhere out there a million miles away, Rikki Beck was probably sound asleep in her nice, warm, secure bedroom in Dallas. He wondered if she had received any of his letters. Maybe she had . . . probably she hadn't. Tony knew Rikki would have at the least received a letter from the army saying he was missing in action. He could see tears welling up in her eyes when she read the letter; he knew she'd think the worst.

Rikki had a tender heart that had drawn him to her early on. He closed his eyes and tried to bring her face into clear focus. Tony could almost smell that lovely scent she always carried with her. He started remembering how much she cared about him and the miles blurred together. Tony recalled the evening he'd told Rikki he'd be leaving for Europe.

"Want some more potato chips?" Tony pushed the plastic basket across the table. The Veasey Drug had always been one of Dallas's best hamburger and malt shops, and the couple ate there once a week. "I can ask the waitress to bring us some more."

Rikki shook her head. "No, I'm fine." She laid her fork down and brought her hands up under her chin. "Tony, you look so handsome in that army uniform . . . almost like a movie actor making a picture with John Wayne or Gregory Peck. I bet everybody in here is jealous of me."

Tony felt himself blush. "Aw, come on!" He looked nervously around the malt shop, hoping someone else was wearing a uniform. He didn't see a soul in military dress. Tony craved her every word, but at the same time flattery made him squirm. "I'm just another soldier."

"Oh, no you're not!" Rikki shook her head and the brown hair bounced off her shoulders. "You're the man I'm going to marry someday. In fact, I'm ready right now!"

Tony grinned. *"All right!"*

"I'm serious, hon. I didn't know it was possible to love anyone as much as I love you." Rikki leaned forward. Her eyes twinkled like they always did when she felt particularly romantic. "Maybe we ought to run off and let a justice of the peace say the magic words."

"Think so?" Tony kept grinning. "How about tonight?"

Rikki laughed. "I guess my mom would shoot me if we did. She's got her mind set on one of those big 'walk-down-the-center-aisle' kind of weddings with the flower girls and all."

"I'm sure she does." He winked. "And that's what you want, too."

"Sort of, but I want most to simply be with you."

The phrase "be with you" set off a rumbling in his mind. Tony had avoided telling her the full truth, but there wouldn't be any better time than right now. He took a deep breath. It was now or never.

"Honestly, Tony. The only thing that counts with me is being with you. I'll go wherever they send you."

Tony bit his lip. "Rikki . . . you can't."

"I don't understand."

Tony laid his fork down and pushed the plate back. "You see . . ." He stopped and looked down at the tabletop for a moment. "Rikki, I'm being sent to the war in Europe."

Rikki had started to say something, but the words never came out. Her mouth hung slightly open. Her face twisted. "W-w-hat?"

"I wanted to tell you earlier, but I simply couldn't bring myself to do it." Tony ran his hands nervously through his hair. "Yeah, headquarters is going to ship me off rather quickly and . . ."

"No!" She put her hand to her mouth. "No, you don't mean it."

Tony nodded. "I'm afraid so. The army thinks I've got special ability to figure out how to use a bazooka accurately and shoot for the greatest effect. They want me to instruct the British on how to use that weapon. Of course, the whole assignment is top secret. You're the only person who can know about what I'm doing. Understand what I mean?" He gestured feebly. "You see if . . ."

Rikki reached up and took his hand. "When . . . when are you leaving? What day?"

Tony looked down at the table. He didn't want to say the words, but there wasn't any alternative. This was the moment he had been dreading for two weeks. "In three days."

Rikki caught her breath. Tears formed in the corner of her eyes, and she dropped back against the seat. "Three days!" Her voice faded away.

Tony nodded his head and didn't say anything. He swallowed hard and felt a knot form in his throat.

Rikki put her hands on her forehead and started slowly rubbing her brow. "Three days," she repeated. "Good Lord!"

"I'm so sorry. I didn't have any idea this would happen. At the camp I loved shooting that steel thing and simply got the hang of hitting everything I shot at. Before I knew what happened, the officers were talking about using me as an instructor. I got promoted fast. You know . . . one thing led to another and before long I got the overseas assignment."

Rikki nodded her head. "I knew this would come sometime . . . someday, I guess . . . but I put off facing the fact it would come . . . so soon."

"I'm sure I won't have any problems." Tony knew he was lying, but it seemed the only thing he could say. "I'll serve my time, and then I'll be back quickly."

Rikki studied his eyes as if trying to read some meaning, find some direction, discover a purpose beyond his words. She looked more perplexed and hurt than anything else.

"I'm so, so sorry," Tony said.

Rikki reached across the table and squeezed his hand. "I am, too, but we can't do anything about it. When you joined the military, it became an inevitability." She started crying.

Tony pushed the plates aside and leaned over the table, kissing her more passionately than he had ever done in his life. Rikki stopped crying and kissed him back with the same fervor. He finally slipped back across the table and sat down. Only then did he notice everyone in the place was watching them.

"Let's get out of here," Rikki said. "We need to be alone."

"Yeah," Tony answered. "I'll pay the ticket." He got up, still noticing that most of the people in the cafe were eyeing them. He tried not to notice.

Rikki held his hand as tightly as anyone ever had when they walked out of the malt shop. He didn't want to leave her . . . ever . . . but there was no alternative.

"Hey, Tony!"

Irving looked up from his bed. Damiaem Van Doorninck walked into the room. "Been talking to Fowler. He says he's ready to help us."

Tony nodded his head. "He overheard you talking with Stooge. Bill's a good man and keeps his mouth shut."

"Excellent." Van Doorninck ignored the jab. "I've been over in the canteen, studying the manhole cover lock." He held up a piece of metal twisted on the end. "I'm not sure, but I believe this key will open it."

Tony studied the key. "Looks rather simple."

"Manhole covers are. You only need to turn a single latch. I think this will work. As soon as you get the approval of the toasting committee, we'll be on our way."

"What about the front door lock? I have to get into the canteen at night."

Van Doorninck nodded. "I believe the addition of Fowler to our little team is all I need to wrap this up."

CHAPTER

SEVENTEEN

Snow had begun to fall, and a gentle breeze blew the white flakes in a swirl of disarray around the inner courtyard. November had become a harder month of winter than usual, forcing the prisoners to spend more time indoors. New prisoners were arriving with some frequency, and the concentration camp had settled into a fairly predictable groove. With no major attempts at escape being tried for several weeks, life at Colditz appeared to be degenerating into nothing but a boring routine.

Tony Irving stood next to the entrance of the chapel, watching across the courtyard as the old German sergeant tried to unlock the camp canteen. The two men next to Irving kept the collars on their coats turned up to protect their necks from the cold wind.

"Okay," Damiaem Van Doorninck said. "As soon as the guard opens the canteen's front door, the three of us go charging over there and make sure we are the first people inside. Don't give the old geezer time to get his wits together."

"We've got to get him addled enough that he's not paying close attention," Bill Fowler added, pushing his black horn-rimmed glasses firmly against his face.

"Look!" Tony pointed. "The door's unlocked."

"Let's move." Van Doorninck took a long stride and led the way.

The three prisoners walked into the canteen before the elderly German soldier had even crossed the room. He turned and stared. His long, sagging white mustache hung over his upper lip, and the military uniform dropped off his shoulders. His hand shook slightly.

"Top of the morning to you." Fowler saluted the German. "I trust you are feeling well this morning."

The old man turned around slowly. "Vat?"

"Hey, it's another wonderful November day," Fowler said. "The snow makes it feel like Christmas is coming."

The sergeant squinted outside the window for a moment. "It's snowing . . ." He blinked several times.

Tony walked over to the glass display case and looked inside at the candy. Van Doorninck stood nonchalantly, looking around the room with an indifferent air.

"Thought you Krauts always liked the snow."

The German blinked several more times as if he didn't quite understand what Fowler meant.

"I say," Tony attempted his poor English accent. "I don't see any Camel cigarettes in here."

The sergeant opened a little drawer and dropped his keys inside a small table he usually sat behind. "Krauts?" he mumbled and closed the drawer.

"No," Tony answered. "Camels. Got any *Camel* cigarettes?"

"Kraut? Ca-a-mels?" The old man scratched his head.

Fowler pointed at Irving. "He wants to buy some Camels."

The German sergeant shuffled across the room and stared into the glass case. "Ve got cigarettes." He pointed.

Irving shook his head. "The brand, the B-R-A-N-D I'm looking for is Camels. C-A-M-E-L-S. Maybe you've got some stored in back."

The old man shook his head. "Don't know. Let me look." He dragged around to the back of the counter and disappeared behind a large door. "*Camels? Kreiz!*"

Instantly Van Doorninck stepped into place, blocking the German's view from the storage room door. Bill Fowler quickly slid the little drawer open and grabbed the key ring. From his pocket he pulled out a moist piece of soap and pressed the front door key into the bar of soap. For a moment he wiggled the key around until the impression was definite.

"Don't find nothin'," the sergeant said from the back room.

Fowler pulled the key out and made a quick swipe on his coat before dropping the key back into the drawer. Just as he closed the drawer, the sergeant came into the room.

"No Camels," he said.

Without turning around, Irving pointed to a bottom shelf. "Okay, give me one of those packs."

"*Ya.*" The old man bent over and pulled out a pack. "You got the *lagergeld?*" He held the cigarettes back until he saw the money.

"Sure." Tony started digging through his pockets, taking forever to find the money. "I know I have several *lagergelds* in here somewhere."

"You git nothing until I see the *lagergeld.*" The German's eyes narrowed and he looked suspiciously at Irving.

"Aw! Here it is." Tony pushed the money across the top of the counter. "We're fine."

The sergeant still held the cigarettes back, making sure the money was authentic.

"You act like you don't trust us," Tony said.

"Harrumph!" Only after the old man had put the money in a container behind the merchandise case did he hand the cigarettes to Tony.

Fowler and Van Doorninck were standing by the door with their hands in their coat pockets. "We're finished," Fowler said and nodded slightly at Tony.

"Well, I hope you have a good day." Tony saluted the German again. "Trust all goes well."

The sergeant kept squinting at the men with a distrustful look in his eye. *"Auf wiedersehen sagen,"* he growled.

"See you around." Tony walked across the room and put his arms across the backs of the two men. "Let's go outside and enjoy the winter weather."

"Certainly," Van Doorninck said with his usual austere voice of Dutch propriety. The door slammed behind them.

The cold November wind hit the three men in the face, and snowflakes bounced off their coats. "That was close," Fowler said. "If grandpa hadn't been older than dirt, he'd caught me with my hand in the drawer. Let's get back upstairs as quick as we can. I don't want anything to happen to this soap."

"You got the imprint?" Tony asked.

"I think so, but I won't know until we take a closer look."

Van Doorninck looked over his shoulder. The German stood in the window watching them talk outside.

"The Kraut's over there watching us," Damiaem said. "He has that look on his face like we've done something bad, but he can't figure out what it is."

"Nothing like keeping the Germans on their toes," Fowler said. "Let's get out of here." The men hurried toward the dormitory.

The threesome bounded up the stairs and into the bedroom. They dropped onto Irving's bed.

"Let's see!" Tony said.

Bill Fowler carefully pulled the bar of soap out of his pocket. He adjusted his glasses and stared at the imprint. "Hey! Looks good."

Van Doorninck bent over. "Yes, you have done well. Bill, I think I can make a key out of this." He traced around the edges with his fingers. "There's enough depth to get a feel for the thickness of the key. Excellent."

"*Yes!*" Irving pounded his fist with his palm. "We're in!"

"At the least, I think we've laid the next stone on our path."

"I'll get to work immediately," Damiaem said. "I have a piece of a bedstead that will do just fine."

A couple of hours passed while the three men diligently worked on turning a rusted old piece of metal into a key. Van Doorninck used several pieces of metal, filing against the longer end and attempting to notch the key at the right points. Only after three hours of rubbing was he able to use a piece of a file he kept hidden as one of his treasures.

"Where'd you get the file?" Irving asked.

"Stole it from a German plumber," Damiaem said. "The Nazis were working in here one day and the plumber dropped it on the ground. When he turned around, I grabbed it and walked away."

"You're almost there," Fowler observed. "Think the metal is strong enough on the other key for the manhole cover?"

"That's the big question," Van Doorninck said. He held the key to the front door up to the sunlight and examined it carefully. "Those drain covers don't have to be very exact. The locks aren't really meant to do more than to keep the covers in place." He turned the lock slowly. "Yes, I think the key will fit the front door."

"And it's strong enough?" Fowler repeated. "The manhole cover key?"

"Probably," the Dutchman drawled, "unless the lock has rusted."

"*Rusted?*" Irving's voice squeaked.

Van Doorninck nodded his head. "Unfortunately, they often rust shut."

EIGHTEEN

Night had fallen and the last *Appell* of the day had been taken. Resolutely, the prisoners filed back into the dormitory for the night and silence fell over Colditz Castle. Shortly after eleven o'clock three men slipped out of bed and started down the stairs.

"The guards won't be expecting any action this early at night," Bill Fowler said. "Wardle told me that our only significant problem is the machine gunner on the roof between the kitchen and the canteen. We've got to crawl approximately a hundred feet along the wall, and then after that he won't be able to see us."

"Obviously, total silence is the name of the game," Van Doorninck said. "Not a sound."

"I'm ready," Tony Irving assured the men, "and I promise to be as quiet as the moon rising over South Texas."

Fowler beckoned and the men followed him out into the courtyard. The three men slipped down the side of the dormitory wall, pressing against the stone wall as tightly as possible and moving south. Far above, they could see the outline of a machine gun, but it didn't look like anyone was sitting behind it. Still they didn't take any chances and moved silently. As soon as they reached the front door of the canteen, Van Doorninck started working on opening the lock. After several attempts, the tumblers clicked.

Motioning with his fingers in front of his face, the Dutch captain nodded and slowly turned the doorknob. In seconds, the three men scurried inside. Van Doorninck locked the door again.

"Hey, that was easier than I thought!" Irving shook his fist in the air. "Okay!"

"Easy nothing!" Damiaem spit. "You were lucky the Nazi up there on the roof was apparently taking it easy, or they might have killed us on the spot."

"He's right," Fowler whispered. "We could have gotten hit as easy as knocking pigeons off a telephone line."

"Well, I'm ready to go," Tony said impulsively.

"If!" Damiaem held his long bony finger up in the air. "If . . . the lock on that manhole cover can be turned."

"Oh, yes." Irving sighed. "Let's pray the thing still works."

The Dutchman walked to the middle of the room and knelt down over the metal manhole cover. He pulled out of his pocket the long piece of a worn bedstead that now looked like a strange key. "Here goes nothing," he said and knelt down over the drain cover. Slowly, he stuck the key into the lock and started trying to turn it.

"It's moving!" Irving exclaimed too loudly.

"Shut up!" Fowler warned. "A sentry could walk by."

"Ah!" Van Doorninck stood up and started pulling. "Here the cover comes."

"You've done it!" Tony whispered as loudly as he dared.

"Apparently our little project has worked so far." The Dutchman laid the cover to one side and looked at Tony. "You ready to crawl down into that dirty hole?"

"I guess."

"Here's your chance to make the big time, kid," Damiaem said to Tony. "As soon as you go down that hole, we'll slide the lid back nearly in place. Then we'll hide behind those sacks over there in case anyone comes by and shines a light in a window." He handed Tony a flashlight. "Be careful."

"I-I'll do my best," Tony said, uncharacteristically hesitant.

The Dutchman nodded back, and Tony started edging his way down inside the drain. "We'll be here when you come back up."

For a moment Tony had to stop and catch his breath. The hole felt more narrow than he had ever expected, and the stench was nauseating. He started breathing harder.

Taking a deep breath, Tony started lowering himself into the hole, but his heart had started to beat so hard and fast, he was almost afraid he'd crawl out of his skin. Several times Tony worried that the smell would make him vomit. He looked up at the faces of Fowler and Van Doorninck staring back at him. No matter what had been said negatively earlier, expectancy was in their eyes. If he even whimpered, they'd never forgive him. The lid slid shut over the hole's entrance.

Tony exhaled deeply and felt his feet edging down into the black hole. Before he completely disappeared into the darkness, Tony flipped on the flashlight and held it in his mouth. His teeth gritted against the cold metal, and for a moment he was afraid it might slip out of his mouth.

Tony couldn't tell how far it was to the bottom, but he kept inching down the hole. The cold, clammy pressure of the narrow space squeezed him like a vise biting into a lead pipe. Perspiration started forming on his forehead. The full meaning of imprisonment began wrenching at his gut. He could die in this hole and no one would ever hear of him again. While his past attempts at escape had been somewhat on the light-hearted side, this experience was packed with a terrible realization of death. Any trace of frivolity dried up like a North Texas drought in August, and there was no recourse but to inch his way to the bottom without stopping. Pressing his knees against the sides of the hole, Tony slowly descended into what felt like nothingness.

Tony's heart pounded so hard he felt out of breath and dizzy. "God help me," he kept muttering over and over under his breath. "Please keep my mind on track." Suddenly Tony no longer felt anything around or underneath his legs.

I've come to the bottom of the shaft. But how deep is it? A foot? Three feet? Tony swallowed hard. *Ten feet?*

The idea hadn't occurred to him earlier. Tony had assumed there would be a tunnel at the bottom, but what if there wasn't? He couldn't move his head, so the flashlight didn't throw any light on what was beneath him. If he flinched and didn't press on, Fowler and Van Doorninck would think him a coward.

For a few moments, Tony dangled his feet in the open space but felt nothing. He didn't have any other alternative but to keep on going or face total humiliation. Taking a big breath, he let go and went flying down into whatever was below him.

Tony crashed into the cement basin in a heap about five feet beneath where he had been. For a moment he lay on the concave pipe, trying to get his breath. He still felt the wooziness of claustrophobia, and his heart hadn't stopped the incessant pounding. Wiping the sweat from his forehead, Tony shined his flashlight around him. He had been right. The drain was large enough that it would easily allow a man to crawl down the length. He flashed his light behind him and could tell that other drains from the kitchens ran into this one. He looked up above him at the hole he'd dropped down to make sure he had a true sense of north and south, and then ahead where the drain ran in a straight line.

"That must be near the eastern edge of the castle," Tony said to himself and felt the rocks above his head. "The pipe has to run under the foundations. I've found the way out!"

Immediately Irving started hustling straight along the drain pipe. After thirty feet, he reasoned the foundations of the castle walls had to be directly above him. The drain surely led to an exit just in front of him. Tony shone his light straight ahead and stopped short. *The end of the tunnel was bricked shut.*

Tony stared, almost unable to comprehend the obvious. The Nazis had cemented the exit shut to prevent exactly what he was attempting to do. Apparently, the pipe's draining contents flowed down through cracks around the bottom of the bricks, but no humans were going out through this exit.

The only hope was possibly to tunnel vertically and hope to come up in the small grassy area at the back of the wall, but that probably would put escapees right in the face of the *Kommandantur*, where the colonel stayed when he was on the grounds. In addition, they would have to go in and out of the canteen endlessly to dig such a hole. Sooner or later someone would catch them. As much as he hated to admit it, the bottom line on this project was clear. Retreat was unavoidable. No one was going to escape through this drain system.

Tony plopped down on the cement and wanted to cry. An escape had seemed so right, so possible, and now he had no choice but to turn around and get out of there.

Hurrying back through the drain, Tony had to stop and close his eyes as the walls started pressing in on him again. He knew the phobia was all in his head, but pushing the emotion back was the most difficult thing he had ever tried. His heart pounded, making him gasp for air. Tony's hands shook as he stumbled forward.

Getting back up the vertical drain pipe proved to be much, much harder than coming down. Tony felt the rocks rubbing raw on the skin on his elbows and his knees ached. He pressed against the wall with all of his might because what he didn't want to happen was to slip and fall back down the long chute. Tony was sure he didn't ever want such an experience again in his life.

"I'm back," Irving whispered loudly at the bottom of the manhole. "Please move the cover."

Tony didn't even hear their footsteps or the cover move. He simply saw a small light and felt a draft of fresh air. "Thank God," he moaned.

"Let us help you out." Bill Fowler stuck his hand in the hole.

"Get a tight hold," Tony answered. "I don't want to fall back down this toilet drain again."

The two men pulled Irving up slowly and carefully. He rolled over on the floor, struggling to catch his breath. His body ached.

"You smell like an outhouse," Fowler said.

Tony pushed himself up into a sitting position and shook his head. "I'm sorry, guys. My plan failed."

NINETEEN

After leaving the canteen exactly as they had found it, Damiaem Van Doorninck carefully locked the door behind Irving and Fowler and led the other two men back along the stucco-covered castle wall. He glanced up at the roof. This time he saw the outline of a man wearing a German metal helmet sitting behind a machine gun far above. He withdrew and grabbed Irving's arm.

Without saying anything, Van Doorninck pointed up and shook his finger. He put his mouth next to both men's ears and said the same thing. "If shouting or shooting starts, run for the dormitory."

Taking a deep breath, the Dutchman started edging his way along the base of the wall. Only once did he look up. The German's helmet hadn't moved an inch. Maybe the man was dozing. It was a good sign. He kept crawling.

Ten minutes later Bill Fowler brought up the rear, and the three men inched inside the dormitory.

"Whew!" Irving sighed. "That was close!"

Fowler kept peeking around the doorjamb. "Doesn't look like anyone saw us."

Van Doorninck sat down on the stairs and pulled his knees up against his chest. "You're sure the bricked end of the drainpipe can't be torn down?"

Irving nodded. "It would take a truck to pull that pile of bricks out of there, but even if we worked on it little by little, we'd have to be going in and out of that canteen every night for months. I think we'd eventually get caught."

The Dutchman nodded. "Yes, you could make that particular run a couple of times, but beyond that you'd be pushing your luck."

Irving shook his head and rubbed his forehead. "Afraid so. I failed."

"Don't feel so bad, Tony." Fowler slapped him on the back. "You tried! We'll do it again."

"I guess so." Irving started trudging up the steps. "It all seemed so easy yesterday."

The men creaked back up the stairs, but Damiaem stayed on the landing for a moment and looked out into the night. The moon hung in the sky like a glowing pearl pendant. Somewhere far out over those distant hills, his wife Hendrika was hopefully with her family up in the north near the town of Leeuwarden, close to the Frisian Islands. If it was cold in Colditz, it would be freezing on the North Sea.

Van Doorninck hadn't heard a word from her during the months he'd been in the Colditz prison camp. Probably she had no idea what had become of him. Maybe Hendrika thought the Nazis had killed him in the bombing of Rotterdam. Maybe, but probably not. Hendrika had always been a strong woman. Her name literally meant "she rules the house," and Hendrika did have a strong hand when it was needed. Her long-legged family were all Frieslanders and naturally tall people. They had been dairy farmers for a hundred generations, and every morning she was probably out milking the cows with the rest of the clan.

But Van Doorninck knew on a night like this one with the moon shining like it did at harvesttime, Hendrika would be awake, looking out the window and thinking about him. She had always been a faithful member of the Reformed Church and would drift off to sleep praying for his well-being. Well, he wasn't where he wanted to be, but he was in a secure dormitory with a warm bed. God had kept His hand on this poor Dutchman, and in the midst of this fierce war that was no small blessing.

What am I thinking? Damiaem thought. *I don't know that God has provided anything! The faith Hendrika and I grew up on was habit, the expectation of the people, our parent's faith. I haven't seen any justice in this place. Tonight had not appeared for our escape. Another example of the failure of God!*

Van Doorninck cursed under his breath and ground his fist into his palm. He could feel the anger churning inside but didn't dare let it explode. During his childhood, his parents had chastened him whenever he released an emotional outburst, so Damiaem no longer could express what rolled around in his soul. He sighed and slipped up the stairs. The night was moving on and he needed the sleep.

Tony Irving stripped off his smelly clothes and piled them at the foot of the bed. Some of the stench had faded, but Tony knew he still smelled like that awful sewer pipe. He probably wouldn't get a chance to take a shower for an entire day. With resignation, he crawled into the straw mattress bed and pulled the covers up. He kept shaking. From the second story, he could see completely across the inner courtyard. The delousing shed and the solitary confinement cells stood on the other side. Beyond them was the entry gate from the ramparts area. High above them in the sky a magnificent bright moon cast dark shadows in every direction.

The moon looked like it always did during those magical, romantic fall seasons in Texas when he had gone out driving with Rikki Beck down by Lake Lewisville on the northwest end of Dallas.

Tony hadn't heard from Rikki yet, and he knew that she'd be looking in the mailbox to see if any word had come about him. Of course, nothing would be in there yet, and she would shut the box sadly and wander inside, worried sick that he was ill or maybe even shot, lying somewhere in a dirty foxhole unattended.

Tony had almost been that bad off down in that dark, forbidding sewer hole. Even remembering the trip down that long, stinking pipe made his skin crawl. If there was a next time, he might collapse. Tony no longer felt like an invisible warrior. He had to push the memory away, and that was possible only by thinking about Rikki Beck.

Rikki would be sitting down at her parent's kitchen table and pouring herself a glass of milk. Her flowing brunette hair would settle around her shoulders and she would be as beautiful as ever. Her red, heart-shaped mouth would leave lipstick stains on the rim of the glass . . . he missed those lips.

From out of nowhere, fear abruptly exploded and Tony's heart started pounding wildly. He caught his breath and felt perspiration break out on his forehead. Doubling his fist, he cursed this phobia that kept haunting him.

"Got to stop," he mumbled to himself.

At 7:30 the next morning the German NCOs stomped through the dormitories demanding the men stand for the first *Appell* of the day. Once they were satisfied with the head count, the sentries retreated.

Stooge Wardle sauntered over to Tony. "Understand you didn't escape last night?"

"Ha-ha," Tony said with a flat tone in his voice.

"Hey, it happens. All of us have tried exit doors that wouldn't open. I'll let the toasting committee know that the exit down there is bricked up."

"I *really* thought it would work." Tony shook his head dismally.

"That's why Eggers and his boys bricked up the exit. If an escape route seems obvious, the Germans have probably already slammed the door and have guard dogs on the other side."

Irving shrugged. "I guess so."

"You've got to come up with an idea that's highly unusual, dark, and hidden. See what I mean?"

"Oh, I get the point. That manhole cover seemed to fit into the order of things. Can you give me an example of what you and that blasted approval committee would consider to be a truly unique idea?"

Wardle rubbed his chin. "Really unique, huh?" He grinned as usual. "Well . . . maybe I'll have to talk with some prisoners, but let me see what the boys might say. Watch for me after breakfast."

TWENTY

Tony Irving knew there wouldn't be much to eat for breakfast, so to pass the time he needed foot-dragging and plenty of slow sipping of the terrible coffee that tasted like boiled roots. Today everything tasted worse, and he hadn't thought that was possible.

Near the end of the meal, Lulu Lawton sat down beside Tony. The Royal Air Force captain swished the coffee around inside of his cup. "Not much worth drinking, I'd say, old man."

Tony didn't look up. "Sure isn't."

"The boys are saying you did a good job last night, trying to find a way out of this place."

Tony turned and looked at him in surprise. "Where'd you hear about that?"

"For better or worse, word travels fast." Lawton took a long sip.

"Thank you." Irving ran his hands nervously through his hair. "What are you hearing about how the war's going?"

"If you listen to the Nazis, you'd be convinced they are about to swallow all of Europe. They want us to think that London is burning down and the *Luftwaffe* is shooting the English out of the skies."

"What's the truth?"

Lawton smiled. "You have to tune in the BBC to get a . . . shall we say . . . more accurate picture."

"I suppose you'd have to have a radio of some sort hidden around this castle to get those programs."

Lawton nodded with a gleam in his eye. "Or you'd need to know how to construct a simple radio out of coils of wire, a crystal, something of that sort."

Irving smiled. "What might you hear on such a machine?"

"The picture the BBC paints is that the British are advancing in Africa and the Russians are stopping the Nazis, holding those green-uniformed swine in Stalingrad."

Tony blinked several times. "Is that right?"

"I think so. We have plenty of reason not to lose heart." Lawton patted Tony on the shoulder again. "Don't give up the fight."

"Lulu, I want to ask you a question. When I made that impromptu escape in a mattress, you gave me twenty *Reichsmarks*. Not only was that generous, you did a brave thing. What's your definition of bravery?"

"I don't know." The Air Force captain frowned. "Never thought much about it."

"Look, you fly around in the sky like a bird, but you also crashed. Zooming toward the ground would have to terrify you. It would anyone."

"Sure." Lawton shrugged. "I thought I was going to die."

"And you did it anyway," Tony insisted. "How come?"

Lawton shook his head. "Our country was under attack by Hitler and his boys. If they won, the Germans would have ripped Britain to shreds. No citizen who is loyal to the Crown could allow that to happen without putting up a fight."

Tony didn't see any particular emotion in Lawton's face. "I must conclude you took those chances because of what you believed in and supported."

"Certainly. I don't consider myself a brave man. I simply am faithful to what I consider to be important."

"Very interesting."

"Interesting? Come on, Irving. This place is getting to you." Lawton stood up to leave. "You still did well last night," he said, and turned and walked off.

Irving felt slightly better and was surprised. After all, Lawton had not only given him German currency, but a piece of black bread when he was hungry. He was a good man.

Tony got up from the table and started across the courtyard, walking toward the chapel. His usual custom was to spend time in the sanctuary praying each morning. If nothing else, the quiet restored his emotional compass and made him feel more serene in the midst of the constant chaos.

"Going over to pray?" a voice said behind him.

Tony turned around to see Donald Wardle standing there with the usual innocuous look on his face that always meant the wheels in his head were turning.

"You've decided to join me?"

Stooge grinned. "Let's take a little stroll around the courtyard. Maybe something will come up if we talk in nice, quiet, subdued tones."

Tony started walking. "You talked to the two other men involved in my super-duper authentic escape plan?"

"Funny that you'd mention that." Wardle stuck his hands in his pockets. "Getting more than a little cold out here for November, wouldn't you say?"

"I'd say that I want to know what you have come up with."

Stooge grinned. "Now you do understand why everything we do is confidential? The reports spread quickly." He poked Irving in the ribs. "Don't want you snitching on us."

Irving stopped and glared. "What do you mean?" he said threateningly.

"I'm only kidding you." Wardle poked him again.

"Yeah, well it ain't funny."

Wardle smiled. "I love it when I can get under the skin of one of you Yankees. You boys puff up like an old bullfrog."

"You'll think bullfrog if you pull that one again."

"I'll tell you what I'm going to do to encourage you a bit. I'm going to let you in on one of the most imaginative plans operating around this little camp."

Irving glanced at him out of the corner of his eye. "Yeah?"

Wardle stopped. "Tony, you don't look so good this morning. Your smile is gone, and you're walking around like a wilted lily. I think last night got to you more than you realize."

Tony took a deep breath and rubbed his temples. "Maybe so. Sometimes I don't know how I feel until I sit in that chapel for awhile." He shrugged. "It's the only way I keep going."

Wardle started walking again. "I want you to know that we all understand and the men appreciate you. Don't be so hard on yourself. You're working hard at getting out of here."

"I'm trying . . ." Tony's voice trailed away.

"I think we simply need to give you a little more encouragement. That's why I've been able to get permission to let you in on a big secret. You ready for a truly amazing sight?"

"I guess so."

"Okay. First, we go into the chapel like it's worship time. You sit there until I tell you what to do next."

"Whatever you say."

The two men walked into the chapel. Several men were praying, and Tony sat down by himself in a center row. Wardle walked around the chapel and finally sat down on the very front row. After a couple of minutes the other men left. Silence again settled over the sanctuary. Tony took a deep breath and for a moment felt like he had retreated into a vast, primeval forest with only the sounds of celestial peace surrounding him.

In the silence, the words of Luke in the Bible came back to him; one phrase kept sticking in his mind: *Enter through the narrow door.* The words seemed so important and yet they didn't fit anything Tony could see. *Enter through the narrow door.*

Five minutes later, Donald Wardle got up and went outside. Tony heard the door shut and closed his eyes to pray. Almost immediately the back door opened, and he heard the sound of feet hurrying up the aisle.

"Come on," Wardle demanded. "We don't have much time." He turned toward the back of the chapel.

Irving ran after him, but Wardle didn't slow down. At the back of the chapel by the large entry door, Stooge pushed a small curtain aside, revealing a set of stairs.

"Stay close," Donald said. "We've got to move fast." He bolted up the staircase.

The narrow spiral staircase wound tightly upward, and Irving had to jump two steps at a time to keep up with the Englishman.

"We're going to the top," Wardle said over his shoulder. "If you hear anyone entering downstairs, freeze and don't make a sound." Stooge kept on climbing.

At the top of the stairs, a large door was locked shut. Wardle instantly turned in the opposite direction and pushed on a small wall panel. The piece of wood fell backwards.

"In here!" Donald scampered through the hole in the wall.

Tony darted in behind him. Wardle put the panel back in place, and for the first time both men stopped running. The room smelled dusty and seemed to be vast.

"Okay," Stooge said, "you are now in the attic above the chapel. You must watch your step."

"The room feels huge. You got a flashlight?"

"Yes, but before we go further, I want to tell you about what we're working on up here." Wardle leaned against the wall they'd come through. "Sit down and catch your breath."

"Sure."

"One afternoon a couple of intelligent men that you probably don't know were paying careful attention to how the wind blows around these buildings. Bill Goldfinch and Tony Rolt are a couple of England's finest. Very observant fellows."

"I know who they are."

"They were sitting in a room overlooking the town of Colditz when it started to snow, and the men noticed that the snow didn't come straight down. Because of the height of the castle, the wind blew the snow up and over the top in a steady, smooth flow of air. Know what does well in such an atmospheric pattern?"

"Nope."

"Gliders."

Tony blinked his eyes. "You've got to be kidding."

"Goldfinch always had extraordinary ideas about constructing a biplane type of kite and making a getaway. He even thought about the idea when he was locked up in Stalag Luf 3 before he came here. Bill figured this roof would be a perfect place to launch a glider."

"My gosh! What an idea!"

"Look, Tony. I wanted you to see this area to encourage you. There have been a billion escape attempts, and most have failed, but no one knows what will work until they've tried it. You shouldn't be discouraged. At the least, you guys made a couple of keys, and Van Doorninck can always get back in that store if we need supplies for another escape attempt. That's no small accomplishment."

"I guess not," Tony said grudgingly.

"Now, let's take a look at what we've been working on up here." Stooge switched on the flashlight, shining it across the room. Lying on the floor were the ribs of an airplane wing as well as other pieces of wood. Pieces of fabric were piled up around the floor. "Our glider will have a wingspan of about thirty-three feet. What do you think, Tony? We think we can put two men inside the glider and catapult them out over the trees. Goldfinch has his eye on a nice little open space down there by the River Mulde."

"Wait a minute," Irving protested. "We're standing up here in an attic. You can't fly a glider through these tiles."

Wardle laughed. "Come on, where's your imagination? The night we're ready to fly, we'll tear a hole in the side of the roof and push a platform out there. Then, we will attach a rope on the glider and tie the other end to a bundle of concrete and dirt weighing about a ton. When we drop the weight, the glider will go shooting off into the night like a hawk chasing a mouse."

"But are you sure it will fly?"

Wardle shrugged. "Goldfinch and Rolt are. Unfortunately, we don't have the time or the opportunity for a test run. It's got to work right because the roofline is a long way up. We don't want those boys plunging to the ground."

"Jiminy Christmas!"

"Our biggest problem is that we don't have any way to drill holes," Wardle explained. "We've got a hacksaw and a file, but we've got to come up with wood that already has holes in the right place. Not an easy task!"

"I guess not."

"It's going to take us a considerable amount of time to get this craft built and functional, but it's one of the projects I'm working on along with the other men. No matter how long it takes, we'll be up here knocking it out."

Irving sat down on the floor and stared at the pieces being assembled into a wing. Parts of the body were stacked together. Wardle had allowed him to see an extraordinary secret.

"Sooner or later, we'll knock a hole in this place and send this little gem sailing off into the wild blue yonder." Wardle smiled.

Irving looked straight into his eyes. "I'm overwhelmed that you've shared this secret with me."

"Look, Tony. We appreciate you, and I don't want you to get worn down by these German jerks. You've got nothing but friends in this camp."

The warmth in Wardle's words touched Tony. For the second time that day, his English friends had offered important words of encouragement. A weight of depression began to slowly lift from his shoulders.

CHAPTER

TWENTY-ONE

*T*ony slipped through the wall panel and quickly descended the spiraling steps down to the chapel, looking around carefully. No one was in the chapel. Tony immediately walked out the front door and onto the inner courtyard, falling in with the men walking over the cobblestone pavement. A strong breeze whipped across the courtyard and signaled that winter wasn't far behind. The air was cold, but his steps now felt more lively. At the least, he knew Wardle truly trusted him. Other men in the camp cared about what happened to him and that felt good.

As he marched along at a good clip, Tony thought about how his experiences had affected him. When he had landed in England, he felt like a thirteen-year-old kid escaping from home. The great adventure had begun, and all he had to do was ride the tide. Meeting those strange-sounding English people had been fun, and much of their food was different from his usual Tex-Mex diet. It was like a paid vacation trip and quite a departure from what he had grown up knowing.

Tony's family had always been physical people of the working class who made it clear that as soon as he turned eighteen it was time for him to hit the street. During his youth, Tony's father had been a farmhand and expected hard work to be the norm for everyone else. Although Tony knew that his dad loved him, there had always been a considerable distance between them. Mom had been much closer, but she shared the conviction that age eighteen was the time to hit the front door for good.

Even though he would never have admitted the fact to Rikki, the army offered an alternative to college, which he couldn't afford anyway. And why not? Tony was big, strong, and adept at running the military course. He had excelled and quickly gone to the top of his class.

But the truth was, he was still young and brash. Looking back, Tony could now see how careless he had been the day he and the British were captured near Calais. He had been like a child playing in a game where the bullets were real. Once the Nazis marched him and the remnant of the British Royal Army Service Corps down the road toward Germany, he appreciated how tough they could be, but not once did he really think that the Germans would kill him. The thought simply hadn't penetrated his mind then, but now his thinking had changed radically.

Getting caught inside the mattress and spending those frighteningly cold nights in solitary confinement had shaken Tony to the core. At first he wouldn't admit it to himself, but the attempt to plunge down that manhole in the camp canteen had smashed his outer emotional shell into a thousand pieces. Tony knew that inside him lived a frightened little boy hiding under a blanket of fear, and that blanket now felt like a shroud.

He kept walking and tried not to look at the men around him. His depression returned with a vengeance. It wasn't so much that he had failed but that the failure had cracked something within him. He no longer saw the Germans as only his enemies but now as opposition with the capacity to kill him. A cold, sober sense of death jarred Tony and rearranged everything into a different perspective. His life was expendable.

Tony started walking more slowly and felt an icy weight slipping back on his shoulder. Sure. Stooge had shown him the secret glider, but he would never fly in one. The truth was that he would probably spend his entire life locked up in this empty, lonely concentration camp. Hopelessness swallowed his dreams.

Tony kept walking.

The wind picked up and a few snowflakes flew past. Tony turned his collar up and pulled his coat closer. After a couple of rounds, he noticed Damiaem Van Doorninck had taken up his usual station, standing next to the building and staring out over the yard as if he owned the place. The arrogance of his posture irritated Tony. On the next round he stopped.

"Colder, isn't it?" Tony said.

"I like the cold," the Dutchman answered with no emotion in his voice.

"Winter's coming."

"Yeah."

"We didn't make it last night," Tony said.

"Works like that sometimes."

Tony studied Damiaem's face. No eye contact. The man wasn't looking at him in any way. The man seemed and sounded totally indifferent. Maybe Tony should simply go on and drop it, but that wasn't easy to do today.

"You sound indifferent," Tony asserted. "Unconcerned."

"Really?" Van Doorninck smiled out of one corner of his mouth. "You giving out awards for nonchalance?"

"I simply thought that after last night's escape attempt you might have some more obvious reaction."

"Reaction to not making it?" the Dutchman laughed. "You cowboys are an interesting lot. You expect me to go into a dissertation on failure?" He squinted one eye and looked angry. "What do you want? A parade because you tried but couldn't get out of here?"

Tony could feel anger creeping up in his throat. The man's cold indifference made him want to hit Van Doorninck. "You're truly a big mouth, Damiaem."

"*Big mouth?* You're the big mouth who has for no reason come around here bothering me. Shove it!"

Biting his tongue to keep his fury from exploding, Tony put his hands on his hips and confronted the Dutchman. "Who do you think you are? You strut around here like you're God Almighty and not simply one of the prisoners!"

"God Almighty?" Van Doorninck spit on the ground. "You back to religion again, cowboy? Is that what this anger is about? You want to get in a religious fight with me?"

For a moment Tony didn't know how to respond. He started trying to order his thoughts, but really he just wanted to hit the man.

"Who do you want to discuss?" Van Doorninck's voice was hard and controlled. "Would you like to go for the ancients and talk about men like Hyppolytus or Augustine? Maybe you'd like someone modern like Schleiermacher or Nikolai Berdyaev." He crossed his arms over his chest. "I bet you can't even spell those names."

Tony swallowed hard. He hadn't even heard of those people.

"Look, you ignorant American, I was standing here minding my own business and you came up looking for trouble. My strong suggestion would be that you go back to walking. I've forgotten more theology than you ever learned, so don't start chewing on that subject with me unless you want me to eat your ears off."

Tony felt himself doubling his fist. The Dutchman's eyes immediately fixed on Tony's hands, and then he shifted his weight into a slightly crouched position. If there was anything Tony didn't need, it was to get in a fight out here in the middle of the exercise area. He forced himself to relax and unclench his fist.

"You're an angry man, Damiaem," Tony said.

The Dutchman exploded in laugher. "*I'm* angry?" He laughed again. "I'd say you're about the most irritated little pip-squeak in this camp." He turned his back. "Go away. You bother me."

Tony backed away and started walking again, but the pace was hard and defiant. Van Doorninck had thrown every switch in him, and he wanted to kill somebody. Irving started walking faster and refused even to look in the Dutchman's direction.

After thirty minutes of hard walking, Tony glanced toward where Van Doorninck had been standing. He was gone and the space was empty. Tony had started out thinking about how the war had affected him and ended up in a fight with Damiaem because he wanted to say something positive about God. How crazy could he get?

The castle was getting to him, and Tony didn't like it.

CHAPTER

TWENTY-TWO

Snow continued to fall throughout the day, and the Allied soldiers stayed inside the castle's dormitory. The woodstove in the corner of the large room put out some warmth, but hardly enough to combat the freezing temperature creeping in from outside. It didn't appear that the weather would change throughout the evening.

"They say Eggers came back this morning," Tony Irving said to the other two listening to him. "I heard Schadlich joking with some men, and he told them they'd better shape up since the boss was back."

"Boss?" Bill Fowler grimaced. "I thought this Glaesche character ran the place." He pulled his coat more closely around his body.

"Ever see him?" Irving asked.

"In any case, Eggers is the guy we have to deal with," Fowler said. "We need to figure out how to keep him and the front office distracted while we work on a way out of here."

"I think you've got the right idea," Lawton said. "We need to get something new going around this place. The winter's going to be long as it is."

"Isn't today the twentieth of November?" Irving asked.

"Yeah," Fowler said.

"In the United States we have a big holiday in a few days. We call it Thanksgiving."

"Thanksgiving?" Lawton rubbed his chin. "Any possibilities in using a holiday as a ruse to set up an escape?"

"Well," Fowler thought out loud, "Christmas is only a month away. That's a better day to work on. Thanksgiving is an American thing, but everyone celebrates Christmas."

The men kept talking, but Tony was thinking about Rikki Beck and what she would be doing this Thanksgiving. Would she be staying at home with her family? Going over to the Irvings' house? The entire family would feel the strain of his "missing in action" status. Hopefully one of his letters had gotten through, but probably not. He didn't have to think about it long to know what would happen.

Rikki would sit down at the table. Everyone would be jolly, laughing about the holiday, talking, maybe making plans for later in the afternoon. She'd try to be casual, a good guest at an abundantly filled Thanksgiving dinner table.

Then it would come time to say the blessing. Someone would be selected. The prayer of Thanksgiving for the country, the day, God's blessing would start and then the intercessor would ask God's hand to be on Tony, to keep him safe and out of harm's way. Rikki would start to cry. Other people would weep. His mother, for sure. Finally, Rikki would jump up and run from the table. Everyone would be crying by then but his father. Rikki would go into a bedroom, but it would be too late. The joy and frivolity would have gone down the drain.

"Tony," Lawton asked, "what about planning a break around Christmas? *Tony!*"

"Huh?" Tony jumped slightly.

"You listening to us or not?" Fowler groused.

"Sure. Sure. I just got distracted."

"Look," Fowler said. "There are three of us. We came in together, and by God we're going to get out of this place together. We may have to use some other men, but I'm determined to break through these walls one way or the other."

"Me, too," Tony insisted. "I think I'm ready to do whatever is necessary . . . no matter how difficult it is."

Lawton leaned back against the wall. "We've got to be clever, more clever than any of us would think possible. I've already learned how difficult it can be even when you have a good plan."

"How'd you get a ticket down to this little vacation spot?" Irving asked.

"I was flying a reconnaissance mission over the French coast back in December of 1941," Lawton said. "On the thirtieth to be exact, when a Nazi Messerschmitt 109 fighter caught me from behind and opened up on me with machine fire. I tried to crash-land my Spitfire, but the impact turned out to be rougher than I expected. The Spitfire actually crashed in a field and it broke my right foot. You should have seen the side of my face. It was seared black."

Irving looked at Lawton's face. "That's why your skin is still pinker than usual?"

"I'm lucky I didn't end up well-done. The Germans grabbed me and hauled me off to a detention center where I had time to let my foot heal." Lawton rolled his eyes. "Interesting days, though. The boys in that center taught me a little something about picking locks and paying attention to the guards. I started learning how to function as a prisoner."

"He started learning to be a *bad boy*," Fowler added. "You can see how his personality became warped."

"I became quite rotten, actually," Lulu said. "One of the prisoners knew all about the layout of cockpits in German aircraft. I learned how you fly the instruments in a 109 as well as a Ju 88 and a Heinkel bomber. At least, I learned how the controls operated."

"Wow!" Tony inched closer. "What happened?"

"My plan was to steal one of those airplanes and fly it back to England. Sounds good, doesn't it?"

"You bet!" Irving grinned.

"Unfortunately, they caught me sneaking across an airfield after I busted out of the detention center. Nailed me about fifty feet from one of the 109 fighter airplanes. The end result was I got a formal promotion to these relaxing accommodations at Colditz Castle."

Bill Fowler grinned. "You see, Irving, you're dealing with big-time criminals in this place. Stealing an airplane is no small crime. Ever know anyone who stole one?"

"I think that's the sort of idea we need to come up with," Irving said. "Something unique, unexpected. Anybody got one of those creative thoughts?"

"They aren't easy to come by," Lawton said, "but you're right. There's a lot of brainpower floating around this place. We simply need to pay careful attention to some detail the Nazis have missed."

"See, Tony," Fowler said, "your idea about the manhole cover in the canteen was actually excellent. The mattress attempt wasn't bad either. Unfortunately, it just didn't take you where you wanted to go, but it was still very good."

"I guess," Tony said soberly. "I truly wanted those ideas to work."

"Okay," Lulu Lawton continued, "now is the time for us to turn over a new page and start again. Let's agree that the three of us will discover some sort of plan that will work. If we can't use Christmas as a backdrop, we can still make it the target date."

Night had fallen and the last *Appell* of the day had been called. The prisoners trudged back to the dormitory and prepared for bed without saying much to each other. The long, dreary gray sky had turned into a black night, and snow covered most of the ground in the courtyard; the wind bit at their heels. Nothing felt good or seemed right. The men climbed into bed lost in their own thoughts. Each man had a private world no one was ever invited into, and tonight seemed to be a time when that hidden domain felt more inviting than a talk with another prisoner whom they had seen every morning and night for what felt like an endless aeon.

Tony kept thinking about the conversation earlier in the day. Most of his thoughts gravitated toward the possibility of tunneling out of the castle, but he hated that idea. Then he wondered if he might have been too quick to conclude that the tunnel under the canteen wouldn't work.

After several minutes of kicking the idea back and forth, he concluded his first assumptions were right. The Germans wouldn't have spent all that time and energy bricking the drain shut if all he needed to do was have a couple of guys help him push and pull on the bricks. He knew tunneling up vertically wouldn't work because they'd have to make too many trips back and forth at night. Sooner or later they would get caught or shot.

The truth was, tunneling turned into impossibly difficult work; it had been discovered virtually every time the prisoners tried it. Tony remained impressed by the glider idea, but that project was closed to him. They had more than enough men working on it. There had to be another way!

Once again an old idea started floating through Tony's mind. The Bible passage he'd read in the chapel months ago returned to his thoughts. *"Enter through the narrow door."* It sounded so simple, so straightforward. That brief passage had to mean something, and Tony desperately wanted to know what it was.

Lulu Lawton sat on the edge of his bed looking out the window long after the lights had been turned out. He had spun the story of the crash of his Spitfire casually, easily, as if it had been nothing more than an automobile stopping for a slight bump at the end of the road. He preferred to keep the story on the simple side rather than evoke the feelings of terror that the story always raised in him, or to at least keep a lid on it in front of the other prisoners. The truth was the crash had proved to be the most terrifying experience of his life. Each second of the encounter filled his mind again. . . .

He could still smell the flames exploding inside the cockpit and remember grabbing the fire extinguisher. His airplane was spinning crazily out of control, whirling and swirling toward the earth. He tried to keep the airplane under control, but the flames kept licking at his flight jacket and crawling up the side of the cockpit. Fire burst up the side of the seat, and his face stung with a sudden burning sensation. Swinging the fire extinguisher around inside the airplane, Lulu stopped the flames around his seat, but his face didn't stop aching.

Lawton stared at the ground coming straight up at him. He was sure death was only seconds away. A cold sweat broke out across his forehead and ran down the side of his face. His entire body felt like it was going to convulse, and he tried to make himself relax.

"God help me!" Lulu gasped under his breath. He held the stick back and felt the airplane start to level out, but he was only feet above the trees. "Please help me to keep from dying!"

The airplane kept tilting back and forth. "Got to get the plane stabilized," Lulu said to himself. His face was burning, and all he could see were treetops. "Keep it level." He tried to slow the Spitfire, but it was racing above the forest far too fast for a simple landing. If he hit a tree, the impact would tear him to pieces.

"Need an open space . . . a field . . . a road." Lulu tried to drop the airplane's wheels.

Out of the corner of his eye he saw the Nazi 109 flying far above him, probably checking to make sure it was a kill. Suddenly the forest ended and cultivated fields lay in front of him. To his left, the captain saw the English Channel.

"Now or never." Lulu aimed at a freshly plowed field and hoped the wheels had dropped.

Bracing himself for a crash landing, Lawton knew the airplane had barely cleared a stone fence and had to be only a few feet off of the ground. The Spitfire hit with a terrible thud and spun forward before smashing into the ground again. The impact threw Lulu forward with a violent twist, and then the world turned black.

When Lulu awoke, he could smell smoke and thought the airplane might be about to explode. He pushed the canopy back and started to jump only to discover his foot was caught somewhere near the bottom of the seat in a mass of wires. For several moments he tried to pull it loose, but the pain became so great, Lulu thought he might pass out. Finally, he broke out of the entanglement only to confirm something bad had happened to his foot. He couldn't tell what, but the pain kept increasing. Pushing himself up to the edge of the cockpit, he immediately discovered the only way out of the airplane was to tumble over the side and slide down headfirst. Lawton slowly eased out of the cockpit, inching his way down, but suddenly he dropped onto the wing and rolled to the ground. When he hit the field, pain shot through his body like a jolt of electricity and everything faded again. He had no idea how long he was unconscious until the sounds of men walking around him jarred him awake.

"*Hallo*," a voice said.

Lulu opened his eyes and saw two young German soldiers standing above him with their rifles pointed at his body. He remembered that they didn't look vindictive or dangerous—just boy soldiers doing their job—but they were still quite capable of shooting him. . . .

The memory faded, but the cold chill of death lingered. In that one crash, he had faced death three times: the 109's attack, the crash landing, and the soldiers, who could have killed him at their whim. Only the hand of God had kept him from death, but the recollection still left him feeling depleted and empty. He hated the sense of loneliness the memories always stirred in him.

Lawton looked out the window again. In the morning, he would start on a new approach, a new angle. He needed to discover some aspect of the castle that no one had yet noticed. Possibly, he could start keeping a record of when new prisoners arrived. Something unexpected might be hidden in that monotonous, daily routine.

Lawton laid back in his bed and pulled the blanket up around his neck. The snow kept falling. Hopefully, during the night no one would call an *Appell* in this weather. Lulu closed his eyes, but he didn't find it easy to sleep.

PART THREE
A Path in the Darkness

CHAPTER

TWENTY-THREE

After a two-week absence, Major Reinhold Eggers returned to his office in the castle high above the surrounding courtyards. He had only been there a few minutes when the door opened and Corporal Otto Schadlich walked in, saluting smartly.

"Welcome back. I trust you enjoyed your leave."

"Thank you, Otto." Eggers returned the salute. "My wife especially relished our holiday in Mannheim." He straightened some papers on his desk. "The reward for finding the escape route was certainly appreciated. We spent time with both of our families and even saw several people you know." He smiled. "The Goritzhans. The Konigsteins. Remember them? We even took a trip down the Rhein and sailed past the Lorelei."

"Good! Excellent! May I say that you certainly had a vacation coming."

Eggers smiled slightly. "I'm sure Colonel Glaesche wouldn't agree," he said almost in a whisper. "Must have galled him to see us rewarded for a job well done." He walked around from the back of the desk.

Schadlich grinned. "At the least, the reward set back any plans he had to run you off."

"Can't ever tell. We have to live in this concentration camp not so unlike the prisoners. It's a one-day-at-a-time operation. We're only as good as what we do today. One bad day, and we're all in the soup."

"Yes, that's most certainly true." The corporal leaned forward into Reinhold's ear. "Have you heard anymore about that nasty business I told you occurred in Warsaw?"

Reinhold put his finger to his lips and walked across the room. He abruptly jerked the door open and looked outside. A sergeant working at a desk across the room looked up in surprise.

The man blinked several times. "May I help you, Major?"

"Nothing right now," Eggers said to the young man. "I'll be with you shortly. Go back to work." He closed the door again and walked briskly across the room. Eggers whispered in Schadlich's ear. "No one is listening."

Otto nodded. "We're safe?"

"I think so, but we can't be too careful," Eggers murmured. "You never know when one of Himmler's dupes or Reinhard Heydrich's devious spies will have their ear to the door."

Schadlich nodded. "I understand."

Eggers beckoned with his finger for Otto to follow him to the window. "I'm not sure exactly what is happening, but matters are not good in Poland." For a moment Reinhold watched the large flakes of snow drift down. "The world has become a cold place, Otto," he said quietly. "I learned that thousands of Jews were starved in the Warsaw ghetto in April, and many, many others have been deported. The stories you heard are apparently based on fact."

"What do you make of this?"

Eggers replied, "I don't know for sure. No one is saying much more than what I've told you. Apparently, the Gestapo is keeping the facts covered up as if they are state secrets. At the least, it sounds to me like hatred of the Jews is getting out of hand."

Schadlich rubbed his hands together and inhaled deeply. "That's what I'm hearing. How about matters on the battlefield? The war is going well?"

"I don't know. Goebbels is pumping out the propaganda, but I don't think we're moving at the rate he claims. I believe the *Wehrmacht* could be struggling in some areas. I know Rommel is losing ground in Africa."

For a moment Schadlich twisted his lip and stared out the window. "What does this all mean? Where is the Third Reich going with this Jewish problem?"

"I don't know." Eggers shook his head. "Frankly, I don't want to think about the issue. It's not our responsibility. We do our business like good soldiers and leave the political issues to politicians. Isn't that the German way?"

Otto nodded. "*Ya*, always has been. I suppose we should drop the subject."

"Definitely." Reinhold turned around and walked back to his desk. "Anything happen while I was gone?"

The corporal shrugged. "Not to my knowledge. The place has been relatively quiet as far as escape attempts have gone. Of course, the prisoners have not stopped their goon-baiting exercises. That nonsense happens every day."

"Oh?" Eggers laughed. "I'm sure that's been interesting."

"Not really," Otto said sternly. "We had one little incident the other night. The security officer Priem decided to call a surprise *Appell* at one o'clock in the morning. Frankly, I think the man had been drinking."

"Sounds like Priem."

"He ran the inmates out in the snow while he checked their beds. Obviously, the night was cold and the prisoners weren't happy. Apparently, before the men left the dormitory a number of them grabbed handfuls of gray ash. After the dormitory was searched, the prisoners came back in, but they left a large 'V' made with the ash out there in the snow."

"A 'V'?" Eggers frowned.

"Our men were baffled, but we knew it was meant as an affront. We came to the conclusion it was the first letter of their word *victory.*"

Eggers nodded. "Yes, Churchill is always making that sign with his fingers. I've seen his picture in the newspapers with his hands up in the air."

"One of the soldiers erased the mark with his feet, and the prisoners went back to bed. The matter was closed, and life went on."

Reinhold turned back to the window and looked out again, gazing over the outer courtyard. He could see the snow was getting deeper. "I believe times will become harder, Otto. Our job certainly won't get any easier, and Glaesche won't stop watching. We must observe these prisoners carefully. They are capable of any kind of crazy behavior." He turned around and looked his old friend in the eye. "*Understand?*"

The corporal nodded and saluted. "I most certainly do!"

Eggers saluted. "Good day, Corporal."

Schadlich turned on his heels and disappeared through the door. Reinhold watched the door close for a moment before sitting down at his desk. He looked at the mail that was piled in a stack next to the register of new prisoners who had entered the prison during his absence. He had plenty to do simply shuffling through the paperwork in front of him, but he found it difficult to get started. What he had heard whispered between German officers about the stories of German aggression concerned Reinhold far more than he had admitted to Otto.

During his entire adult life Reinhold did what the public anticipated a teacher should do, and in turn he expected the Kaiser, or whoever was in charge of the government, to do what he was appointed to do. Everyone did the right and respectable thing expected in a Christian society. In fact, Germany was the most advanced scientific culture in the world. Never would he have believed that such atrocities were possible.

Reinhold didn't like the attacks Hitler and his troops were making on the Jews, but they weren't his concerns. These pogroms of Jewish persecution had come and gone, moving from one country to the next, for far longer than a thousand years. He anticipated nothing more than another little upheaval that would soon settle down. Instead, he had heard unpublished stories of concentration camps being constructed solely for the execution of these strange people.

CHAPTER

TWENTY-FOUR

During the five days following the prisoner's discussion around the dormitory heating stove, each man kept looking for new angles and details on prison life in the castle. Tony walked along the walls, checking the foundations, and Fowler kept watching the kitchen doors for some slip. Captain Lawton had started keeping meticulous notes on the new prisoners brought into the camp. He discovered the new prisoners didn't seem to arrive on any predictable schedule but were hauled in at a wide range of times each day. Nothing worked for an escape plan.

Tony Irving and Bill Fowler stood out in front of the mess hall while waiting for lunch. "We've got to get out to exercise more often," Irving told Bill. "We can't let this cold weather keep us inside the castle or the monotony will drag us down emotionally."

"Yes, we don't want to turn soft either."

"And moving around is the only way we're going to discover some exit out of this joint."

Stooge Wardle walked up to the two men standing in front of the entry to the mess hall. "You being 'good boys' today?" He grinned his silly smile.

"Of course!" Irving said. "What else could we be?"

"Just checking." Stooge winked. "Never know about prisoners like you."

"Anything going on?" Fowler asked.

"Always is," Wardle said.

"I mean in the near future?"

Stooge grinned. "Keep your eyes open, boys. Surprises are possible at any moment in this tunnel of love and fun!" He strolled into the mess hall. "You're in a laugh-a-minute entertainment park."

"Now that's interesting." Fowler watched Wardle walk away. "Sounds like our old buddy is working on something right now."

"Wardle knows more than he ever says." Irving rubbed his chin. "Sounds like something big is unfolding in here somewhere."

"Hmm, keep your eyes open." Bill Fowler pointed to the door. "Let's go in and have another one of those scrumptious meals they prepare for us every day."

"You mean more boiled water and cabbage?" Irving grimaced. "How much weight you think you've lost?"

Fowler ran his hand up and down his ribs. "Feels like more than I'd like to admit." He walked into the mess hall, looking for the food line. "I don't want to guess."

Men were sitting at the long tables with cups of the poor coffee in front of them and bowls of soup on the table. Each man had a piece of black bread.

"What a surprise!" Fowler said cynically. "Another meal of watered-down cream of leftover soup."

"What's this make? One thousand endless days of awful soup at noon?" Irving looked at the prisoners nibbling at the bread to make it last as long as possible. Many of their faces looked worn. "I think our boys are taking it on the chin."

Fowler nodded and lined up for a bowl of soup. "These Nazis certainly don't err in being too generous."

The two men found a place at a table and slipped in next to several other prisoners. They ate silently. A few of the prisoners smiled, but most didn't make eye contact. Resolute determination seemed to be their only discernible emotion. After the soup was gone, some of the men used their bread to wipe the bowl clean.

"Gentlemen!" Bill Fowler suddenly stood up. "May I have your attention?"

Stillness instantly settled over the quiet mess hall. Several German soldiers moved into the doorways as if they were ready to stop any nonsense before a demonstration got out of hand.

Fowler held up his coffee cup as if proposing a toast. "In the United States today the Americans have a national holiday called Thanksgiving. They celebrate the abundance with which God has blessed them. Shouldn't we salute our compatriots and wish them the best?"

"Here! Here!" echoed around the room. The Germans pulled their rifles off their shoulders and frowned. "To the Americans!" someone shouted.

Fowler kept turning around to address the men on all sides. "Here we are in our own festive environment. Well fed. Confronted with more than we can eat. Our own bellies filled to the brim. I propose a toast of solidarity with President Roosevelt and all our American friends. Here's to freedom!"

The mess hall erupted into a roar of shouting and cheers. The prisoners suddenly turned into guests at a bridal party. "To our comrades!" a Pole shouted in slurred English. "The best to our celebrating American brothers!" a Dutchman hollered.

"Indeed!" Fowler drank his coffee and noticed the Germans starting to inch their way along the mess hall walls. "Quiet!" he said. "Quiet!"

The uproar settled as the inmates waited to hear what Fowler might say next. "We are surrounded by such supportive German friends."

Fowler pointed around the room so that the prisoners would be aware that the guards looked worried and had their rifles in hand. "Shouldn't we also drink to our guards?"

Total silence dropped over the room.

"They probably can't understand the King's English," Wardle said to the group but turned to the guards, saluting them with his cup and a pejorative wish.

The room broke into an uproar of laughter and boos with hisses. The guards stared stone-faced, unsure of how to respond.

Fowler slowly sat down and grinned at Irving. "A little toast for your friends at home. You can tell them that they were remembered on this Thanksgiving in Colditz."

Irving laughed. "Did you see the look on that guard's face? The man had no idea what to do. They knew something was wrong but they weren't sure what."

"We must throw a few logs on the fire every now and then," Fowler said. "Gives our boys something to laugh about. You gotta chuckle occasionally or you get swallowed by this dump."

Irving nodded. "Fowler, you're a genius. You've turned a depressing lunch of 'nothing soup' into a time to remember!"

"You look better today, Tony. For several days we were concerned that those two failed escapes had gotten to you, but you've pulled through. At least, Wardle told me to keep an eye on you."

"Wardle, huh?" Irving ran his hands through his hair. "I don't know why, but he's been good to me."

"Stooge is a funny guy. I suspect a very serious man is behind his silly smile."

"At least he knows where the serious stuff is happening."

"Tony, have you ever walked down there in the park area on the other side of the stream?"

"Strange as it sounds, I haven't. Been too concerned in finding a way out of this castle."

"There's a nice little walk down there on the south side of the castle with even a bridge over the stream. It's not nearly as steep a drop as it is behind the chapel and the dormitories."

"Lot of snow out there," Irving said.

"Some of the men have already trampled it down a tad. For awhile the Germans wouldn't let us walk in the park, but it's open again. How about a stroll?"

Irving smiled. "Sure. Why not? I don't remember having a crowded schedule this morning."

"Yes, we must check our datebooks to make sure we don't have any appointments hanging over our heads," Fowler pointed to the back door. "We'll have to go out the rear exit. Follow me."

The two men passed by the other inmates, noticing that the atmosphere had completely changed. Prisoners were joking, laughing, and talking. Silence had disappeared and been replaced by a lighthearted casualness that must have confounded the German soldiers pacing back and forth along the sides of the mess hall.

"That was fun," Fowler said and stepped out the back door. "Nothing like confronting the Germans! A little goon-baiting goes a long way." He looked out over the flat area covered with snow. "They say when the spring comes this area will be filled with grass."

Irving looked up at the catwalk running down the steep slope. "The Nazis are certainly up there waiting for spring *and watching us.*"

"Always are, but don't let that bother you." Fowler pointed to the south. "Follow that path through the snow and you'll find your way."

"Hey, you're the guide. I'll stay behind you."

The men walked past the parapet wall that opened to the road down to the park. Next to them stretched a metal fence with long strands of barbed-wire. The prisoners walked the length of the castle walls until they came to a gate in the fence.

"Over there are the quarters for married guards." Fowler pointed to the south. "We'll take the path that goes down to the river. They tell me some of the prisoners have gardens down here in the summer. Wardle said it really was quite a lovely place, but we may find too much snow along the way. It's really been coming down."

"Lead on," Irving said.

At the bottom of the hill they crossed over the Hohnback Stream, which was mostly frozen with piles of snow lying on the ice. Ahead a number of men were walking around the exercise area.

"How is it, boys?" Irving called to them.

"Snow fairly deeply," a Czech answered in poor English.

"I think so!" Tony said. "I'd wait a couple of weeks until the enthusiasts get this place trampled down."

"Think an escape could happen down here?" Fowler's voice abruptly shifted, sounding intense and serious.

Tony looked more carefully and slowly around the exercise yard. The area was certainly surrounded by sentries with a high wall behind them. He studied the barbed-wire fence. "Wouldn't be easy, but it is certainly worth thinking about."

"Not a bad thought."

"Who knows? Probably the hard part would be getting through the canteen at night."

"Or finding an alternative route."

"Yeah." Tony pulled his coat collar up around his neck. "I'm freezing. You ready to walk back?"

Fowler nodded. "Sure. Let's stay with those men in front of us. We'll let them stomp through the loose snow first. Keeps our feet drier."

Tony grinned. "Fowler, you don't miss a trick." He looked up and saw a woman walking toward them. For a second Irving stared, unsure of what he was seeing.

The woman seemed unusually tall and stout, but German women often had such a build. Decked out in her best and with bright red lipstick, she wore a straw hat that had an artificial rose in the center. The *frau* kept her pocketbook tucked under her arm, holding it tightly with her white gloves. Her black skirt swished beneath her knees as she passed. Without looking anywhere but straight ahead, she resolutely marched through the prisoners at a fast clip like a proper woman avoiding taunts from a band of fresh soldiers. When the woman walked around Tony, she avoided all eye contact.

Tony stopped and watched the woman briskly walk by. Just as the woman stomped beyond the two men at the end of the line of prisoners, her watch slipped from her wrist into the snow. She didn't stop but kept pressing on.

"Hey!" one of the prisoners called out. "You dropped your watch! *Die Uhr!*"

The woman walked faster.

"*Uhr!*" the man shouted again.

Without looking back, the woman hurried on toward the bridge over the Hohnback.

"Wait a minute," the prisoner holding the watch said. "Is that a woman?"

Instantly a German guard ran up the hill from the exercise yard and started shouting. The woman took off like a track runner, sprinting with great strides toward the park wall. All gentility disappeared.

"There's one of our guys!" Tony whispered. "He's dressed up like a woman, but he'll never get beyond the wall."

Two other Germans suddenly appeared near the end of the barbed wire with their rifles pointed at the escaping prisoner.

"*Stoppen!*" the guard warned. "*Nun!*"

The inmate stopped running and held his hands with the white gloves in the air.

"Good Lord!" the prisoner holding the dropped watch gasped. "He would have escaped if I hadn't shouted at him and alerted the guard."

"Who is it?" Tony asked Fowler. "Who's the guy."

"I don't know."

Three German sentries slowly surrounded the escaping prisoner. The inmate didn't move but stood resolutely straight, looking out over the exercise yard as if he owned the area. One of the guards reached up and grabbed the straw hat off his head.

"Why that's Lieutenant Boule!" a prisoner behind Fowler said. "My gosh, he came up with his own ingenious disguise and no one knew it."

The guards turned Boule around and started marching him up the path toward the castle. Boule stepped along with a swing of his hips and a grin on his face. When he reached the prisoners gawking at him, Boule smiled politely.

"Hi, boys," Boule said in a high falsetto. "Be careful out there on the trail. A girl can never tell who'll turn up."

The men started laughing and clapping while the German soldiers kept marching Boule on up the hill toward the castle's isolation cells.

CHAPTER

TWENTY-FIVE

With Christmas only ten days away, Major Reinhold Eggers stood at the window, watching the sentries march the inmates out of the dormitories into units lined up on the inner courtyard. For some reason, the prisoners seemed on the insolent side and kept irritating the NCOs.

"What's going on out there today?" Major Eggers asked Corporal Schadlich. "Why all the confusion?"

"I'm not sure, but I think the cold weather and the lack of sufficient exercise is causing some rebellion. These French inmates always tend to be quite individualistic." Otto Schadlich looked nervously over his shoulder. "When is Colonel Glaesche supposed to arrive?"

"Any minute," Eggers said. "He's not going to be happy with this bunch of rowdy rapscallions."

"How come we're having this big *Appell* for him?"

"For some reason the colonel was quite upset with that soldier dressed as a woman who tried to escape a couple of days ago. He wanted the French prisoners lined up out here where he could review them."

"But we caught the inmate before he even got close to escaping!" Otto protested.

"I think Glaesche was seeking an escape attempt to have sufficient reason to jump us," Eggers said quietly. "I expect to be treated shabbily today."

Schadlich rubbed his chin. "I'm sure the men have heard the colonel is coming today. That's part of the problem."

Eggers glanced at his watch. "Glaesche should come rolling across the moat about now. We've got to keep this mob in order. Tell the sentries to be alert. If there's any nonsense, they are to strike first and ask questions later."

Corporal Schadlich saluted and hurried off to instruct the guards about a quick response to any nonsense. At the least, Glaesche's delay gave Eggers a few more minutes to snap the prisoners into line. The major watched Otto walk from guard to guard giving instructions, then he turned and hurried out of his office to greet the colonel. The sentries took their rifles off their shoulders, but the men continued to be difficult.

As the major anticipated, Colonel Glaesche came in the entrance gate through the ramparts area. Acting more like a general, Glaesche strutted into the courtyard wearing an overcoat that stretched down to the top of his long black boots. Under his arm the colonel carried the leather riding crop he inevitably enjoyed banging on his desk. The gold buttons on the front of his double-breasted coat with embossed bars on the shoulders set off the thick, darker-colored collar and the Iron Cross hanging around the colonel's neck. His high-topped officer's cap with the Nazi insignia and gold braid made a formidable contrast with the camp's soldiers in their plain green uniforms. Edgar Glaesche obviously meant to leave an impression.

Eggers snapped to attention and saluted. Glaesche barely acknowledged his presence.

"The prisoners know I am coming today?" the colonel asked in a sharp, demanding tone.

"We presume so," Eggers answered.

Glaesche pulled his riding crop from under his arm and began thumping his gloves. "Their attitude seems significantly less than appropriate."

"Yes, sir." Eggers remained standing at strict attention.

"Why?" The colonel turned with a sneer on his face. "I would have expected a more subservient and respectful response."

"We are dealing with difficult men, sir. The winter has only increased their restlessness. Frankly, they have the capacity to be quite difficult."

"I will not tolerate insolence." Glaesche smacked his glove with the whip. "If there is the least disturbance, I will have the man shot."

Eggers stiffened. "We are already fully prepared for any difficulties."

"Good, because I am not going to put up with these imbeciles!" The colonel crossed his arms over his chest, looking at Eggers as if he were one of the inmates. "I will not tolerate resistance *in any form.*"

"Of course." Eggers nodded his head subserviently. The wind came up and blew a swirl of snow through the air. "Are you ready for me to call the men to attention?"

"At once," Glaesche snapped.

"*Aufmerksamkeit!*" Eggers shouted. The German sentries immediately stiffened in place, but the French inmates only stood at ease.

"Apparently, the men don't take you seriously," Colonel Glaesche taunted. "You must not frighten them enough." The German turned toward the units of men and whipped his riding crop under his arm. "*Aufmerksamkeit!*" he screamed.

The prisoners didn't react any differently. Abruptly, they started shouting loudly without moving their lips. From across the rows of French soldiers came a wave of responses, but no speaker was identifiable.

"*Ou sont les Allemands?*"

"*Dans la merde!*" another Frenchman answered.

"What's going on out there?" the colonel demanded.

"The French are good at a call-and-response chant, sir."

"*Enfoncez-les?*" a French voice called out.

"*Jusqu' aux orielles!*" some Frenchman responded.

German NCOs ran up and down the lines demanding that the French soldiers stop, but the calling continued to echo through the columns of men.

"I demand these fools stop!" Colonel Glaesche slapped his glove with his riding crop. "*Now!*"

Major Eggers fought to keep a smile from erupting. "The prisoners call this behavior 'goon-baiting,' sir. It's a form of taunting our guards."

The back of Glaesche's neck started turning red. His eyes narrowed and the colonel clenched his fist. "They will not treat me in this insulting manner! I demand they stop!"

"*Stoppen!*" Major Eggers called to the sentry. "Put an end to this nonsense."

"*Ou sont les Allemands.*" The chant started over again.

"*Dans la merde!*" The answer came from another section of the inmates.

Suddenly shouts erupted from prisoners standing in the French side of the dormitory windows. The courtyard burst into a chorus of jeers and shouts, the whooping echoing off the walls and bouncing around the camp. Men appeared in the windows of the dormitory, shouting and shaking their fists at the Germans.

"I'll show you how to handle this pack of pigs," the colonel growled. Glaesche walked quickly to a group of soldiers standing by the delousing shed. "I want this riot to stop," he shouted at the guards. "Prepare to shoot!"

The shouting of the inmates only increased. Men laughed, booed, jeered. Other nationalities joined the goon-baiting, driving the austere German soldiers wild.

"Fire!" the colonel shouted.

A volley of Gewehr 98 rifle shots blasted the side of the dormitory. Glass splattered and pieces of shattered cement showered in every direction. Silence instantly fell over the prisoners. For a second nothing happened, and then a French soldier slumped forward in the third-story window. Colonel Glaesche stared at the limp form with a surprised look on his face.

"A prisoner was shot?" Major Eggers's voice took on an agonizing quality.

The German NCOs ran back and forth shouting at the silent prisoners. No one moved or said anything.

"Get the camp doctor there to check out that prisoner," the colonel demanded. "I want a full report immediately."

Eggers turned to Corporal Schadlich, now standing next to him. "Get the doctor!" the major snapped, and Otto ran across the courtyard.

"I would suggest that we get these men back inside the dormitory," Major Eggers told the colonel. "It would be the quickest way to break up the current hostile atmosphere."

For a moment the colonel looked unsure. He glanced back at the brooding, silent mob of prisoners. The atmosphere felt like a ticking time bomb. "Y-e-s," Glaesche concluded. "Send them back inside and don't tolerate any nonsense."

The roll call ended without a head count being completed. The colonel stood silently watching the dispersement, tapping his glove with the riding crop.

Major Eggers stood to one side watching the colonel. Glaesche looked almost like he would explode. Everything had spun out of control, and the colonel was the ringmaster, trying to control a runaway circus. While no one would probably report it as such, the shooting of the prisoner was not only irresponsible but totally unnecessary. Some fool sentry had simply missed the mark or something of that order. Eggers knew that whatever intentions the colonel had, his entire plan had gone awry.

"Follow me!" Colonel Glaesche's voice cracked. "We will go to the *Kommandantur's* office and discuss this problem at once."

Reinhold Eggers maintained his stiff posture and walked briskly behind his commanding officer. Even though Glaesche's behavior had been arrogant and stupid, the man was no fool. The rebellious prisoners had obviously thrown him off stride, but Eggers knew by the time they reached the *Kommandantur*, Glaesche would probably be back on course.

But by the time they walked into the colonel's formal office, Glaesche had become even more angry. Without saying a word, Edgar Glaesche banged his riding crop on the top of his desk and poured himself a whiskey. He didn't offer a drink to Eggers. The major stood at attention, seemingly impervious to the emotional volcano erupting in front of him.

Someone knocked on the door and opened it. "Sir, I am Doctor Ernest Heinz. You asked for a report immediately."

The colonel looked up slowly from his desk. "Yes, what did you find?"

"Apparently, a bullet ricocheted and struck one of the Frenchmen in the back of the neck," Dr. Heinz reported. "We are treating the man and believe he will recover."

Colonel Glaesche's composure didn't change. "Thank you. I will expect a continuing report on his condition."

"Yes, sir." Dr. Heinz clicked his heels and walked out.

"I want you to understand something." Colonel Glaesche began lecturing Major Eggers in a slow, deliberate manner as if he were talking to one of the prisoners. "If I have to shoot every one of these swine, I'll do it!" He walked from behind the desk until he was only inches from Eggers's face. "We are not going to run this concentration camp as if it were a vacation experience for these Allied dogs!" He leaned closer. "Do you understand me?"

"We have always maintained order in accord with the Geneva convention."

"To hell with the Geneva convention!" Glaesche shouted. "We are going to run this camp like a prison."

Major Eggers did not answer but looked over Glaesche's shoulder to avoid eye contact.

"I am the supreme commander here, and that is my order! Do you understand me?"

"Of course," Eggers answered, "but we must both be aware that injuring or killing an Allied soldier simply because of disrupting behavior puts us in jeopardy."

"I don't care what it does! We are the *Wehrmacht* and the Army of Germany is beholden to no one. *Are we clear?*"

"Yes, sir!"

"Then run this prison in that manner!" Colonel Glaesche turned on his heels and marched back to his desk. "I have squads of SS men in the town of Colditz, and they are ready to descend on this castle and kill these prisoners if the need arises. I will not hesitate to use them all if necessary."

Major Eggers did not answer but stood at attention.

"Now get back out there and make sure no other problems have developed."

The major saluted, turned on his heels, and marched out of the room. He walked back down the stairs and said nothing to anyone. In a few minutes, he was back on the inner courtyard now clear of prisoners. Eggers walked around the cobblestone street for a moment and then lit a cigarette.

No matter how loud Glaesche shouted or belligerent he acted, Eggers knew that shooting a prisoner by accident could be serious business. The colonel's screaming and shouting was his little attempt to cover his own actions, but he had still painted himself into a corner. Yet, it could turn into a larger problem, and Eggers didn't want to be any part of such a quandary. The possible intervention of SS fanatics sent shivers down his spine. Possibly, Glaesche really was crazy enough to turn the Gestapo loose on the unarmed prisoners.

Eggers blew a long puff of smoke above his head. Probably the inmates were watching him and he needed to appear in charge. The truth was Glaesche's arrogant behavior had nearly given complete control to the prisoners.

Corporal Schadlich abruptly walked out of the sick ward area.

"I've been checking on the shooting victim," Otto said. "I hope the man will recover, but the bullet hit him in the back of the neck."

"Not a good situation, Otto."

The corporal shook his head. "Not good at all." He pointed toward the sick ward. "I want to show you something else. Follow me." He walked into the narrow entryway between the stairs leading down to the cellars and the wall in front of the sick ward. "Look here." Otto pointed to the wall.

Reinhold Eggers leaned forward. Someone had hastily scrawled across the wall, "Remember Holzminden." Eggers stiffened.

"What's this mean?" Schadlich asked.

"Holzminden was a World War I POW camp where the commandant murdered one of the prisoners. Following the war, he was hanged. One of the Brits wants us to remember the incident."

"What'll we do?"

"Otto, wash it off one way or the other, then write up a report and send it to Colonel Glaesche. The reminder will be good for the man."

Otto grinned. "As you say, sir." He saluted and hurried away.

"We will not forget Holzminden," Eggers said to himself as he walked back to his office.

CHAPTER

TWENTY-SIX

Nearly two weeks had come and gone since Colonel Glaesche's visit to the concentration camp and the shooting of the French prisoner. Even though the man was recovering from the wound in his neck, he had lost the ability to use the fingers on his left hand. The incident caused increased hostility and belligerence. Periodically "Remember Holzminden" would appear scrawled on the walls. Inmates kept taunting the Germans that they had crossed the line of all legal and moral decency. The guards didn't seem to know how to respond to the goading and warned the prisoners to shut their mouths. If Glaesche returned to the castle at all, he stayed out of the prisoners' sight.

As Christmas Day approached, the insolence subsided somewhat, and both the Germans and Allied prisoners sensed a truce was unfolding. By Christmas Eve the confrontations ceased, and both the prisoners and their guards took on a new sense of propriety. As the sun slid into the horizon, a cease-fire finally fell into place.

A gentle snowfall slowly drifted over the castle under the evening stars that sparkled in the black winter sky. The stillness of the night settled over each man, whether prisoner or guard. The meaning of Christmas Eve transformed the usual hostility between the German guards and the Allied soldiers into cordiality and friendliness, permeating even such brief exchanges as "Good evening" or "Merry Christmas." Major Eggers had allowed the French chaplain to hold a midnight service, so at eleven o'clock the prisoners began walking toward the chapel.

Tony Irving and his British comrades strolled quietly across the snow-covered courtyard. The wind had stopped, and the briskness of the night felt invigorating. Even though it was in a concentration camp, Tony had never seen a more meaningful setting for Christmas than the beauty of this evening.

"Takes your breath away, doesn't it?" Bill Fowler said.

"Yeah," Tony answered. "We don't get much snow in Dallas. Makes tonight sort of extra special."

The men entered the chapel silently. Much to Irving's surprise, the entire sanctuary lay bathed in candlelight and the pews were filled. Tony quickly slipped into the final seat on the aisle near the back. From the choir loft a pipe organ began playing a prelude.

Tony had not heard music in such a long time that the beauty of the old organ touched him deeply. The sound of the *Dominus*, so often used in a midnight Christmas Mass, fell over him like the calm snowfall settling outside. In its own unique way, the prelude resounded across the chapel with a promise of peace that felt like the calm winds blowing through the pines in the forest.

Tony didn't know Father Jacque Le Brun, the priest captured during the war in France, but he watched the clergyman incensing the altar. Apparently, Major Eggers had allowed the priest full use of the regular supplies for the chapel. Le Brun walked back and forth in a white chasuble, stately swinging the thurible and sending large puffs of incense up above the altar.

Because Tony had grown up in an evangelical church, much of what he was seeing seemed foreign, but it struck him as imparting a deep sense of reverence for the meaning of the birth of Christ. The pungent smell of the smoke set the room apart in an aura of holiness.

The organ shifted and began playing "O Come All Ye Faithful." Men stood and began singing joyfully, *O come let us adore Him, o come let us adore Him, Christ the Lord.* Tony looked around. Prisoners were lined up across the back with German guards standing in the corners, but each person was singing, *Christ is born of Mary.* The verses echoed with a unity, transcending national boundaries and the war raging so far away. In this moment, the world's problems appeared to vanish, leaving behind nothing but the sanctity of an ancient manger still resting in Bethlehem.

The men sat down and prepared to hear the Christmas story. The priest picked up a Holy Bible and held it above his head, slowly lowering it to the wooden stand. Le Brun first read Matthew's Gospel in French and then again in English. His voice sounded firm and confident.

... And she will bring forth a Son, and you shall call His name JESUS, for He will save His people from their sins.

So all this was done that it might be fulfilled which was spoken by the Lord through the prophet, saying: *"Behold, the virgin shall be with child, and bear a Son, and they shall call His name Immanuel,"* which is translated, "God with us."

The words kept resonating long after the sound of the priest's voice drifted away. "God with us." Tony kept thinking about the promise. From that first moment in Bethlehem to the end of history, God had promised to be with them, and tonight every word was being confirmed in his heart.

Back in Texas, Rikki would be in a church somewhere. God had promised to be with them as well. No matter what happened or how difficult their circumstances became, God *would be* with them.

The service continued, but Tony sat transfixed, not wanting this moment to end. The promise had been too personal and enduring. God would stay with them no matter whether the snow was piled deep or the sun blazed in the sky. He had promised.

"And not far from here is where on this very night Hans Gruber wrote 'Silent Night,'" the priest explained, jarring Tony's wandering mind back to the reality of the service. "Yes, 'Silent Night, Holy Night' began on a cold winter's night exactly like this one. Let us go forth singing this hymn and thanking God for the Child offering us our redemption."

The men stood and the old organ began the beloved hymn. Tony was one of the last to stand. The candlelight, the incense, the Christmas carols, and most of all the promise of God's constant presence had touched him deeply. He couldn't sing the first line and only barely managed to hum. With tears rolling down his face, he tried to get out the words of the second verse, but only a few words came here and there. By the last line, Tony knew it was impossible to sing further and sat down in the pew. The hymn ended and the men filed past, but he didn't move. Only after the sanctuary was nearly empty did he leave.

The rancor quickly picked up again when Christmas passed. The cold, gray winter days wore on and reduced the prisoners' exercise time.

One afternoon in mid-January, Tony Irving, Bill Fowler, and Lulu Lawton gathered again around the stove in the dormitory, standing next to the fire and warming their hands.

"Months ago we vowed to find a way out of this place and nothing has happened," Irving said. "I think it's time we did *something.*"

"You got something in mind?" Lawton asked.

Irving shook his head. "I came up with better ideas during the first weeks than I have the last several months. No, I've been thinking about a new way to tunnel out of here, but I haven't found any angles that would really work, and I'm not crazy about narrow spaces. Obviously, tunneling is a long, hard route."

Fowler nodded. "You're right. It's little more than a way to kill time."

"Anyone know how the war is going?" Irving asked.

"I think the Germans are getting run out of Africa," Lawton said. "At least, that's what I get from the BBC broadcast. The story seems to be that General Montgomery has backed Rommel's *Afrika Korps* across the desert. More Allies have landed in Morocco and Algeria, but the battle is still raging."

"Algeria is a long way off," Irving said. "A long, long way from here."

"Yes," Fowler agreed. "And it will be a *long* time before the Allies get us out of this camp."

"I guess we haven't discovered anything yet." Irving sounded disgusted.

"Maybe, maybe not." Lawton grinned slyly. "I've been keeping a record of how prisoners are hauled into this dump, and most of it has been on the boring side. The Germans run new guys in at every possible time of day, but I've noticed that they usually show up in the early morning, around seven o'clock. I did discover an interesting fact: The prisoners always come up to the castle *exactly the same way*. No one gets into this place except through a narrow side door that is carefully watched by a German NCO."

"What are you saying, Lawton?" Fowler pushed.

"As bizarre as it sounds, we might be looking at the most possible way out of this camp—*leaving by exactly the same route we entered*."

Tony blinked several times. "I'm not sure I understand."

Lawton grinned mischievously. "What if we simply walked out of here?"

"How in the world would we do that?" Irving asked.

Captain Lawton's grin widened. "I think I have an idea how to do just that."

The next day the winter wind felt particularly biting, but the prisoners still tried to exercise outside. Midafternoon sunlight bounced off the snow and left a gray haze in the sky. Captain Lulu Lawton walked with the parade of prisoners marching around and around the inner courtyard. The men said little but kept up their steady pace. Cold nibbled on his ears, and Lulu had to periodically put his hands to his head to fight the chill. He didn't like the slightly painful sensation, but he knew walking was important. On the sixth time around the oddly shaped yard, he noticed Stooge Wardle standing next to the building, looking at him. On the next turn, Wardle walked up and fell into step with Lawton.

"I hear you got a new idea about how to get out of this lovely little city," Stooge said.

"My, my, where would you ever hear such a thing?" Steam rolled out of Lawton's mouth. "What a strange rumor!"

"Being on the toasting committee does have its advantages." Wardle looked around to make sure no one was listening or walking too close behind them. "What can I do to help your cause?"

"I need a map of the castle. I haven't decided yet on how to approach an escape, and I don't want to talk about the possibilities until I have more data, but I think I'm on to something significant."

Stooge kicked at the ground. "*Significant*, huh? Sounds good enough to me. It won't take long to find a map. I'm sure someone on our committee has access to a diagram of this place."

"After I've had time to study a map of the castle more carefully, I think I'll have something to submit to your buddies."

"Good. I'll take a hard look."

Lawton nodded. "Let me know." He walked on by himself as Wardle fell back and eventually disappeared into the dormitory.

By the time Lawton had made a few more rounds, the cold became too severe and he retreated to his own dormitory. Like the rest of the men, Lulu had no choice but to wait for the evening mess hall to open, but he didn't stop thinking about the strange plan rolling around in his mind. The idea seemed so extreme and unexpected it might just work, but he had to take a hard and careful look at how the castle's grounds were laid out.

Eventually the Germans started ringing a bell, and the men migrated toward the mess hall. Lawton fell in with the other prisoners and lined up behind one of the Poles.

"Vat you tink we ave to eat tonight?" the Polish soldier asked with a twinkle in his eye. "Steak dis night?"

"Probably a porterhouse," Lulu snickered. "Surely not soup again!"

The two men laughed, avoiding the fact that the meal would be soup. Lawton picked up the predictable piece of black bread and shuffled on through the line. No one seemed to be saying much, and conversations remained on the low, quiet side. Even though he tried to string out his time at the table, supper went by fairly quickly. Lawton kept considering what he might do that evening. Probably he would watch the entry gate again. Nothing else to do. Lulu got up to take his utensils back.

"Going anywhere?" a voice said behind him.

Lawton stopped. Stooge's voice was recognizable under any set of circumstances. "I suppose it depends on you."

"Why don't we stroll back to the dormitory?"

"Sure," Lawton said without turning around.

"I'll meet you in the doorway." Wardle disappeared as quickly as he had appeared.

Lawton continued his slow, easy ramble out of the mess hall, walking obtusely in the direction of the dormitory. He could see Stooge standing casually inside the doorway.

"You got something for me?" Lawton asked.

"When you go upstairs, lie down on your bunk. Under the cover you'll find a map of Colditz Castle."

"Fantastic! You didn't waste any time."

"Your local toasting committee is an efficient group of bad boys. Let me know what you're planning when you get to the stage of making definite decisions."

"I will." Lawton edged past his friend and then turned around. "Thanks, ole buddy."

"Think nothing of it." Stooge walked away.

Lawton strolled upstairs, trying to look indifferent. He didn't speak to any of the other inmates but stretched out on the bed. It wasn't that he distrusted the other prisoners, but he didn't want to talk about what he was thinking until every aspect of the plan was clear in his mind. Talking to other inmates would only be confusing. After several minutes of staring at the ceiling, Lulu rolled over and started fishing under the covers. His fingers felt the smooth surface of a piece of paper. Making as little noise as possible, he pulled out a map of the castle grounds. The layout had been drawn in pencil and looked like it had been traced off another map, but it was a clear, scaled diagram of the entire floor plan of the castle. With his index finger, Lawton traced the path of where he had seen the prisoners enter the castle. He followed their journey through the narrow door into the confines of the castle.

Just as I thought, he mused to himself, *my idea is workable. All I need to do is find the right place to start from, and we can simply stroll out of here.*

Lulu folded up the diagram and slipped it back under the covers. The light went out but he kept staring into the darkness. If a few more pieces in the puzzle fit together, his audacious scheme would let them walk right out of the stinking prison. He had found the door out of Colditz Castle.

PART FOUR
The Door Out

CHAPTER

TWENTY-SEVEN

A warm wind from the west had blown into the castle's grounds, slightly melting the snow. The prisoners had begun exercising outdoors again. Any reprieve from the cold weather helped.

In the middle of the afternoon, Royal Air Force Captain Lulu Lawton walked out of the entrance to the dormitory and stopped for a moment to watch the men hike around the courtyard. Above the mess hall kitchen on the roof, the iron-helmeted sentry sat behind a machine gun, poised to fire down on any possible insurrections; other guards stood around the area with rifles hanging from their shoulders. Lawton smiled at the predictability of the scene.

Standing across the large, stone-covered courtyard outside the mess hall, Dutch Captain Damiaem Van Doorninck appeared indifferent to the increased number of prisoners out on a tramp. At around forty years of age, Van Doorninck was numbered among the older prisoners. He had allowed his red beard to grow, giving him the appearance of a gangling pirate preparing to sail the open sea. Damiaem seemed to be cleaning his fingernails and paying no attention to the men walking by.

Lawton fell in with the marching parade and started the long walk around the courtyard so that any conversation with Van Doorninck would appear more casual. When he marched by the opposite side of the courtyard wall, Lawton stepped out of the line and stopped next to the long-legged Dutchman.

"You're looking healthy today, Damiaem."

The Dutchman looked up without moving a muscle in his body. "What's on your mind this afternoon, mate?" Van Doorninck answered in a perfect British accent.

"You're quite good with languages, aren't you?"

Damiaem abruptly smiled. "I once lectured in English while teaching higher mathematics at our university. Interesting you should happen to notice."

"I bet you can speak German as well as anyone in this castle."

"Sprechen Deutsch?" Van Doorninck puckered his lips. "Hitler might think I was his personal valet."

Lawton rubbed his chin for a moment. "You're exactly the man I'm looking for. I think I know a way out of here. Want to come?"

"Escape?" the Dutchman whispered. "You're on."

"I need someone who can speak German like a local country boy." Lulu stepped closer. "Also, I need an inmate who can pick a lock. From what I've seen, you're the best at both."

"Interesting you should mention this little hobby of mine. I've been working on a new tool, a type of homemade micrometer, to help me quickly open these cruciform locks they use around here. The pistons inside of those gadgets are rather complicated."

"How accurate is this micrometer you've made?"

Van Doorninck grinned. "Oh, I'd say I can measure down to within a tenth of a millimeter."

Lawton's mouth dropped slightly. "You're kidding!"

"Nope! I've reached the place where I can probably open any lock in this entire castle in short order."

Lulu's eyes narrowed. "You are *exactly* what I'm looking for, Damiaem. The only problem I can foresee is that you'll have to shave that beard and mustache before we actually escape."

"My mustache?" Van Doorninck felt the long, pointed end of his eloquently waxed whiskers. "I'm not sure I could bear leaving my object of art behind in this dismal place." He grinned. "Probably take me thirty seconds to cut it off."

"It'll be awhile before we're ready to go. We've got to get a number of the pieces of the puzzle in place. Just go about your business as usual, and I'll be back in touch later. Of course, this is still a secret at the moment. Only two other people are aware of my intentions."

The Dutchman nodded slightly. "Excellent. I hadn't planned on going anywhere soon *anyway*." He winked.

"I'm sure you'd enjoy a little jaunt over to Switzerland."

"Most certainly!" Captain Van Doorninck dropped his head as if answering royalty. "At your service." He made a sweeping gesture with his hand.

Lawton stepped back into the line of walking soldiers. He'd made the first move, and the right pieces were coming together.

Evening had fallen when Lulu Lawton huddled with Tony Irving and Bill Fowler in the dormitory. German sentries had already checked the rooms to take the evening head count, and the men didn't expect an *Appell* to follow.

Lawton pointed over his shoulder. "I've lined up Damiaem Van Doorninck to be part of this attempt."

"Why him?" Irving asked. "He's an inconsiderate jerk."

"Because he can open any lock in this castle," Lawton said. "Got it?"

"A lock?" Irving frowned.

"Here's the scoop," Lawton whispered. "I noticed that on many evenings the Germans billet small groups of Polish prisoners in the town of Colditz. They usually march them up here to the prison around seven o'clock in the morning." He nodded his head in the direction of the entry gate. "At the same time, the Nazis change their sentries at the entry gate at seven o'clock. Get where this is going?"

"You are suggesting that shortly after seven in the morning would be a good time for us to try to get through that front gate," Fowler said.

"Exactly!" Lawton grinned. "Several inmates dressed in Polish uniforms along with someone who speaks excellent German could walk out straightaway."

"Van Doorninck!" Tony Irving gasped.

"You got it," Lawton answered. "He sounds as authentic as Eggers does. We're going to dress Damiaem like the German soldier in charge of this little exit party and let him march us out of here."

"Wow! What an idea!" Fowler leaned closer to the group of men. "But we can't walk a group of disguised men out of this dormitory, or the Germans will be all over us. Where can we assemble this group?"

Lawton nodded. "I've thought about this and studied the problem using a map of the castle I obtained from Stooge Wardle. I think we've got to find a way to get our group of men somewhere in the vicinity of the storeroom and the office that the Nazi sneak Heinz Gephard occupies."

"Gephard's office, huh?" Bill Fowler said.

"How do you plan to do that?" Tony Irving asked. "Sounds like we're talking about digging a tunnel." He shivered.

"A tunnel?" Fowler shook his head. "I don't know . . . they haven't worked well."

Irving shook his head. "I hate that idea. Narrow places make me feel crazy."

"Who said anything about a tunnel?" Lawton answered. "Tunnels are for rabbits. I think we need a little more imagination than digging burrows."

"Imagination?" Tony scratched his head. "What have you got in mind?"

"Unlocking the front door and walking in," Lawton said.

Tony stared. "I don't see how . . . ," his voice died out. "*That's* why you talked with Van Doorninck!"

"Yes, sir! Damiaem Van Doorninck . . . the best locksmith in the whole world or, at least, in this prison."

TWENTY-EIGHT

Stooge Wardle sat down at the mess hall table across from Captain Lawton. He winked and began talking slowly. "The toasting committee thought about that idea you shared the other day. Understand?"

Lawton nodded. "Sure."

"We think you ought to act on that possibility as soon as you can. You certainly have our approval."

"Good." Lawton looked down at the watery bowl of soup. "I'm going to need some help."

"We thought so. Some of our most trusted men are already working on coming up with some of the items you will need." Wardle looked over his shoulder in both directions and could see no one was listening. "We can supply some identity papers and help put together the Polish uniforms as well as civilian clothes for after you're out."

For the first time Lawton grinned. "Most excellent and deeply appreciated. Can you help me build two wooden boxes?"

"Boxes?" Wardle shrugged. "Sure."

"They need to be able to be dismantled and put together quickly."

"Okay." Wardle looked up at the guard walking toward them. His tone changed. "Yeah, I think the snow is going to be gone before long. We'll be back to walking up and down in that exercise field."

Lawton saw the guard. "Maybe we can come up with a soccer game or a tournament."

"Great idea!" Wardle said loudly. "A spring sports event. Of course, we'll probably get more cold weather before it truly turns warm around here, but we could at least start planning."

The German guard paused, glanced at the two inmates, then walked on.

Lawton watched the German's back going down the aisle between the tables. "Hitler's little buddy is gone. Thanks for the help, Wardle," he whispered.

"You bet." Stooge Wardle got up and moved on to the next table.

Lulu Lawton sat quietly at the table, thinking about the plan. Other good schemes had come and gone, and some of the best strategies had backfired at the last minute, but everything about this plan seemed to be falling into place. He didn't want to get excited yet, but Captain Lawton felt his idea was working out in a way that was almost too good to be true. He pushed back from the table and walked out.

———

Tony Irving had finished his meager meal and sat by himself in a corner of the mess hall sipping the bitter coffee. He watched the prisoners and noticed that most of them seemed brighter. Probably yesterday's warm-up had settled into their bones and they felt a new vigor. The food certainly wasn't anymore plentiful, but the men seemed to be more hopeful. A good sign.

"You staying here any longer, mate?" Bill Fowler asked.

Irving shook his head. "No, I think I'll go over to the chapel. There are a number of things that I should pray for today. Know what I mean?"

Fowler raised an eyebrow. "Most certainly. We could use some divine assistance."

"Yeah." Irving stood up. "I'll be back in the dormitory after awhile."

Fowler walked over to another group of men talking together while Irving hurried out of the mess hall in the direction of the chapel. No one ever chided him about praying so often. All of the men wandered into the chapel at some time or the other. They knew how desperately each one of them needed God's help.

Tony slipped in the back door of the chapel and closed it behind him. The hush of the sanctuary wrapped a cloak of holiness around him. Shadows drifted across the pews, deepening the sense of human struggle that always emanated from the camp. Nevertheless, the awareness that God waited for him in the shadows comforted and encouraged Tony. A couple of men were sitting around the sanctuary, and a candle was burning near the front. Tony walked to the nearest pew and sat down. Almost immediately he entered into the silence that always restored his soul.

For ten minutes the young American silently prayed and soaked up the consolation. Tony had no idea what was ahead, and his claustrophobia worried him. Hopefully, he wouldn't get crowded into some narrow space that might resurrect the anxieties that stayed hidden in the back of his mind. Tony didn't want another panic experience. He certainly didn't want any of the men to know about this disconcerting problem. He prayed fervently for God's intervention to settle his anxiety. Tony took a deep breath and relaxed. He could feel his worries and anxieties start to float away as new confidence replaced them.

At the end of the entry near the east end of the chapel, Sergeant-Major Gephard's office was across the way from the sick ward. The prisoners often called the large, arrogant German "Mussolini." Tony was sitting next to the exact place Lulu Lawton had talked about using as part of their escape route. Could he possibly be actually perched right next to an exit out of this castle? The immediacy of the present possibility felt unreal.

The predictable, daily routine of prison life had worn its ruts in him, causing Tony to develop his own set of expectations that followed, one after another, the same way every day of the week. In a matter of hours that world of the expected was about to be blown away. Tony wanted to be prepared for what lay ahead for him. Life in the camp had periodically left him feeling addled. Tony knew what it was to have his carefully constructed plans destroyed.

The relief he had felt moments earlier suddenly disappeared, and once again inner turmoil began churning. During his years in Dallas, Tony hadn't ever felt a quaking sense of insecurity. He looked down and discovered his hand was shaking slightly. The time in Colditz Castle had infused him with a previously unknown sense of insecurity and uncertainty. His arrogance and cockiness had disappeared.

Tony peeled the little black Bible out of his pocket and thumbed through it until he found the thirteenth chapter of Luke's Gospel. The words were exactly the same as he remembered them. *"Make every effort to enter through the narrow door . . ."*

"The *narrow* door?" Tony said under his breath. "God, please fulfill this promise whatever it means. I hate the word *narrow*. We want to recover the freedom You have given us. This castle is tearing me apart."

The words once again took on the same urgency he had experienced previously. The line almost seemed to stand up and march off the page.

Sliding down to his knees, Tony prayed silently for God to confirm in some way what the Bible said. He wanted to make sure the path now opening before him was truly one the hand of God had ordained. No more mistakes or nonsense. No surprises. Tony wanted only what God had chosen for them. He certainly didn't want to get caught again and spend anymore time in that stinking isolation cell. That was for sure!

After fifteen minutes of praying, Tony stood up and walked back outside. The sun was shining brightly and the snow continued to melt.

More men were walking around the courtyard. The prison scene was changing. Maybe, just maybe, he was coming to the end of his tenure in Colditz prison.

TWENTY-NINE

*L*eaving the chapel behind, Tony Irving returned to the dormitory. Some of the inmates were playing cards while others stood around the room, talking and generally trying to pass the time of day. Boredom hung in the air like stale smoke.

Captain Lulu Lawton looked up and motioned for Tony to come over to him. "You certainly look bad," Lawton began. "A little peaked, in fact. Your eyes seem dull and your skin looks flushed."

"What?" Tony frowned. "I feel fine!"

"That's exactly how these things start." Lawton raised an eyebrow. "One minute you feel okay and the next you're sick as a horse. Happens every day."

"But I'm telling you that . . ."

"No," Lulu said firmly. "I'm telling you that you need a visit to the sick ward. You need to spend a couple of days in those beds, and while you're there invest a little time checking the locks on the doors."

"Now that you mention it, I'm starting to feel on the weak side."

"No question about it. The next step in this illness is feeling run down. I think you need to get to that sick ward as quickly as you can walk. You might collapse."

Tony nodded emphatically. "I might not be able to travel in a few minutes."

"Certainly." Lawton said. "Your feet are likely to slide out from under you. Boom!" He clapped his hands. "Why, we'd need to carry you over there."

"You think it'd help if you went with me?"

Lawton's grin took on a sly twist. "I'd be able to stabilize you . . . as well as *point out which locks* we need you to thoroughly examine."

"Even as I stand here, my stomach has started to hurt. I think we need to get on our way immediately."

Lawton slipped Tony's arm around his neck. "Definitely. Let's move on before you die on the floor."

The two men hurried down the stairs and out into the inner court-yard where prisoners still milled around the stone pavement. Slowing down, they trudged across the exercise area toward the hallway leading into the sick ward. Tony groaned softly and limped, hanging on to Lawton.

"Got a sick man for you," Lawton told the guard seated at the door. "I think he needs to be put in bed quickly."

The guard's eyes narrowed. "Let me see." The plump German leaned over the desk and glared into Tony's half-open eyes. "He dost not look *too* sick to me."

"We got him here early before this man vomited all over the dormitory. I'd suggest you get him in bed or you may be sorry."

Shaking his head in disgust, the guard stood up. "I'll check and see what's open back there. Dis isn't a flophouse for you prisoners." The little man walked briskly out of the room. "Don't forget it."

Lawton pointed to the front door. "We need you to study this lock carefully." He whispered and motioned toward the sick bay. "We must have an accurate picture of how to get out of that room back there. Got me?"

"What's my objective?" Tony asked.

"We must know how to sneak out of here, steal across the outside corridor, and break into Heinz Gephard's office."

"Mussolini's place? The German fat boy? I'll do my best."

The guard walked through the door. "Take him back to one of de beds next to the east wall. Drop him der."

Tony doubled up as if fighting stomach cramps. "Th-th-thank you," he muttered.

"What caused dis problem?" the guard snarled.

"I think he's been eating too much at lunch," Lawton quipped. "Probably ate all that steak last night. Maybe the dessert was too rich."

Eyeing him suspiciously, the guard motioned with his head. "Don't push your luck. Get him out of here."

Lawton straightened Tony up and started walking Tony back toward an empty bed.

Moving along gingerly, the captain spoke sympathetically. "A little rest will do wonders, Tony. I don't imagine you'll need to stay long."

Two days later Irving hobbled out of the sick ward and walked back into the courtyard. Once he got past the entry door, Tony stood up and walked faster. At the other side of the cubicle, Damiaem Van Doorninck stood leaning against the stone wall, staring ominously out over the prisoners with his dark, intense eyes and his long mustache twirled to a point at the ends. Irving nodded and walked up to the Dutchman.

"Your health improving, cowboy?" Doorninck asked with a perfect American accent.

"I took a little stroll last night, Damiaem. Even walked back to the end of the corridor by Sergeant-Major Gephard's office and looked at the door for awhile. I instantly started feeling well."

"What did you learn about Mussolini's office?" Doorninck's voice remained as emotionally empty as always.

"I noticed cross-shaped keyholes both inside and outside of the sick bay," Tony said quietly. "They looked much like Yale locks but had four arms."

"Yes." Van Doorninck continued using his American accent. "Inside the cylinders are tiny pistons. To open those locks requires accuracy to one-thousandth of an inch."

"Humph! Sounds extremely difficult to me."

"It will take a visit or two to the sick ward, but I'll have it worked out in no time."

Irving blinked several times. "Really?"

"You Americans are *so* easily surprised," Van Doorninck said, switching to his usual Dutch accent. "I'll let you know how it works."

Irving watched the Dutchman walk away with the nonchalance of a peddler ambling down a country road. He hadn't veered an inch from the indifference Tony had experienced in the past, and his callousness still made Irving's blood boil. Damiaem had not made any acknowledgment of or apology after their verbal clash. Tony had tried to share encouraging words about God, and the Dutchman had virtually hit him in the mouth. Van Doorninck's mood still remained irritating, but Tony wasn't giving up on that little talk he had planned for him.

Tony walked into the entry of the dormitory and hurried up the stairs, thinking about the plan that was about to unfold before him.

"Hey!" Lulu Lawton called out. "Our sick boy has returned!" The men around him clapped. "Welcome back."

"Amazing that it only took a couple of days," Tony replied.

Lawton put his arm around Tony's shoulder and walked him toward the window. "How about that other little matter we discussed?"

"I just got through talking to Van Doorninck downstairs. I gave him the information."

"Excellent!" Lawton slapped him on the back. "Well done, mate."

"I don't like that man," Tony said. "He's a cold fish."

"Yeah, but we need that fish to swim in our pond. Don't worry. Damiaem will come through for us."

"How soon are we going to pull off this exit?"

"Soon," Lawton said. "Very soon."

CHAPTER

THIRTY

Night had fallen, covering the castle in blackness. Even the moon had disappeared behind opaque clouds. Shortly after midnight, Dutch Captain Damiaem Van Doorninck and his colleague Colonel Jacob Sas crept out of the dormitory into the murky darkness of the courtyard, crawling along the inner side of the castle toward the sick ward.

Both men could see the outline of a German sentry sitting on top of the prisoners' kitchen. Periodically the soldier lit up a cigarette, revealing the distant outline of his face. At those moments, Sas and Van Doorninck moved quickly. As soon as they inched past the chapel, the Dutch prisoners found it easy to slip inside the hallway leading to the sick ward and Gephard's office. A quick peek inside the infirmary revealed the guard was fast asleep at his desk.

"Just as you predicted," Sas whispered. "The old fool is sawing logs."

Damiaem nodded. "We shouldn't be bothered by anyone at the end of this dark alley." He hurried toward the door to Sergeant-Major Heinz Gephard's office.

"Why did Lawton want to get into this godforsaken hole?" Jacob whispered in his friend's ear. "Mussolini's office is a foreboding place to fool with."

"I'll tell you in a minute." The Dutchman dropped to one knee, inserting a long, thin probe into the locks. With his ear near the last fastener, he carefully wiggled the thin rod back and forth in the most complicated of the locks.

"What are you looking for?" Sas asked.

Damiaem didn't answer but only listened. After several minutes, he exclaimed under his breath, "I've got it!" He stood up and carefully opened the door.

The two men rushed in and Van Doorninck shut the door behind them quickly. "We've made it. My invention worked!"

"Invention?" Jacob Sas stared at the strange little device with a long metal rod sticking out at the end. "The contraption looks like a darning needle machine."

"Made it myself," Damiaem said. "It's a homemade micrometer that will measure down to a tenth of a millimeter."

"You're kidding!" Jacob leaned forward to look even more carefully at the small metal device.

"I can open any lock in this place with my little friend." Van Doorninck carefully slipped the device into his pocket. "Even ugly old Mussolini's office is now open to us."

"That's what I don't understand," Sas said. "Why in God's name are we breaking into this dangerous suite?"

Damiaem grinned. "That's exactly the point. Gephard's abode is no doubt considered safe—it would be far too brazen for a prisoner to attempt an escape out of these quarters. For exactly that reason, Lawton and his party want to break out through here."

Sas blinked several times. "Amazing!" He rubbed his chin. "An astonishing idea."

"Yeah, but now we've got to find out how to use this place. Let's check it out carefully." Van Doorninck began moving slowly through the office.

"Unfortunately, the windows are covered by iron bars," Sas said, observing the surroundings. "In addition, the window is right in the line of sight of the sentry that usually stands out there by the precipice. We can't climb out."

Damiaem nodded. "Hmm, yes I see." He stared out the window. "You'll notice there's a shed down there under this window where they store clothing, old uniforms, underwear, clogs—stuff like that."

"Yes," Sas said thoughtfully. "The shed is directly below us."

"Which means," Damiaem thought out loud, "all we need to do is to get under the floor of this office, and we can drop into that shed—a perfect way out of here!"

"May take a night or two to dig the tunnel," Sas concluded. "But if we put people in the sick bay, they could break away during the night and get this job done easily."

"I think so, but I'll need to make a key for them to get in this office. They would have to leave this room in perfect condition. We cannot leave a clue about what we're doing."

"Right!" Sas kept rubbing his chin. "We need at least two men to work this job."

"That's Lawton's call. He's been planning the escape, and I'm sure Lulu will know who is best to send over here."

"Okay," Jacob said. "Then let's get out of here and report what we found to him."

"Take it slow and easy," Damiaem said. "The Kraut with the machine gun is still up there on top of the kitchen."

Three nights later at one o'clock in the morning, Jacob Sas and Bill Fowler huddled with Lulu Lawton and Tony Irving out in the hall of the dormitory to report how the excavations had gone.

"What did you accomplish?" Lawton asked.

"Fortunately, the stupid Nazi guarding the door to the sick bay sleeps like a rock. He didn't move a muscle through any of our comings and goings."

"Good. Good." Lulu smiled. "Went as I expected."

"We worked the boards loose under Mussolini's desk," Fowler said. "Ole fat Gephard's floor proved easy to use as an entry to make a short tunnel down to the shed."

"Yes," Sas added, "we covered the tunnel with blankets to muffle any sounds of our movement. No one had a clue."

"Excellent!" Lawton grinned at Tony. "See what you started with your little trip down to the hospital?"

Irving laughed. "Amazing how these little ideas spread to other, bigger things."

"We used the chisels and spikes, but we found the mortar between the stones to be old and worn," Fowler added. "Moving the stone blocks was no problem."

"You got down to the shed then?"

"We found the back side of the plaster wall but put the stones back in place to cover up our tunneling," Sas said. "When we came back up the last time, we even sealed the cracks in Gephard's office floor with a dust-colored paste we made."

"Yeah," Fowler said, "and the second night we enlarged the tunnel. Everything is ready for an escape break down to that old storage shed."

"Gentlemen, you have paved the first mile out of this hole," Lawton answered. "The people on the escape committee are preparing uniforms for us. In a few hours, they'll have Polish and German uniforms finished as well as the wooden boxes we need. I think this escape will happen in the next two days."

Sas grinned slyly. "What if we're ready to leave sooner?"

Lulu nodded. "If the Nazis would open the front gate, I'd bet we could empty this castle in five minutes. Well, I hope in forty-eight hours at least six of us vacate our beds. I believe we're in excellent shape to break out soon."

"How are they making uniforms that the Germans won't notice are obvious fakes?" Tony asked thoughtfully.

"Our people have made a sewing machine out of wood," Lawton answered. "Darnedest thing I ever saw. One of the Polish prisoners carved wheels out of lath, but that little machine whips along like it was steel, making seams like a haberdashery shop in London. You wouldn't believe it."

"A wooden sewing machine?" Tony shook his head. "We've certainly brought the twentieth century to this medieval castle!"

"Now our job is to deceive these Nazis right out of their drawers." Lulu pointed into the dormitory. "Let's get a good night's sleep, men."

THIRTY-ONE

The prisoners living in the *Furstenhaus* awoke at their usual hour and prepared for another boring, meaningless day in the Colditz concentration camp, but three of the inmates crawled out of bed with an unusual sense of anticipation. If all the pieces of the puzzle were in place, this could prove to be a good day, an exceptional day . . . a final day.

At precisely seven o'clock, an unexpected black Mercedes drove through the front entrance of Colditz Castle. Pulling his black leather overcoat close, Colonel Edgar Glaesche stepped out of the car and walked briskly into the officers' quarters where Major Reinhold Eggers maintained his office. As he intended, Glaesche arrived early enough to find all the offices empty. He walked confidently through the outer offices and into Eggers's inner headquarters.

For several minutes Glaesche inspected every inch of the room. Checking every item on the bookshelf and thumbing through the files, he looked for some small mistake, some object out of place, some entity missing, but he found nothing worthy of a personal attack on Eggers. The office seemed to be in remarkably good condition, which only irritated the colonel. Glaesche sat down in Eggers's desk chair and began thumping on the desktop with his riding crop.

"Nothing amiss!" the colonel said to himself. "Got to be something wrong!" Glaesche pushed his riding crop across the papers on the desktop, but saw nothing and cursed.

Glaesche didn't like Eggers's predictable efficiency. The major seemed to be *too good* at his job, and it agitated the colonel. If he couldn't find anything wrong, then Glaesche had no other excuse but to move back into the administration area. It wasn't his preferred route to accomplish his purpose. He would have much rather acted because of Eggers's incompetent behavior, but Eggers hadn't given him any ammunition.

At ten minutes before eight o'clock, Major Reinhold Eggers opened the front door and walked into his office. "*What?*" he exclaimed in shock, staring at the senior officer sitting in his chair.

"I have been here waiting," Colonel Glaesche said with cold indifference.

"I'm sorry. I wasn't expecting you."

"You should *always* be expecting me!" Glaesche sneered. "I am the commandant of this prison."

"Of course." Reinhold bowed politely.

"I have decided to take some direct action in this camp," Glaesche sounded like a lecturer. "I believe greater efficiency is possible."

"Yes . . . ," Eggers said slowly, removing his officer's cap and hanging it carefully on the hook attached to the wall.

"I want this camp to be run with maximum efficiency as should be true of every German installation. *Am I communicating?*"

"Certainly." Eggers hung his overcoat beneath the hat. "Of course, our last attempt at such . . . as you call it . . . efficiency . . . ended with a man being accidentally shot."

Glaesche's face flushed. "Next time I'll kill every one of those swine!" The colonel stood up and walked around the desk. "Yes, I am aware that some pig-headed prisoner wrote a few words about the former

Holzminden situation, trying to intimidate *me*." Glaesche beat the palm of his hand with the riding crop. "But the war is changing. It makes no difference! I don't want to hear anything more about this situation again. Do you understand?"

Eggers tipped his head. "Of course."

Glaesche felt rattled by Eggers's cool comments and it made him even angrier, but he knew it was important to keep from exploding. He took a deep breath. "I will be here in my *Kommandantur* office this week and will be in complete charge."

"Yes, sir."

"I expect *all matters and details* to be run through my offices. I am the commander. Understood?"

"Of course." Eggers bowed again.

For a moment the colonel thumped his palm again, studying Eggers's face. The man appeared passively obedient and compliant. He couldn't find anything to attack, which made this encounter all the more deplorable.

"Anything else, sir?" Eggers's face remained completely passive.

"I'll let you know." Glaesche stomped out of the room and marched off to his quarters in *Kommandantur,* not liking anything about this *too perfect* situation. He would eventually catch Eggers in something or the other, and then the ax would fall.

The three prisoners from the *Furstenhaus* ambled through breakfast, checking with each other as well as some of the responsible officers to make sure every aspect of their escape plan was in place. Near the end of breakfast, Wardle sat down across from the three men.

"You gentlemen look chipper this morning," Wardle said with his usual, carefree air. "Must be enjoying the scrumptious buffet."

"We think this might turn out to be an important day," Tony answered.

"I believe so," Wardle said. "Everything is ready."

Lawton's eyes narrowed. "You're speaking of those extra uniforms and the pieces of wood?"

"Exactly." Wardle's cavalier attitude disappeared. "The wood will be smuggled into the sick bay today, but the uniforms have already been stashed in the back of the shed. The necessary documents are with the uniforms."

Irving leaned forward. "Why don't you go with us, Stooge?"

Wardle's smile returned. "I'd love to, mate, but that would be against the rules of the game. Thanks for the invitation."

"Will anything change the timing?" Fowler asked.

"Hard to say," Stooge said. "You know unexpected events can always toss the best plans into the trash can. We're still checking all the angles, but I believe tonight is good."

"Have you checked with Van Doorninck?" Tony asked.

"Yes." Wardle nodded over his shoulder. "He's downstairs at his usual post, holding up the building." Wardle grinned. "Both he and Sas are in good spirits. They're ready."

"What's the next step?" Tony inquired.

Lawton leaned forward. "Each of you is to make a visit to the sick ward. As soon as you get the opportunity, crawl under any bed and hide. Stay there."

Tony's eyes narrowed. "We're going to hide in the sick bay through the entire evening?"

"Exactly," Lulu said in a low, intense voice. "Our break tonight begins right under their big Nazi noses."

At two o'clock in the afternoon, Corporal Otto Schadlich knocked on Major Eggers's door.

"Come in," Reinhold called out from his desk.

Schadlich walked in, taking his cap off. "Do you have a moment, sir?"

"For you I have all day, old friend." Eggers stood up and walked around his desk. "What's going on?"

Schadlich cleared his throat and looked nervously around the room. "This tip has to be completely confidential." He lowered his voice and glanced suspiciously around the office again.

"As always." Major Eggers pointed to the chair in front of his desk. "No one has the skill you do, Otto. You float around this prison like a butterfly picking up data and tips that allow us to keep ahead of these 'bad boys.' I am grateful you are my comrade."

"I am here because of our relationship." The corporal looked pained. "You are a good man, Reinhold. I don't want to see you hurt by some egocentric idiot."

The major frowned. "I don't understand."

"I noticed that Glaesche showed up early this morning. He didn't see me, but I watched him walk into these offices as if he owned the prison."

Eggers nodded and looked pained. "Yes, the man was trying to catch us off guard. I think he came in here to investigate my office without me having any idea he was coming."

Otto shook his head. "Yes, I followed Glaesche when he left and went over to the *Kommandantur's* offices. I figured something must be afloat."

"And you moved in to find out what it was!"

Schadlich rubbed his forehead. "Yes, I started monitoring the colonel's phone calls."

"Dangerous business," Reinhold said. "If he had caught you, I'm not sure I could have done anything to help."

"I understand." The corporal fidgeted nervously in his chair. "But shortly after he left your office, he made a private call to Heinz Gephard."

"Heinz!" Reinhold leaned forward. "Why in the world would he call him?"

"Glaesche learned about the 'Remember Holzminden' message scribbled on the wall from Heinz," Otto said. "It turns out Gephard is his secret source of information within our ranks. Heinz relays information to Glaesche at virtually every opportunity."

Eggers dropped back in his chair. "I can't believe it! Why, I thought Heinz was an excellent soldier, a friend, a good colleague."

Schadlich whispered, "Heinz wants your job."

"What?"

"That's why the colonel was so difficult from the beginning. It is his intention to replace you with Gephard."

The major took a deep breath. "I am astonished."

Otto shook his head. "The colonel knew Gephard before he arrived here. I fear Glaesche will stay in control inside the castle until he finds some angle, some problem he can hang around your neck. Then you're on your way out and Gephard will sit behind this desk." He rapped his knuckles on the desk.

Silence fell between the two men. Finally, Eggers spoke. "We must be very careful and not let anyone know about what you have discovered, but you must keep probing."

"I know of no plans in the mill for an escape," Otto said, "but Gephard might be planning something devious. I must watch the man closely."

"And keep your eyes on Glaesche! We must not inadvertently walk into a trap."

Schadlich got to his feet slowly. "I will do my best to watch every detail unfolding in this castle." The corporal started walking to the door. "But it is not easy to second-guess everything happening in a place this large."

"I understand." Reinhold watched Otto close the door behind him. "Take care," he called out almost as a second thought. Eggers trudged back to his desk and slumped in the chair. "And don't let the wolf bite you," he said to himself.

CHAPTER

THIRTY-TWO

Although the ceiling in the hall was relatively low, the ancient ball-room at Colditz still conveyed the magnificence of Germany's for-mer imperial glory days. Carvings on the ceiling and frescoes across the walls emanated visions of splendorous women in expensive floral gowns gliding across the polished wooden floor on the arms of noblemen, who were wearing the uniforms of heroes of war as Kaiser Wilhelm had once been. The scene reeked with an ambiance of the kind of power Glaesche needed to establish his authority as the *sole* commandant of Colditz.

Only a day had passed since Colonel Edgar Glaesche's unexpected arrival at Oflag 4C concentration camp, and he had already ordered the staff to assemble as the first business of the day. Officers filed into the once-elegant ballroom and took their seats. The colonel stood alone before them as if to emphasize his singular command over the castle. Carrying his riding crop under his arm, Glaesche made himself appear as formidable as possible.

Major Eggers sat on the edge of the front row next to the wall, giving him a view of the rest of the group. While the colonel lectured, Reinhold studied the soldiers carefully, observing how they reacted to Glaesche.

"I am now ready to take this prison camp to a new level of effi-ciency," Glaesche began, standing at rigid attention. "No longer will we allow the sloppy behavior of prisoners that I have observed on many occasions." He held the riding crop behind his back, pushing his chest forward and giving him a more forceful appearance. "These Allied Forces incompetents consider themselves to be exceptions to all the rules of war established in the past by the *Wehrmacht*. We will no longer allow this predisposition."

Eggers slowly let his gaze turn to Sergeant-Major Heinz Gephard, sitting in the middle of the front row. Gephard was looking up at the colonel almost like a man seeing a vision. He stared with an intensity and admiration Eggers had not seen in this soldier before.

How interesting, Reinhold thought. *As usual, Schadlich's report was right on target. Heinz has never radiated such admiration for anyone before. Gephard is playing a little game, but I'm sure the colonel is lapping it up like a dog at his feeding bowl.*

"I will expect a new level of performance from every officer." The colonel paced back and forth. "You must attend to details with precision. If not, you will be replaced. Many other soldiers would be glad to take your place."

Glaesche is obviously setting the stage for dramatic change, not in the camp, but with the staff, Eggers thought. *Glaesche will be searching for some reason to ax everyone he doesn't like, and I'm sure he's put me at the head of that list.*

The colonel kept clicking his heels against the wooden floor, broadcasting an ominous sound like thumbscrews being tightened. His voice rose and fell, as if Glaesche was imitating one of Hitler's speeches. Whatever Glaesche lacked in ability had been compensated for by the fire and fury, which he was quite good at manufacturing.

Eggers kept watching Heinz. The man's eyes sparkled and danced as the colonel raved. Glaesche kept looking straight at him as though Gephard was his singular audience. Reinhold instantly realized he must do something to upstage this impertinent upstart before Gephard made some dramatic gesture at the end of Glaesche's emotional speech.

"Therefore," Glaesche's voice lowered, signaling that he was coming to the end of his speech, "I will expect resolute response from every officer and complete discipline. Is this understood?"

Uncharacteristically, Eggers sprang to his feet. "Colonel, we pledge you our total and complete support. We are your loyal officers." Reinhold shot his arm straight forward in a rigid salute. "*Heil* Hitler!"

Officers sprang to their feet, following the major's example. Unprepared for Eggers's sudden salute, Heinz was completely caught off guard in the backwash, and Glaesche appeared equally surprised. The rest of the officers broke into clapping and slowly returned to their seats.

How's that, Edgar? Reinhold thought to himself. *You want to be the big cheese? You are! I'm more than glad to give you all the credit . . . and the responsibility . . . for what happens around Oflag. Let's see how big a dog you are when these prisoners start biting you!*

Late that afternoon the first party of British Royal Naval officers arrived at Colditz. Never before in the history of Colditz Castle had a group of British sailors been held as captives. When the naval prisoners walked into the inner courtyard, the inmates exploded in shouting and applause like a victory celebration had been unleashed.

Colonel Glaesche rushed into the courtyard with a contingent of soldiers carrying rifles running along with him. "Stop these fools!" he demanded. "Restore order to this pig mob!"

Like a pack of angry police dogs, the German soldiers fanned out across the yard. Rather than retreat, the prisoners only screamed back at them. Guards hoisted their rifles in the air, threatening to shoot, but the Allied officers seemed obstinate and unafraid.

"Greetings to our new visiting colleagues!" a Brit yelled down from a window. "Welcome to *our* camp."

Prisoners yelled and jeered while the Navy officers stared in amazement as if they had marched into the middle of a riot. The prison looked more like a madhouse than a concentration camp.

"*Stoppen!*" Colonel Glaesche kept demanding. "*Stoppen! Nun!*"

From the windows of the dormitory and across the inner courtyard, prisoners screamed back contempt and hurled pieces of paper from the windows.

On top of the roof of the prisoners' kitchen, Reinhold Eggers watched from the sentry's machine gun box, looking down on the courtyard. Corporal Otto Schadlich stood next to him.

"Looks like the good colonel is having a bit of a problem today," Otto mused.

Eggers smiled. "You can't treat men like animals without eliciting animal behavior." He raised an eyebrow. "No respect for the prisoners only brings forth no respect for us."

Otto pointed to a heavyset officer running up and down in front of the prisoners screaming at them. "I don't think Sergeant-Major Gephard would understand what you just said." Schadlich leaned closer to Eggers. "You know the prisoners call him *Mussolini.*"

Eggers watched Gephard bouncing around like an out-of-control monkey and chuckled. "Gephard does seem like a crazy Italian today," he said. "He looks a bit on the agitated side."

Tony Irving stood behind several prisoners, shouting as loud as the rest of the inmates. The men kept booing their Nazi captors, and the German guards in steel helmets continued jabbing at the mob with the tips of their bayoneted rifles. The scene had risen to a fever pitch on the verge of exploding in disaster. Standing near the rear of the prisoners, Tony kept screaming as passionately as any of the prisoners. Captain Lulu Lawton walked up behind Tony and spoke in his ear.

"Irving, this diversion is exactly what we needed. No matter what follows this demonstration, we leave tonight."

Irving turned around and grinned. "Man, am I ever ready!"

"You've got to get into the sick bay and hide under one of those beds. Don't waste any time. Make sure they don't arrest you if this uproar gets any further out of hand."

"Think it will?"

Lawton shrugged. "Can't tell. We've got that crazy fool Glaesche up front, and we know he likes to shoot. The demonstration could explode, and the guards could start throwing our boys into the isolation cells. It could happen. Be ready."

"I understand." Tony started walking backward out of the crowd. "I'll get out of the turmoil and start preparing for tonight."

Lawton grabbed his wrist. "Tonight's the big one, Tony. Be ready."

CHAPTER

THIRTY-THREE

The creaking noise of a wooden board only inches above his face abruptly awoke Tony. For a moment Irving had no idea where he was, but he seemed to be wrapped in a cloud of blackness. Inches in front of his face the prickly ends of pieces of straw protruded out of holes in a tattered blanket. The suffocating closeness of the sticky pieces of stubble and the large flat surface bearing down on him hit all of his panic buttons. Tony's claustrophobia exploded, and for a few moments he nearly bolted out from under the bed.

The bed? Why . . . a bed?

Tony realized where he was. Earlier in the evening he had jumped under the prisoner's bed in the sick ward and had drifted off to sleep. He knew how vital it was not to make a sound. Ill-timed, impetuous movement could jeopardize the entire escape mission.

Relax, Irving thought. *Take a deep breath. Don't let yourself panic. Slow down. Inhale. Don't let your emotions go crazy.*

Slow deep breathing eased his panic and helped push back the fear. He made his clenched fists ease and shook his fingers to loosen them. His toes slackened and his entire body relaxed. Maybe he wouldn't have a panic attack after all.

Somewhere far off in the distance, Tony could hear footsteps and guessed the German officer in charge of the night shift was making his final rounds of the evening. After what felt like thirty minutes, the noise disappeared. The entire hospital ward returned to silence, but Tony guessed at least three other men had to be stashed around the room under other beds.

Sergeant Irving had no other choice but to wait for a signal from Captain Lawton before he slid out from under the bed. He could fantasize about his situation in any way he might choose, but until Lawton gave the sign, Tony knew he shouldn't move, regardless of how his bones ached from lying on the hard floor. He had to stay put.

Taking another deep breath, Tony closed his eyes and tried to reorder his thoughts. He could be lying under the bed for hours and needed to find somewhere else to focus his attention. For the first time in days, Rikki Beck's lovely face came back to mind.

Tony was startled to realize that he hadn't thought about this woman who was so important to him *in days*. Planning the escape had pushed all thoughts of Rikki and home out of his mind. He cringed. Not remembering Rikki made him feel uncomfortable. Colditz Castle had started to take the toll other prisoners had warned him about. The castle's constant regulations, procedures, and surveillance had quietly intruded into his thinking and he felt undermined. The fortress certainly carried its own subtle but unique capacity to destroy his best thoughts.

For the first time in days, Tony's mind allowed him the luxury to dwell on Rikki. Although it was hard to realize, two years had passed since they had last seen each other. Two long, agonizing years! Would she still be his? Was she still there? Did she still care? He had to struggle to bring Rikki's face into focus.

He could remember that glorious dark hair. Because the German soldiers had confiscated his picture of Rikki in the last concentration camp, Tony strained to see her brown eyes once more. The sparkle of her gaze returned along with the memory of her heart-shaped mouth. Tony could easily recall her tall height, but he no longer knew how to compare her stature to anything else. The picture in his mind was only hazy at best.

The strain of recall bore on his mind like a heavy weight, and Tony realized that time had dulled his memory. The boredom of each long, pointless day had been like a grinding wheel, silently cutting away bits and pieces of his reflections. The passing of days, weeks, and months must be working on Rikki in the same way. Maybe she had simply given up hope that he'd ever come back. Although he had written to her from Colditz, not one letter had yet arrived from Rikki. Of course, the Germans could be cutting off the mail, and the truth was, his letters probably hadn't reached her.

The more Tony thought about this painful situation, the more his loneliness increased. He had to get his mind off any thoughts that could destroy the aggressive mental attitude he needed for this night. Rikki had always said she loved him, and he had no reason to doubt it. *That* was all there was to that! He had to trust her.

God help me, he prayed silently. *I know the battle is in my head, and I can't let myself be torn apart, obsessing over problems I can't control. Please help me be ready to bring nothing but my best to this escape. Strengthen me and . . . and don't let fear destroy me.*

Suddenly, Tony heard a prisoner somewhere out in the ward snap his fingers. A second later, someone tapped the end of the bed. Lawton's signal! Instantly, Tony started scooting out from under the bed. The prisoners were ready to run!

THIRTY-FOUR

Irving slid out from under the bed and stood up cautiously. Much to his surprise Tony saw four other men getting to their feet. In the darkness, he recognized Bill Fowler's horn-rimmed glasses and knew Captain Lawton had to be one of the men. He watched a tall, thin man walking toward him. Even with his mustache shaved, Tony instantly recognized the enigmatic Dutchman. Damiaem Van Doorninck's long strides gave away his identity across the dark silence. But the fourth man?

"Sh-h-h," a prisoner whispered, sitting down on a man's bed. "Everyone over here!"

Tony inched his way across the room toward the bed.

The prisoner struck a match and motioned for the men to gather around him. Tony saw in the light of the tiny glow the face of Stooge Wardle.

"I took a little trot down to the head," Wardle said. "You men are in good shape. No one's out there." He blew the match out.

Lawton nodded and whispered. "We'll be on our way."

"God bless you," the prisoner in one of the sickbeds said. "The best to you and don't worry when the sun rises. We'll take care of any problems that come up."

Tony and the four other men hurried toward the door and tiptoed down the dark hall leading to Heinz Gephard's office. Already waiting at the door, Jacob Sas had crawled across the inner courtyard under the nose of the sentry with the machine gun on top of the prisoners' kitchen. He gave the men a "thumbs-up."

Van Doorninck dropped to one knee and started working on the locks on the door. The simple locks popped open quickly, but one required more effort. The Zeiss Cruciform remained the most complex lock in the castle, but Damiaem's homemade micrometer silently jimmied the keyhole until he heard the pistons inside the lock move. He quickly pushed the door open.

"Inside!" Damiaem whispered. "Quick!"

Six men scurried around the corner and into the office. Van Doorninck secured the locks, sealing the men inside Gephard's office.

Tony grabbed Stooge Wardle's arm. "What are you doing here?"

Wardle shrugged. "Sometimes life plays its little tricks on you. We discovered that the Nazis got some kind of tip that I was on the escape committee. Looks like the Germans will be working on my case in short order, so I had to get out of the castle. Surprised you, didn't I?"

"Certainly glad you're with us," Tony said. He couldn't see Wardle's face in the dark, but he knew that strange grin would be there. "Adds to the fun."

"Okay, men," Lawton spoke quickly, "let's get down to business. Get closer to me so you can hear the plan without my having to speak loudly. We have to be ready to walk out of the castle by seven o'clock in the morning, and we've got to work our way downstairs under Mussolini's desk."

Tony leaned into the tight-knit circle ready to do whatever Lawton said. He glanced around at the faces only inches from his own. Each man looked determined and ready.

"Because Damiaem speaks fluent German and looks enough like the Krauts to be one, he will be the senior German NCO to lead us out in the morning. Van Doorninck will wear a German uniform." Lawton pointed to Sas. "Jacob's our other Heinie who'll bring up the rear of the parade. The rest of you are Polish prisoners of war. Got it?"

Each man nodded.

"You haven't heard the entire plan before now because I didn't want anyone to be jeopardized if you got caught, but here's what we are going to do . . ." Lawton stopped and listened.

The sound of two Germans talking floated down the outside hall. The men froze, listening as if they were about to be captured by a squad of Germans.

The prisoners couldn't hear everything he was saying clearly, but the first voice belonged to Corporal Otto Schadlich. His words became clearer. "You're saying Colonel Glaesche sent you on this midnight chase around the castle?"

"*Ya*," the other man answered. "Look, Otto. I don't like this any better than you do, and I don't know why the colonel selected me. I've always been a nobody around here." The men stopped in front of Gephard's door.

"Look, *Herr* Priem, level with me," Schadlich said. "Are you into some special arrangement with the colonel?"

"I don't appreciate that question," Hauptmann Priem answered briskly. "All I'm doing is performing my job. Now open the door to *Stabsfeldwebel* Gephard's office so we can check it."

Tony felt his heart almost stop. He looked at Lawton with the frightening question written all over his face. *What would they do?* Lawton froze in place. No one moved.

Schadlich cursed. "There's more locks on this door than there are in the rest of the entire castle," Schadlich complained. "It will take all night to open Gephard's office."

"Do you have the keys or not?" Priem demanded.

"Oh, somewhere in this ring I'll find the right keys, but you're going to have to wait. I don't often get pulled out of bed in the middle of the night to tramp through this godforsaken castle because the colonel's suddenly got a wild hair about security."

Tony could hear the rattle of the keys and knew Schadlich would soon have the door open. Would they jump the two men . . . if there were only two men? Tony took a deep breath and clenched his fist. The prisoners had always avoided physically attacking the Germans when they got caught. The Krauts had guns, which ended any debate, but Irving was ready to grab those two Heinies outside the door.

"Can't you find the keys?" Priem demanded.

"Look," Schadlich snapped. "You know no one would break into Gephard's office. The room is the center of security in this castle. Nobody forces their way into the *Stabsfeldwebel's* domain unless Heinz invites them in." Otto kept jingling the keys, searching for the right one.

"Oh, forget it!" Priem quipped. "Gephard's a special friend of Colonel Glaesche anyway. Let's move on."

After a long pause, Schadlich answered. "*Special friend?* Whatever you say."

"I'm telling you again, Otto," Priem said. "I don't know anymore about this midnight excursion than you do. Honest. I simply want to make my rounds and report that the castle is in order. Nothing more. I want to be back in bed as bad as you do."

"Whatever you say." Schadlich repeated to himself. Once more the jingle of the keys echoed down the stone hallway. "Let's move on. We've still got to backtrack and check the solitary confinement cells."

"*Ya,*" Hauptmann Priem growled. "Let's get the job done and get out of here."

Tony listened to the sound of their leather boots clopping down the hall and out of the stone corridor.

"Whew!" Lawton wheezed. "That was closer than I want to get to those German swine."

Sweat was running down Tony's neck. His shirt had begun to feel damp, and he had almost quit breathing even though his heart pounded like a defective well pump.

"I don't know if Colonel Nazi is on to something or if the old fool is only reacting to this afternoon's demonstration, but I don't like a surprise of this order," Lawton said. "Our job is to move Gephard's desk and get down into that tunnel under this floor. We must drop into the German's clothing storage shed underneath. So, let's go!"

Without a word spoken among them, the six men quickly pushed the desk back and removed the floorboards. Peering down into the black hole, they could see nothing but darkness.

"Remember," Jacob Sas said, "we lined the tunnel with blankets. You shouldn't make a noise making your way to the bottom."

"Excellent," Lawton answered. "Gentlemen, we're ready for our descent to the next level. Remember, we've got to get out of the castle before Mussolini shows up in the morning. He usually gets here well after eight o'clock. Let's hope he sleeps late tomorrow."

"Yeah," Tony said. "*Real* late."

Lawton stepped up to the hole. "I'll go first. You boys follow and Irving can bring up the rear. Give me a minute to shove the stone blocks out of the way and open the hole in the wall downstairs." He dropped through the hole in the floor and disappeared into the darkness.

The rest of the escape crew lined up, listening to the sound of stones being pushed out of the way. When silence returned, they quickly followed suit and entered the tunnel. In a matter of seconds the five men disappeared, leaving only Tony to bring up the rear.

For a moment Irving hesitated, looking around the office the Germans considered so sacrosanct and staring into the black hole yawning in front of him. Once again the suffocating darkness glared back at him. Tony felt his heart start to thump even faster. The empty pit looked more like the mouth of a dragon, waiting to devour him in a single, smoky gulp.

Quivering all over, Tony inched his legs down into the tunnel. He wasn't sure he could allow himself to drop any further. For a moment, Tony thought the Germans would find him in the morning frozen on the floor with his legs hanging down in the tunnel. Sweat on his brow increased, and he was certain that death awaited him only inches below.

"God, please help me," Tony prayed quietly. "I don't think I can get through this small space. O Lord Jesus, put Your hand on me."

Tony began to feel as if indeed an unseen hand was pulling him silently downward. He didn't want to go, but a gentle inner nudge pushed him into the opaque opening. He lifted his head, let go, and dropped into the tunnel. Seconds later, Tony slid out the bottom, landing on his rear.

"We thought maybe you'd decided not to leave with us," Lulu Lawton said into his face. "Having second thoughts?"

"No." Tony shook his head. "I was taking one last look."

"Certainly took you long enough," Lawton groused. "Let's change clothes, boys."

CHAPTER

THIRTY-FIVE

Damiaem Van Doorninck stood by the shed's door, watching to make sure no German showed up and caught them off guard. Tony stretched out in his new Polish uniform, trying to get a few last minutes of dozing before morning broke.

"These loose-fitting Polish uniforms must have been constructed to work on anybody," Tony said to Stooge Wardle, resting next to him.

"They're comfortable enough," Wardle said. "I think I'll be able to sleep for awhile."

"How long do you think we have?" Tony asked.

"At least three or more hours," Stooge answered.

"Hey, knock off the talking," Captain Lawton said. "Let's get some sleep. The clock is ticking."

Tony rolled over and watched Damiaem Van Doorninck peering out into the night. Saying little as usual, the captain maintained his steady look of stoic indifference, but Tony knew the Dutchman had to be thinking of much more than who might be walking up and down a back alley in the middle of the night. He surmised Van Doorninck might be thinking about his wife Hendrika living in some far-off part of Friesland. Maybe he was worrying whether she was still alive or even if she was waiting for him. Tony knew the men didn't mention such fears, but Damiaem's apprehensions had to be like everyone else's. Was Rikki

Beck waiting faithfully for him to return, or had she found somebody else? Each man had his own worries. If the Germans had any idea about the depth of these fears, they'd have a far better tool with which to pry loose the confidence of the prisoners. Why if they knew that . . . if they knew . . . if . . . Tony yawned and the night poured in.

"Wake up!" Lawton said into Tony's ear. "We must assemble the boxes."

Tony blinked several times. "Boxes?"

"We had wood smuggled in here with the uniforms," Captain Lawton explained. "Remember? We've got to assemble the pieces into crates that we'll use to hide our change of clothing when we march out of here."

"Clothes?" Irving mumbled. "Yeah. Yeah, that's right."

"Hurry up," Lawton demanded. "Time is slipping away. Here's the final detail. We're going to take the back way out of this slammer. We'll wind our way along the edge of the precipice that drops down to Hohnback Stream, which means we keep on walking until we are well past the back exercise area. Remember Damiaem will be in charge."

Tony could tell that the sky was clearing. He stood up and watched the men pushing pieces of wood together. Tony got down next to Bill Fowler to do what he could in constructing the boxes.

"Fix that piece of rope," Bill said. "We'll push it through the side. The rope will make the handles that we carry."

Tony tightened the end of the rope into a knot to keep the cord in place. "We'll be able to swing this box between the two of us."

"Exactly," Fowler answered. "Just like we're being good boys, trying to make these Nazis happy."

"All right, men," Lawton said quietly. "We're about ready to roll. Fowler, Wardle, Irving, and I are going to be Polish prisoners, and we'll carry the boxes between us as if we're completing a job for our captors. Van Doorninck and Sas are the German officers leading us back to the village of Colditz. Everybody got it?"

Tony nodded his head.

Bill Fowler raised his hand. "I have something I want to say," he began slowly. "We've all paid a high price to get this far, and I know we all have apprehensions. Fear is normal, but remember why we're here in this old shed. We believe in freedom, and we're not going to let the Germans turn us or anybody into their slaves. When you are afraid, let that thought guide you. We are people who stand for liberty."

"Thanks, Bill," Lawton said. "You speak for all of us." He turned to Van Doorninck. "What do you see, Damiaem?"

The Dutchman looked at his watch. "The guards always change at seven o'clock," he murmured, "but I don't know what's happening. No alternate sentry is in sight."

Lawton quickly crawled over the pile of old clothes and looked out through a hole in the walls. He shook his head. "You're right. Nobody is out there."

The men huddled near the door while their apprehension grew with every tick of the clock. Five minutes, ten minutes passed, but no replacement guard appeared.

"Be ready, men," Lawton instructed the group. "I don't know what's happening. Shouldn't be such a delay. Hope Gephard didn't show up early this morning." He paused. "When this guard change occurs, we've got to come charging out of this hut with those boxes between us. No hesitation."

About another five minutes passed without any change in the guard. Tony felt his stomach knot again. It wasn't like claustrophobia; he was plain terrified. In a matter of minutes the guards at the gates could be shooting at them, and they'd all be dead on the grass. He gritted his teeth.

Irving bowed his head and silently prayed. "Help us, O Lord. Please don't let those Germans kill us. Please guide . . ."

"Seven-twenty!" Van Doorninck said. "There's the new guard taking the other one's place. Get ready. We're about to leave."

The men stood up and Tony grabbed the end of the rope. Damiaem quickly eased the door open slightly. "Stand by," he said. "When I start walking, follow me. Sas, don't forget to shut the door and lock it."

"Certainly," Jacob said. "I'm ready."

"Oh, Lord," Tony said out loud. "Please make sure Mussolini sleeps late this morning. We don't need him showing up early."

"Amen," the men around him echoed.

"Let's go!" Van Doorninck pushed the door open and walked out with the regal bearing of a German general. He kept his long strides to a more narrow pace but marched as if he knew exactly where he was going.

Tony saw the first sentry just ahead. Van Doorninck saluted smartly, and the guard returned the salute without saying anything. The men kept marching around the high, steep side of the castle. None of the Germans gave them more than a casual glance. For the first time, his heart began beating with excitement rather than fear.

Without missing a step, the prisoners stayed straight behind Van Doorninck. The footsteps of Jacob Sas echoed, bringing up the rear. No one hurried, but the pace didn't slacken. Off to his left, Tony could see the practice field where the men played soccer; at this hour of the morning the field was empty. He kept walking with a determined pace.

Van Doorninck turned to the group and said softly, "Easy. The final gate is just ahead. Don't anybody panic." He turned back around and kept walking.

In front of them loomed a large, long barricade, running down into the valley. In the middle of a wall of spiked metal palings stood a narrow door. Van Doorninck kept walking.

Tony stared at the door . . . *the narrow door.* His prayer times in the chapel raced through his mind. The words of Jesus said, "Make every effort to enter through the narrow door," and there it was! *The narrow door out of Colditz Castle!* He was so stunned that the rope almost slipped out of his hand.

Van Doorninck marched up to the metal door. A key was hanging beside the door. He picked it up and turned it in the lock, but nothing happened. For a moment, the Dutchman stared at the lock in astonishment. The lock proved to be much larger than the key hanging by the door.

"Having a problem?" a German NCO called out from a ledge above the party of escaping prisoners.

Van Doorninck turned slowly and saluted. In perfect German he answered, "Yes, I understood I would have no trouble leaving through this door."

"I have the key." The German officer held up a huge key in his hand. "I keep it. Didn't you know that?"

The Dutchman paused for a moment, but the staid expression on his face didn't change. "No," he answered. "We have only been in Colditz for a few days, and the guard at the main entrance told us we could get out by a shorter route through this narrow gate."

"I understand," the German NCO said, walking toward them. "They don't often tell the newcomers about the shortcuts out of the castle." He stuck the large key into the lock and turned it. "I live in the sick bay quarters," he said. "Let me know when you want the gate open, and I'll be here." The narrow door swung open before them.

"Thank you." Van Doorninck smiled and saluted again. "On our way, gentlemen." He marched on straight ahead with the men following him. "*Marsch!*" he ordered and picked up the pace.

After they had walked fifty feet, Tony glanced over his shoulder. The German sentry was still standing at the gate watching them march down the road. The NCO seemed to have a look in his eye as if he wasn't quite sure everything was acceptable, but he closed the gate and locked it.

Tony wanted to shout and clap, but he kept walking silently at the usual pace. The air felt as if it had turned purer and the path had become straighter. They were out! Free! Released!

The party clopped around a bend in the road, and suddenly Van Doorninck darted to his left into the bushes. The prisoners hurried behind him, disappearing into the trees.

"We're free!" the Dutchman exclaimed with an intense, low voice. "Thank heavens! We're out of that hole. We are free!"

Tony dropped his box. "The narrow door!" he said more to himself than anyone else. "*The narrow door was the way out!*"

THIRTY-SIX

*L*awton kept watching the forest as well as eyeing the road off in the distance running toward the Tiergarten while the rest of the escape party crawled out of their Polish and German uniforms and hustled back into civilian clothing. The men moved feverishly, preparing to run.

"The glad rags don't look much like me," Tony said, "but the cloth feels good. I'm . . . I'm . . . a local citizen!"

"Yeah," Bill Fowler answered, pushing his black horn-rimmed glasses back in place. "We look like a pack of German farmer boys strolling in from the fields."

Within minutes the loose-fitting shirt and pants had also changed Captain Lawton's appearance. The escaping prisoners silently finished preparing to run.

"Here are your travel documents." The Royal Air Force captain started handing out passports and travel passes. "You'll find your new names inside along with permission to move across Germany, should get you to the Swiss border in good shape," Lawton explained. "We couldn't come up with much money, but there's a few *Reichsmarks* to help along the way. You can buy a little food."

"We'll have no trouble," Jacob Sas said.

"Easy for you to say," Stooge Wardle quipped. "You speak excellent German."

Sas smiled slightly. "Maybe you can be a deaf mute."

Stooge laughed. "Eh?" He put his hand behind his ear.

"Okay, okay, men," Lawton interrupted the exchange. "Sas will travel with me. We're going to walk to the station at Wechselberg and catch the train running toward the German border. Wardle and Fowler will take a different route, but their objective is the village of Rochlitz. If possible, they will also try to ride a train as well." Lawton turned to Tony. "I want you to stay with Van Doorninck. The two of you will travel to the town of Singen. It's the last place you can get on or off the train without showing an identity card. When you get there, you will be in walking distance to the Swiss border."

Tony nodded, trying not to smile. Damiaem Van Doorninck spoke perfect German. If nothing else, Tony knew traveling with Damiaem would prove relatively secure and should get them over the border.

"I want to thank all of you for trusting me with the development of these plans," Lawton continued. "I appreciate you and wish each of you Godspeed. I certainly hope to meet you in Switzerland and share a scrumptious twilight supper together."

The soldiers heartily shook hands, wished each other well, and within minutes the three groups broke out through the trees on their separate paths out of Germany.

"I'm certainly glad to be with you, ole buddy," Tony said. "*Very* glad."

Van Doorninck only nodded.

At precisely eight o'clock, Colonel Edgar Glaesche walked into his office. Major Eggers, Corporal Schadlich, Sergeant-Major Gephard, Private Hauptmann Priem, and two other officers were waiting and snapped to attention. Glaesche stopped behind his desk and laid down his leather riding crop. Major Eggers saluted smartly.

"At ease!" the colonel barked.

The men relaxed slightly but remained standing.

"Last night I began a new procedure," Glaesche walked slowly around the desk. "I personally decided to send Schadlich and Priem on a surprise inspection of the castle. The practice of doing the unexpected and unanticipated is now part of my standard tactics." He clicked his heels together. "Understood?"

"Yes, sir!" the officers answered in one voice.

"From this time forward," Glaesche continued, "you can expect a new and higher level of security in this prison. I do not anticipate any further successful escapes as long as I am the commandant."

Gephard stepped forward. "Sir, you have our undying loyalty and support."

"Thank you, Heinz," Glaesche said. "Your unequivocal commitment is an important aspect of our work here." He looked slowly into the faces of each man. "Is that true of the rest of you?"

"Yes, sir!" the officers again answered in unison.

Glaesche kept eyeing Eggers. "As I have already pointed out, failure to maintain the highest standard will be met with harsh repercussions." Glaesche shot a glance at his wristwatch. "Time has come for the first *Appell* of the day, and I expect our soldiers to be assembling the prisoners out in the courtyard. We will need to oversee the roll call."

Major Eggers nodded his compliance. "I am ready to take my usual position."

Ignoring Eggers, Glaesche spoke to Otto Schadlich. "Keep a clear and accurate record of all of these proceedings, Corporal. I will personally inspect the *Appell* this morning." He turned and walked out the door with the officers trailing behind.

Schadlich cast a troubled glance at Eggers. The major nodded but said nothing. He brought up the rear, allowing Gephard to walk directly behind Glaesche.

At exactly 8:30 A.M., the colonel marched up on the platform with *Stabsfeldwebel* Gephard standing directly behind him. Major Eggers stood to the back, looking out over the strange behavior of the prisoners.

"What's going on here?" the colonel snapped.

"I don't know," Gephard answered. "The lines are irregular with big holes in the ranks. I don't understand . . ."

Prisoners slowly crumbled to the ground. Others grabbed their stomachs. A few men rolled on the dirt and kicked their feet.

"Get out there and make some sense out of this pigsty mess," Glaesche ordered. Gephard trotted out into the fray of strange behavior. "Bizarre!" the colonel barked in disgust.

At that moment a prisoner swung out the window on the second floor and threw a bucket of water on the German soldiers below him. Prisoners abruptly began jeering and booing. A second bucket of water splashed out the window, spraying prisoners and sentries alike.

"Stop that fool!" Glaesche yelled and pointed with his riding crop toward the window. "Get a riot squad up there and put an end to that nonsense!"

A squad of German soldiers broke into the dormitory, rushing up the steps, but water kept flying out the window. The cheering and applause of the prisoners in the courtyard continued with a roar.

Gephard came running up on the platform. "I don't understand it," he said, scratching his head. "Seems like an epidemic or something has broken out. The prisoners say they are sick."

"*Sick!*" the colonel exploded. "I don't believe it. Send those men back into their quarters, then run them back outside again. I don't care what their condition is! Get them back out here in formation on the double."

Major Eggers stood at the rear and watched the near riot unfold while the German soldiers forced every one of the men back into the castle's dormitory. Forty-five minutes later another *Appell* started to form with some prisoners hanging on each other while others fell on the pavement.

Eggers's eyes narrowed. "They are putting on quite a show," he whispered to Schadlich, "but I don't believe those prisoners are sick at all."

"I don't either," Corporal Schadlich answered, "but I'm not sure what's behind this."

"Did we ever get an accurate head count?"

Schadlich shook his head. "Nothing certain."

"Just watch," the major whispered. "This is the colonel's show. Let's see what our good commandant does next." He glanced at his watch. "It's nearly ten o'clock."

Colonel Glaesche kept pacing back and forth in disgust while beating his palm with the riding crop. No one seemed to be able to line up the prisoners in any kind of proper order. The sentries kept running up and down the rows, trying to get an exact head count. Finally, Heinz Gephard came hurrying back to the center platform.

"Sir," Gephard said, breathing hard. "We keep coming up six men short."

"I don't believe it!" the colonel snapped. "They're playing a little game with us this morning. Well, I can play as rough as they can. I'm going back in my office. You keep them standing in line until we have accounted for every last one of these fools."

Glaesche turned on his heels and stomped across the inner courtyard toward the senior officers' quarters where he kept a small office. Major Eggers and Corporal Schadlich walked silently behind him. The colonel trotted up the stone steps, steaming like a broken hot-water valve.

"I'm not going to put up with this absurdity!" Glaesche whacked the top of his desk with the riding crop. "If necessary, I'll starve that pig-mob!"

Major Eggers stood at attention and said nothing.

"I know no one is missing. They are only trying to rattle me." The colonel started walking back and forth. "This deceptive behavior must stop!"

An orderly walked in the door and began whispering in Major Eggers's ear.

"Stop it!" Glaesche demanded. "You tell *me* what is happening."

"I have just received a phone call," Reinhold Eggers began. "Apparently, the military police in Colditz are reporting some woman found two wooden boxes of Polish and German uniforms near the Tiergarten above the park."

"What?" Glaesche gasped. "What are you saying?"

"Looks like we *did* have an escape last night," Eggers answered casually.

THIRTY-SEVEN

Descending like a gentle blanket of warmth, the bright noon sun covered the escaping prisoners with new promise. Even though the temperature had risen slightly, the air still felt brisk and kept the two men moving at a fast clip through the forest.

"We're avoiding the town of Colditz?" Tony Irving asked.

"Yes," Damiaem Van Doorninck answered. "I hope we have at least several hours' head start on the Nazi search. I don't want to chance some bright-eyed villager giving us a close look if we get near the town. We're making a broad sweep around the village."

Tony kept walking at the fast pace the Dutchman's long legs set, but he barely kept up. "Makes sense," he said. "I'm sure the Germans will attempt a broad sweep of the entire area to catch us."

"You can bet on it! They'll also turn those supersniffer dogs loose on the trail. I fear the German Shepherds more than I do the soldiers."

"Hadn't thought of that angle. Yeah, that concerns me too."

Tree branches brushed past them, catching their clothing and slapping the two escapees on the arms and legs. The forest became thicker with more debris and broken branches blocking their path.

"You know where we're going?" Tony asked.

"You sound a little apprehensive."

Tony shrugged. "I'm afraid this is my first successful break. They caught me at my first prison camp, and this is the only time I've been able to get beyond the front gate at Colditz. Yeah, I'm a bit on the worried side."

Damiaem held out a small compass. "Didn't know I had one of these, did you?"

"Amazing!" Tony stared at the simple round disk. "Looks home-made."

"It is. Made it myself."

"So you know exactly where we're going?"

"I'm avoiding the train stations in the area. I'm afraid we're going to have a rather long hike today."

"No problem with me." Tony grinned. "If I can keep up with your long legs."

Van Doorninck raised an eyebrow. "We all have our gifts, and mine happens to be in the long and lanky department. I also have a good sense of procedures. I hope Lawton knew what he was doing in sending the other guys toward those railway stations so near to the castle."

"You think the Germans will hit those stops?"

"No question about it. The Gestapo is especially good at showing up when trains are coming and going."

"We're going further away? Right?"

The Dutchman shoved the compass back into his pocket and started walking again. "Absolutely. We're going to put as much ground as possible between us and those goons back at the castle."

"Yeah," Tony said. "I knew you'd have insight into what we should do."

"I've spent a considerable amount of time in Germany," Van Doorninck said. "I grew up using German in Holland as well as my native Dutch. Those experiences prepared me for this war. We'll make it."

"You're an unusual person, Damiaem. I've watched you at the castle. You don't say much, but you're always watching."

The Dutchman laughed for the first time in days. "You're finally getting the picture. The Germans are actually quite predictable. Their strict, militaristic discipline turns them into little machines, doing exactly what the senior officers tell them without thinking. In time, they become as predictable as the sun coming up. All you and I need to do is the opposite of what those robots are programmed to do. Get it?"

"You bet!" Tony stretched his stride and walked step for step beside the Dutchman. "The Krauts certainly tick differently from we Americans. Of course, we have military discipline, but our soldiers are far more spontaneous and creative."

"Exactly!" Van Doorninck abruptly slapped Tony on the back. "You've got it, cowboy!" He leaned over and whispered in Tony's ear. "That's why I told Lawton to make you my traveling companion."

Tony stopped. "*What?*"

"You heard me." Damiaem laughed again. "We're old traveling companions. Surprised? Now, let me tell you exactly who we are and what we're about." He jumped over a tree stump but kept talking. "I'm a German architecture student out on a lark, and you are a Belgian laborer. We met by chance in Leipzig and just happened to be going to the same place." Van Doorninck winked. "Singen! Can you believe it? We decided to travel together."

"Excellent."

"You don't speak German, and the Heinies won't expect it from you. If we run into the Gestapo or their troops, I'll speak to you in French."

Tony frowned and shrugged. "I don't speak French, either."

"*You do now.* I'll attempt to make it easy, but you're going to have to fake understanding me if necessary."

"I'll try."

"Your performance must be better than 'try.' You must be perfect."

The men walked on without saying anything for thirty minutes. Finally Tony asked, "*Exactly* how do you know where to go?"

"Two prisoners escaped and made it successfully to Singen before they got caught, but they mapped out how to find the trail. You probably didn't meet Hans Larive and Francis Steinmetz, but they broke out during a soccer match. Didn't get out of the country, but they laid out the path and detailed what to expect on the way."

"And you memorized everything they told you?"

"Every word of it," Damiaem said. "Every last syllable and sentence!"

"How are we going to get across the country so fast?"

"We're going to catch a ride on the back of a truck instead of a train."

"Oh!" Tony raised his eyebrows. "*I see.*"

The two men walked on in silence. Tony and Van Doorninck had certainly faced confrontations in the past, but Tony couldn't have found a better companion for the walk to the Swiss border. Damiaem Van Doorninck was a man who knew the way out of Germany.

CHAPTER

THIRTY-EIGHT

Major Eggers stood to one side of Colonel Glaesche's office and watched the commandant pace nervously back and forth across the room. Eggers said nothing but studied Glaesche carefully. Something not yet completely defined was wrong with Glaesche. As had been true in the past, failure pushed Glaesche toward the edge, but he now appeared even more unstrung.

The door opened and Corporal Schadlich walked in with Sergeant-Major Gephard following behind him. At the rear, Hauptmann Priem appeared to be shirking back.

"Well!" Glaesche immediately demanded. "What did you find?"

Corporal Otto Schadlich stepped forward, standing at rigid attention. "We were able to ascertain that the escape party left through the shortcut path on the north side of the castle by leaving from the back west side of the chapel," he read stiffly from his notes. "We do not have the exact number, but it appears six men escaped."

"Six got away!" Glaesche's eyes widened in fear. "You're . . . you're *certain?*"

"Yes, sir. The escape party was seen coming out of the clothing shed."

"The clothing shed!" the colonel nearly shouted as the words suddenly erupted like a volcanic explosion. "How in God's name could they get into that area?"

"We examined the back wall of the shed," the corporal explained slowly, "and found the stones had been freshly moved. When we pushed the rocks aside we found a tunnel had been dug behind the wall."

"*A tunnel?*" Glaesche's voice dropped to nearly a whisper. "Where in the world would a tunnel go?" His mouth slowly dropped. "A tunnel *upward?*"

"Yes, we crawled into the tunnel," Schadlich continued, "and found that it went straight up underneath *Stabsfeldwebel* Gephard's office. They got into the tunnel by pushing his desk aside and crawling under the floor." The corporal turned and stared at Gephard.

"*Your* office?" Glaesche appeared almost in a daze. "But your office is under maximum security!" Streaks of dark pink shot down his neck, and Glaesche's face began turning red. "How could this be?" He rubbed his mouth nervously.

Eggers silently studied the scene of confusion, noticing that Priem seemed to be trying to fade into the woodwork. "Priem, didn't you check Gephard's office last night?"

Priem's head dropped and he stared at the floor. "The door was secured with several locks," Hauptmann said slowly, but he never looked up. "We didn't go inside."

"*Didn't go inside?*" Colonel Glaesche's voice turned shrill. "The escapees were probably sitting in that room at that exact moment!"

Priem nodded his head silently.

Glaesche whirled around toward Gephard. "And when did you go into your office?"

"Not until a few moments ago," Heinz said in a weak voice.

"Your office was to be one of the most secure areas in this entire complex!" the colonel shouted. "How could anyone break in there and you not know it?"

Gephard shook his head and held his hands in the air. "I-I-I simply don't know."

Glaesche stared intensely with rapid eye movements. His entire nervous system had gone into overload. He wrung his hands and looked panic-stricken.

Heinz Gephard bit his lip and struggled to find some right words to say. "In fact . . . in fact, the doors were locked when we went inside only moments ago. No one should have been able to have gotten in or out." He shrugged and gestured aimlessly.

"You fool!" Glaesche yelled at Gephard. "I trusted you! I thought you were a man of capacity, but now you have created the biggest mess we've ever had in this castle. Never before have so many prisoners escaped at one time."

"But . . . but . . . ," Gephard struggled to find some explanation, but nothing made any difference. "The door was locked," he concluded feebly.

"Idiot!" the colonel screamed at the sergeant-major. "Get out of my office. Get out of here!"

Looking like a whipped dog, Heinz Gephard saluted and quickly backed out of the office, disappearing down the hall.

Glaesche stared at his riding crop lying on his desk. He kept breathing hard and seemed to be on the verge of exploding.

"Sir?" Major Eggers stepped forward. "If I might make a suggestion. We have a standard response to any escape from Colditz." He stood at rigid attention. "Operation Mousetrap involves sending out a squad of four soldiers with police dogs to trail the escapees. In addition, a cordon is thrown up around every railway station within a twenty-five-mile radius of the castle. The escapees have at least a five-hour lead on us, but I believe we should spring Operation Mousetrap at once."

The colonel's frustrated, nervous eye movements had settled down into a blank stare. "Y-es," he said hesitantly. "Send out the alarm at once."

"Thank you." Eggers stepped back with military precision. "Private Priem, you are dismissed until further notice."

Priem cast a nasty look at Schadlich, but backed away. "Yes, sir." He saluted and left at once.

"Corporal, please come with me and we will start the search at once."

"Yes, sir!" Schadlich saluted smartly.

"We will keep you advised, Colonel." Eggers said to Glaesche. "Is there anything else?"

The colonel took a deep breath and exhaled forcefully. "No."

"Of course," Eggers answered politely. "Please follow me, Corporal Schadlich."

Otto fell in behind Eggers, marching out of the commandant's office and down the hall as if they were merely conducting routine business. Nothing was said until both men entered Eggers's office and closed the door.

A smile broke across Reinhold's face. "Looks like we have stepped out of the fire."

Otto looked around the room. "I'll take that drink you offered the other day."

Eggers walked over to the cabinet where he kept the cognac. "As I recall, the colonel instructed you to keep an accurate record of all of these proceedings."

"Yes, he did."

"And that should include a careful explanation that Glaesche was in charge of *every detail* of security during this time of escape," Reinhold said.

"Without question," Otto answered. "I will state that fact in a number of different ways."

"We should also mention the obvious role our *Stabsfeldwebel's* lack of oversight played in the escape." Eggers took out the dark brown bottle and two glasses. "We need to give Heinz all the headline material he can handle. He apparently wanted better exposure, and now Heinz will get more than he can digest."

"I think my report will be quite exact," Otto said, "also noting that the audacious and ineffective colonel completely usurped your normal role during this period."

Eggers offered the corporal a glass and toasted him. "To your health, Otto." Both men clicked their glasses.

"Your report should be at the *Oberkommando der Wehrmacht* headquarters by tonight. I want the German High Command to know exactly what happened here before Glaesche has the opportunity to create some story to cover his tracks."

Schadlich set his glass down on the table and rubbed his chin. "Tell me, Reinhold. What do you think *really* happened to Glaesche today?"

The major put his hands behind his back and started walking back and forth in front of his desk. "I don't know for sure, but I think this inept colonel was preparing a massive shake-up of the staff and replacement of the top officers. Gephard would have taken a short hop into my job. Maybe Priem would have had a nice promotion. Who knows? But I think this morning's escape destroyed Glaesche's plans for the big rearrangement."

"Yes, that explanation makes sense," Schadlich said. "I'm not sure how Glaesche sees me. What do you think the man would have done with me?"

"With you?" Eggers scratched his head. "Hmm, I'm not sure. Glaesche seems to see you in a positive light. He hasn't discovered that we are close childhood friends yet, and the fact that he instructed you to write the report on the escapes would be an affirmative sign." Eggers laughed. "However, when he realizes it was his order that sent your report in today, I suspect Glaesche will feel even more like a fool."

"Well," Otto chuckled, "at least I won't lose any rank over this."

"Oh, far from it. In fact, Gephard has been so discredited by these escapes today that I suspect that he might be leaving us before long.

Who knows? Possibly, the *Oberkommando der Wehrmacht* will recommend him for a stint on the Russian front."

Schadlich took a deep breath. "Oooh! Wouldn't that be a show-stopper!"

"Yes, but not as interesting as having you appointed as the next *Stabsfeldwebel*. Possibly before this is all over, you'll be our new sergeant-major." Reinhold saluted his friend. "I like the sound of those words . . . Sergeant-Major Otto Schadlich!"

THIRTY-NINE

After three days of long rides in the backs of old trucks and hours of walking through the thick woods, Damiaem Van Doorninck knew they had to be close to the town of Singen. His homemade compass told him that they were south of the town, and intuition said they were only kilometers away. Somewhere on the other side of the pine trees in front of them, he could hear the sounds of a stream running.

"Whew!" Tony wiped his forehead. "I thought I had walked before, but nothing like this little hike."

"You're lucky we caught so many rides on the back of those trucks or you'd really be tired."

"I feel like we've walked halfway across Germany."

Van Doorninck grinned. "Come on, cowboy. Where's that spirit of the old West?"

"I ain't stopped yet, have I?"

"A fast walk is good for whatever ails you."

"Look!" Tony stopped and pointed straight ahead. "There's a tavern over there by that stream."

"Yes, and more important there is a motorbike parked next to the pub." Damiaem rubbed his chin. "No one but the Gestapo and the police ride those vehicles in Germany. You can bet there's an officer working inside."

"Let's get out of here." Tony started to run, but Damiaem's strong hand grabbed his shirt.

"No," the Dutchman said firmly. "We need to go in and have a pint. Be one of the boys."

"*What?*" Tony's eyes widened.

"Back at the castle I told Van den Heuvel, our Dutch escape officer, that I'd find out if any special permits were required near the Swiss frontier. We must go in because sitting in that pub is the answer to Van den Heuvel's question."

"Good Lord, Damiaem! We could get captured."

The Dutchman raised an eyebrow. "It's possible . . . but then again . . . it's possible anywhere along this road. Don't worry." Damiaem said soberly. "Let's go inside, sit down, and see what we can find out."

Tony wrung his hands, bit his lip, and looked worried. "I-I-I don't know."

"I do!" Van Doorninck jerked him forward. "Follow me." He walked toward the pub with the same certainty with which he'd broken through the trees in the forest.

The quaint Bavarian tavern, decorated with the trappings and artistic flourishes of a typical German roadside tavern, had empty seats at one of the small wooden tables. Six or seven men sat around the room talking. Tony glanced up at the rough-beamed ceiling painted with Tyrolean scrolls and little country figures.

"See that man standing at the bar next to the waitress?" Van Doorninck pointed toward a heavyset man doing something with the barmaid's hand. "The round one wearing the little Austrian hat. He's Gestapo."

"How do you know?"

"He's taking her fingerprints. The Germans have a law requiring anyone working this close to the border to be on record. Don't worry; *Herr* Big Nose will be over here in a minute."

Tony looked down to avoid any possible eye contact. "God help us."

"Keep smiling, mate," Damiaem said. "Remember you don't speak German so simply play dumb."

"Yeah, that's easy for you to say."

"Ah, I believe Big Nose is through with the fingerprints and has spotted us." Damiaem kept looking out the window. "He should be traipsing over this way momentarily."

"I can't wait," Tony said under his breath.

"Remember. You speak only French."

"Humph!"

The fat man started walking toward the table with an authoritative swagger. "You are traveling in this area?" he asked in a demanding voice.

Van Doorninck smiled. "Yes," he said in his best German. "We've come down from Leipzig."

"May I see your papers?" the agent said in a polite but exacting tone.

"Of course." Van Doorninck pulled out his passport and placed it on the table. He turned to Tony and asked for his papers in French but kept tapping on his passport with his finger.

For a moment Tony looked uncertain, but he pulled his passport and papers out of his pocket and laid them next to Van Doorninck's.

"I met this man I am traveling with," Damiaem rattled off in German, "when I was standing on a train platform. Unfortunately, he only speaks French and doesn't understand German, but he says he's from Belgium." Van Doorninck smiled a broad, friendly grin as if he'd known the Gestapo agent forever. "I trust his papers are in order as I wouldn't want to be part of any action that could prove harmful to the Reich."

For several moments the fat man said nothing, but he scrutinized Irving's papers twice. "No," he said with certainty, "I see no problem with any of these papers. Everything is in order."

"Good." Van Doorninck kept smiling. "Glad to hear it."

The fat man turned around and made another slow stroll through the pub, scrutinizing everyone before he disappeared out the front door. The motorbike revved up and roared down the road.

"What was that little conversation in German all about?" Tony asked.

"Nothing personal," Van Doorninck said with a sly grin, "but I put you at a slight risk for a couple of minutes."

"*What?*"

"Remember? I promised my old friend Van den Heuvel I'd find out if a special permit was required near the border. Should we get caught and returned to the castle, I'll be able to tell him nothing is required. If I don't, I'll send a camouflaged letter."

Tony blinked several times. "You *put me in jeopardy?*"

"Our job is larger than escaping. We must also help set up the conditions for others to follow us. Even if it means that I am captured." Van Doorninck raised an eyebrow askance.

"You'd let yourself be grabbed by the Gestapo simply to convey information back to the castle?"

Damiaem nodded his head. "We're all in this together, cowboy. The boys back at that medieval barn remain just as important as we are out here scampering down this border road."

Irving leaned back in his chair and frowned. "I guess I didn't think of that angle." He noticed a large man in a blue shirt several tables away. The German kept watching them.

"You Yanks are individualists," Damiaem observed. "If there's a fault with the bunch of you, it's that you tend to think about yourselves more than the good of the entire group." He smiled. "I think you'll find worrying about what's best for all the prisoners to be worthwhile."

"Really!" Tony looked down and pursed his lips. "Humph." He shot a glance at the man in the blue shirt still watching them.

"You're an American cowboy, Tony. You think like those old pio-neers out on the western plains that crawled up on their horses and went riding off into the sunset by themselves."

Irving rubbed his forehead and frowned. "Look, people in Texas live like they always have. I don't see anything wrong with that way of doing things."

"Nothing wrong with that, partner." Damiaem slapped him on the shoulder. "We all grow up that way, but along the path we have to make adjustments. One of them is learning to put the well-being of others ahead of ourselves."

"Can I help you, gentlemen?" the barmaid asked in German.

"Give us two pints of the local favorite," Damiaem answered.

"Certainly," the middle-aged woman whirled around and walked away.

"What you just said to me is a Christian principle," Tony said. "Do you know that?"

Van Doorninck's countenance abruptly changed. "Well . . . ," he said. "Whatever."

"You live by more of those principles than you've recognized. Sort of strange for an agnostic, isn't it?"

"Agnostic?" Van Doorninck sneered. "Who said I was an agnostic?"

"Well I thought . . ."

"Here you are, boys." The barmaid sat two large steins on the table. "I hope you like the brew." She winked at Damiaem. "It's a bit on the brisk side."

"I'm sure we will." Van Doorninck slipped the woman one of the *Reichsmarks* he carried with him. "Keep the change."

"Why, thank you!" The woman beamed. "You are a gentleman, indeed!"

The Dutchman nodded appreciatively and winked back. The woman returned to the bar with a broad smile on her face.

"What was that all about?"

"In addition to worrying about our boys back at the castle, we must keep the locals happy. Don't want any irate barmaid calling that fat Gestapo agent for an updated report on two strangers she didn't like. We must tickle her under the chin to keep her smiling. That's part of the scene as well."

Irving nodded. "You don't miss a thing, Damiaem."

"I try not to," the Dutchman said. "We need all the help we can find to make our way out of Germany."

Tony looked one more time at the man in the blue shirt. The German kept drinking his beer and was no longer looking at them. Irving felt relieved.

CHAPTER

FORTY

As the sun slowly set, a gentle haze hovered over the countryside tavern. The breeze picked up, and the brisk air turned cold. Tony pulled his collar up more closely around his neck.

"Starting to feel a tad chilled?" Damiaem Van Doorninck asked.

"I'm not looking forward to spending the night out here in the woods," Tony answered.

"Neither am I. The trick is to make sure we know exactly where the border is."

"You're expecting to run into guards before we get across, right?"

Van Doorninck shook his head. "It's always a possibility, but my first question when we find somebody who knows anything is to find out the details on how the Germans guard the border."

"You bet!"

The two men kept trudging steadily onward in a westerly direction, following the road away from the pub as it wound through the trees toward Singen. They passed a two-story farmhouse, but no one appeared on the graveled road. Not far ahead the buildings of Singen loomed in the distance.

"Think we'll go through the town?" Tony asked.

"I've got mixed feelings," the tall Dutchman answered without slowing down. "I don't like getting close to any place where the Gestapo is bound to be lurking. On the other hand, we could sure use some insight into what to expect at the border."

"You won't get any help from me," Tony said. "I'm as lost as a goose in a snowstorm."

"The truth is that I'm running on automatic control, and the automatic isn't functioning all that well right now." Van Doorninck rubbed his chin. "We probably ought to pump some local Jerry for directions. Let's see what we can find near the edge of town."

In fifteen minutes the two men walked into the outskirts of Singen. The town looked humdrum and rural with German citizens going about their business in self-absorbed function. A couple of children chased each other down the street, and the sounds of talking reverberated down the street. Several large dogs lay sprawled out in front of a bakery as if waiting for anyone to toss them a scrap, but the front door stayed closed and the townspeople kept walking down the street, paying them no attention. No one took notice of the two escapees as they ambled down the road.

"Looks like a pedestrian type of little village," Tony said.

"Yeah, we probably won't see many motor vehicles here unless they belong to the *Wehrmacht* or, at the least, to the government. The town's fairly remote."

"Look over there." Tony nodded toward an old man sitting on the steps of a worn house. With shutters hanging loose and the dilapidated walls needing a paint job, the house reflected the man. "Think he'd talk to us?"

Van Doorninck stared. "We've got nothing to lose. Let's see what the old geezer has to say." He walked boldly in the direction of the house.

The villager nodded but didn't speak.

"*Hallo*," Damiaem said, launching into a conversation in German. "You live here?"

Looking well into his eighties, the old man took a large, curved pipe out of his mouth and smiled. "*Ya*," he said. A thick white mustache hung down over his lower lip virtually hiding his mouth. "All my life."

The Dutchman sat down on the step and sprawled his long legs out in front of him. "Nice evening."

The old man nodded his head and white hair fluffed out from under his Alpine cap. "Weather's getting better," he said without much emotion. "Getting warmer I think."

"How do you think the war is going?" Van Doorninck asked. "We whipping the Allies?"

Squinting one eye, the old man looked askance at Damiaem. "You get right down to business, don't you?"

Damiaem smiled. "I'm always interested in the opinions of people I meet. I only wondered what people around here are thinking these days."

The old man snorted. "What's my opinion got to do with anything? We don't see many soldiers around here."

"What about the men guarding the defense line with Switzerland?"

"Defense line!" The old man exploded in laughter. "Who are we going to defend against? The Swiss?" He snorted. "Ho, Ho! Not them! Anyone can walk straight across the border into their country."

"Really?" Damiaem raised his eyebrow.

"Always been like that! Why, when I was a boy, I walked into Switzerland every day of the week. Singen is in the backwoods. Nobody pays no attention to us."

"I like you!" Van Doorninck slapped him on the back. "You give good answers."

The old man pulled his Alpine cap down low over his forehead. "Frankly, I don't talk about the war much anyhow. Everyone says it's going well and that's all that counts. We've got more money than we've had in years in this town, and people seem to be content." He leaned over and said quietly, "What more could anyone ask?"

"Only the freedom to go where they wish," Damiaem said with a cool tone. "I like to have the capacity to walk where I choose."

"Me, too," the old man said. "Always been a free spirit myself."

"Where would you cross the border if you went out tonight?" Van Doorninck sounded nonchalant and indifferent.

"You're kidding?"

"No," Damiaem said. "I've got to go over there in the morning. What's the shortest route?"

The old man leaned back and pointed down the road back toward the pub. "You go back down the same thoroughfare you came up. I'd guess you'd walk about one or two kilometers." Still squinting, he looked up into Damiaem's long, narrow face. "Remember seeing a two-story house with a walking path running beside it that emptied into the woods?"

"Why, yes! Yes, I do."

The old man kept pointing. "If you'd taken that path into the woods, you'd have been only a few hundred yards from Switzerland. It's simply that easy to cross over because part of the Swiss border juts into Germany at that exact point."

"I guess we walked right past the cutoff."

Puffing on his pipe, the old man grinned. "Sure did. You won't find any signs out there in the woods. Like I say, we've always gone back and forth. This war won't stop us from using that route."

The Dutchman stood up. "You've certainly helped us get back on the right path. Thank you."

With his bushy eyebrow quiver, the old man said. "You boys watch out now. Them rocks out there can get treacherous."

"We will." Damiaem started walking back the way they'd come. "Certainly will." He waved.

The old man waved back and returned to smoking his pipe.

Damiaem waited until they had walked several hundred feet before he explained the details of his conversation to Tony.

Irving listened intently to what the old man had said. "Then we can get across tonight!" Tony's excitement exploded through his words. "We're almost out of the country!"

"If the old man was telling us the truth." Damiaem raised an eyebrow. "When we take this bend in the road, we'll stop and watch him through the trees. I want to make sure he doesn't jump up and run to the nearest police station."

"Good idea." Tony looked over his shoulder. "But he doesn't seem to be moving anywhere. Still sitting there."

"Good." Damiaem pointed around the bend. "Let's get off the road and cool our heels. If he keeps sitting there, we can rest assured that we heard the truth."

The two men pushed through the brush near the road and worked their way behind a couple of trees. For fifteen minutes they watched the old man in the village, but he only sat on the steps and smoked his pipe. Finally, Damiaem smiled. "I believe the coast is clear."

"Excellent!" Tony beamed. "We're on our way out of the country."

"You bet!" The Dutchman slapped him on the back. "We're dancing on the edge of freedom."

FORTY-ONE

Evening had settled over the forest by the time Tony and Damiaem reached the two-story farmhouse. The road remained empty, and candlelights appeared in the windows of the house. Other than the wind blowing through the trees, no other sounds echoed from the woods. Large clouds drifted overhead, covering the moon and making the night darker.

Tony looked through the bushes and peered up and down the road. "What do you think?"

"I don't know," Van Doorninck said. "I never take these situations for granted. A platoon of Germans could be hiding over there or even a better bet would be a pack of Hitler Youth along with the local police, waiting behind the barn."

"You really think so?"

"It's happened before and it could happen tonight. Can't be too careful."

"I'll buy that." Tony dropped down on one knee. "What do we do next?"

Van Doorninck rubbed his chin. "I think . . . ," he spoke slowly and thoughtfully. "I think we should make a sweep around the farmhouse and the outbuildings. The walking trail shouldn't be hard to pick up on the back side, and then we'd almost be in Switzerland if the old man told us the truth."

"I'm ready to move."

"Slowly and carefully," Damiaem cautioned. "We don't want to make a sound."

"Got the message."

The Dutchman pointed toward the far side of the house. "Follow me." He beckoned with his thumb and darted toward a low rock fence.

Crawling on their hands and knees, the two escapees inched down the lane until they came to the end of the ancient rock wall. Van Doorninck worked his way through a break in the fence line and started creeping in the direction of the farmhouse. A dog barked, and the Dutchman hit the ground.

For thirty minutes the men lay on the ground, waiting for someone, anyone, to move out in the barnyard, but nothing happened.

"Okay," the Dutchman finally whispered. "Let's try again, but don't make any noise."

Tony nodded and got up on his haunches.

For the next agonizing five minutes, the Dutchman and the American slid through the tall, wet grass until they reached the back of the fencerow thirty feet behind the house. Van Doorninck raised his head slowly and watched for several minutes.

"What do you see?" Tony whispered.

"Nothing." The Dutchman slipped back down to the ground. "If there's anyone hiding out there, they've done a good job of camouflaging themselves. I can't see anybody."

"Do we make a run for it?"

Damiaem shook his head. "No running. We've got to slip out of here as if we're a couple of worms disappearing in the grass. Not a sound." He abruptly stumbled into pieces of wood and fragments of pipe, nearly falling. "Watch out! Building material is lying all over the place."

Suddenly a door slammed. The two men froze in their tracks, staring at each other without making a sound. They could hear a man walking from the house across the ground, coming in their direction.

Tony slowly peeked through a crack in the wall; his heart nearly stopped. Only twenty feet in front of them a man carrying a pail was ambling through the barnyard. Tony reached slowly for a rock, poised to strike if this character came over the fence.

The man stopped and started throwing grain from the bucket around the yard. From out of nowhere chickens came squawking and grabbing at the spray of grain. After a couple of minutes, the farmer turned around and went back toward the farmhouse. The dog barked a couple of times, and the man pushed him in the house.

"Whew!" Tony gasped. "Man, that was too close for me."

"That's two of us." Damiaem leaned back against the stone wall, breathing hard. "Surely there's nobody around here or the farmer never would have come out of the house."

"We can run now." Tony dropped to one knee like a racer, preparing to make a dash for the finish line.

"Don't run," Damiaem warned again. "You'd be too obvious. Let's walk quietly toward those trees." He pointed toward the edge of the forest. "Remember this place is crawling with debris. This farmer must be building a barn or something of that order. It would be easy to trip and fall."

Tony took a deep breath. "Okay. I'm ready."

The prisoners turned toward the forest and started gliding over the top of the grass.

"*Stoppen!*" a German shouted from behind them.

Tony turned slowly. Two men stepped out from behind the barn with rifles. "God help us! It's soldiers!"

"No," Damiaem said under his breath. "Look again! Notice his hat. That's the Gestapo agent we ran into back at the tavern. He's with one of the men who stayed behind in the pub."

Irving swallowed hard. "Yeah, I recognize the guy in the blue shirt."

The Germans crept forward. "*Schiesen!*" the Gestapo agent warned. "*Gehnich weg beelib stehen wodbist.*"

"They're warning that they'll shoot," Van Doorninck translated quickly. "Those Nazis must have been sitting over there waiting for us to show up. We're caught!"

Tony looked frantically around him. He couldn't let himself be captured again. Anger swelled up in Irving. Regardless of what happened, he wasn't going to go down for the count on this one.

"*Schiesen,*" the Gestapo agent repeated.

Quickly studying the ground around them, Tony looked for something, anything, that he might use to fight back.

"*Schiesen!*" Van Doorninck shouted in German. "They're telling us that they will fire," he warned Tony.

Suddenly Tony saw it—a pipe. A long piece of black drainpipe just about the right footage and width! He bent over and grabbed the pipe, hoisting the drain on his shoulder. "Bazooka!" he screamed. "I'll fire!"

For a moment the Dutchman stared in astonishment, speechless at Tony's brashness.

"I'll fire!" Tony screamed again.

The Germans stopped and gawked in consternation.

"*Gehimiches Gewehr!*" Van Doorninck yelled. "A bazooka! *Lasse das gewehr sailen!*"

Looking bewildered, the Germans hesitated, then lowered their rifles slightly.

"I'll blow you away!" Irving warned. "Drop those guns and get out of here."

"Bazooka!" Van Doorninck threatened.

The two Germans looked at each other and suddenly started running back to the barn.

"Don't stop!" Tony shouted. "Or I'll shoot!"

The Gestapo agent and the man in the blue shirt disappeared behind the barn.

"Get out of here!" Damiaem shouted and started running like a frightened deer. "Run!"

Tony kept the drainpipe on his shoulder until he reached the edge of the forest. With one final heave, he threw the heavy metal pipe to one side and dashed into the trees behind Van Doorninck.

"Darkness will cover us," the Dutchman said over his shoulder, "but don't stop running!"

Irving ran as hard as he could behind Van Doorninck but struggled to keep up.

"We might still run into some soldier out here walking around," the Dutchman said over his shoulder. "We've got to be as quiet as possible."

The two men ran down the back fence line and through the trees behind the house. Staying bent over, they quickly disappeared into the brush and paused for a moment.

"My pants are completely soaked," Tony complained. "The grass is really wet."

"We can't be far from the border," Van Doorninck puffed. "Keep running straight ahead until we know we're in Switzerland." The Dutchman started again. "The trail ought to be to our left."

"Okay." Tony stayed close behind. "It's getting darker and harder to see where we are."

"Keep your eyes open, mate," Damiaem warned. "The bush is getting thicker."

"Absolutely."

After a hundred feet, Tony grabbed the back of Damiaem's shirt. "You think we've missed the trail?"

"I don't know. If we don't find it quickly, we'll have to double back."

"Yeah, because it's getting very dark."

"Yes," Damiaem whispered. "The clouds make it hard to see anything."

"I'm behind you," Tony said quietly. "Don't worry. You won't lose me."

"The ground is getting steeper. Watch the grade."

"Yes . . . ," Tony said, "getting rockier too."

"Yeah, I'm afraid we've missed the . . ." Damiaem stumbled forward. "Watch . . . A-a-a-h!" he screamed. "A-a-a-h," descended into silence. The sound ended with a dull thud.

"Damiaem! Damiaem! Where are you?" Tony froze and dropped to his knees, groping with his hands. Abruptly, he felt the edge of a rock and then nothing but empty space. "Damiaem!" he shouted, reaching out into the nothingness. "Good Lord! Where are you?"

Only silence came back. Tony suddenly realized he had been shouting and stopped. He couldn't hear anyone coming through the forest. Apparently the Germans weren't chasing them. Catching his breath, Irving once more felt around the edges of what seemed to be an abyss.

"God help us," he groaned. "Please don't let anything terrible happen to Damiaem." He felt into the pitch blackness.

The clouds kept moving and the moon came out again, casting a beam of dim light across the forest. Tony blinked several times and tried to adjust his eyes to the blackness. He slowly began to see what was in front of him. Only then did Tony recognize he was close to the edge of a cliff. Looking down into the vastness of a hole, he saw the outline of Van Doorninck's body down at least ten feet below in a pit near the edge of the cliff. The Dutchman had stepped off into a sinkhole situated between the rocks.

Tony flinched and shuddered. The opening of the hole was small, and Damiaem had hit it at the right angle to drop him straight to the bottom. If he was still alive . . . if he was breathing . . . but getting the Dutchman out would be no small task. Tony had no idea how far the drop off the edge of the cliff would prove to be. He could be standing on a precipice, plunging him forever into a pile of unforgiving rocks.

Irving froze in place. His heart started beating harder and his palms became clammy. Tony's lungs gasped for more air. The hole stared back at him like the mouth of a great anaconda, waiting to devour Tony in one gulp. If he dropped into that hole, Tony knew death was waiting for him at the bottom with open arms.

Claustrophobia kicked in with desperate urgency, wrapping the cold fingers of fear around Tony's neck. He doubled over in agony. Tony couldn't leave his friend in the pit, but Irving wasn't sure he had the ability to climb down, much less pull Van Doorninck out. They had been so close to escaping but now were light-years from getting away. Tony's hands started to shake.

"Damiaem!" he cried. "Oh, Damiaem. Please! Please . . . Wake up!" He didn't see any movement in the pitch-black hole. "God help us!"

Tony grabbed his face and covered his eyes. Gritting his teeth, he looked up again and discovered that the clouds had moved once more. The moon hovered above him like a spotlight. He looked at the hole again that was shaped like a door, like a narrow door.

CHAPTER

FORTY-TWO

Tony stared into the black hole. He could not conceive of dropping himself into that dark tube of death opening up at his feet, but neither could he leave the Dutchman behind. Tony's heart kept pounding and his breath came only in forced, hard panting. No alternative existed except for him to climb down into that narrow, seemingly bottomless, pit and attempt to bring Van Doorninck out over his shoulder.

Tony dropped his legs over the edge, searching for a rock to stand on, but his body froze. He wanted to go further but couldn't. Tony's muscles felt as if they had turned to stone and he had become a statue.

"Oh God," he prayed aloud. "I don't think I can push myself down into this cave. I'm afraid I will suffocate in the darkness."

Somewhere off in the distance an owl sent a long, low *whoo*, drifting out over the forest like a moan from the dead. Tony caught his breath and gripped the ledge as if his fingers were melting into the stone.

"Lord, please help me. I have to rescue my friend, but I don't think I can. I must have Your help. *Please.*"

Tony caught his breath again. Probably he was still on the German side of the border, and time remained a factor. Even though he was sitting on the edge of the rocks, *waiting* was an option he really didn't have.

With perspiration starting to form on his brow, a memory abruptly returned. He hadn't thought about this particular childhood experience for years. Once more Tony Irving was a six-year-old boy, living on the Texas sagebrush-covered plains.

On the edge of the family's property was an old windmill, pumping to fill the water tank for the cattle that periodically wandered in from the back forty. In his mind's eye, he could still see that worn, dented water trough that had endured a hundred winter storms. Water from the windmill's pump constantly drained into the overflowing tin tub before running down toward a large pipe that emptied far down below into a small stream that wound through the pasture.

His mother often warned him to stay away from what she called "that nasty drainpipe." If he'd fallen into that moss-covered tube, he might have plunged to the bottom, where his mother was certain that he would be killed.

And her admonition was the problem. While he believed his mother, Tony was always attracted to anything she cautioned him against. In a moth-to-flame attraction, danger drew him toward what he ought to be running from. After all, it was summertime when the plains' temperatures would soar into the hundreds and a drink of cold water could only help him get beyond the dry spell. He would forget her warning.

One afternoon, the temptation was too great. Tony looked around. No one was watching him. Out of the corner of his eye he spotted the trickle of water running into that battered, gray drainpipe. His mother was in the kitchen, thinking he was out playing somewhere on the other side of the house. *Now* was the perfect moment to get a closer look at that drainpipe hole.

Tony crouched closer, wondering what it would be like to peer into the drain. The opening was certainly large enough for him to stick his head and shoulders in and get a good long peek. He knelt down and looked over the edge. The stream of water splashed over the smooth worn spout, dousing his face with a spray of cool water. Far down below, Tony could see the stream bouncing over the distant rocks that looked like they were at the other end of the world.

Suddenly, the wet moss around the edge slipped and he plunged forward. Instinctively, Tony stuck his hand in front of his face and grabbed a broken piece of the drainpipe that stopped his headfirst plummet straight to the bottom.

"A-a-h-h!" Tony screamed. He knew at any moment his hand holding the rough piece of the drainpipe wouldn't stand the pain any longer and he would slip. "Help!" Tony barely gagged the word out of his mouth.

Pain shot up his arm. Far down below the water careened over the rocks, sounding more ominous than he'd dreamed possible. Tony could already feel what was coming. When he finally nose-dived into the sharp pointed pile of rocks at the bottom, his head would split open like a watermelon.

Tony was certain his life would end in only a matter of moments. Terror shadowed his mind, pushing out every semblance of thought. All-consuming horror grabbed at his throat and strangled all reason.

Suddenly, two hands grabbed Tony's legs and jerked him straight up. In a sudden sweep, he was yanked out of the pipe and laid on his back in a pile of dust. Looking up, he saw his mother!

His hair-raising slip into the pipe had planted the fears that still bore fruit in his mind. The terror of slipping into any narrow, confining space had begun with that old drainpipe from the tank on the Texas windswept prairie. The memory faded.

A Bible passage raced through his mind. "Be anxious for nothing, but in everything by prayer and supplication, with thanksgiving, let your requests be made known to God." Sitting on the edge of the hole dropping into oblivion, the scriptural words wrapped themselves around Tony's fears like a warm blanket. He took a deep breath and let each syllable and sentence do their work on his haunting thoughts. Slowly but steadily, he began to breathe easier.

Be anxious for nothing . . . for nothing . . .

For nothing . . .

Tony felt his heartbeat begin to subside and took a deeper breath. The words kept working on him. *Be anxious for nothing.*

He looked again into the black hole and at the form lying down below. The moment had come, and there was no way around what had to be done. Tony must descend through that open, narrow door.

"Help me, God, descend into the depths that I might be a faithful servant," he prayed aloud. He slowly eased into the darkness crowding around him.

CHAPTER

FORTY-THREE

With sweaty palms clutching at the rock jutting out from the side of the boulders, Tony inched downward. Captain Van Doorninck had not moved, and his body lay at a frightening angle.

Night only heightened Irving's fear of the narrow space closing around him. Attempting to push the effects of his ever-increasing claustrophobia out of his mind, Tony searched with his feet for a hold, for any hold, that might ensure his security. The pile of stones heaped around Van Doorninck and Tony's pulsating fear made descending nearly impossible.

Got to concentrate on Damiaem's condition, Tony thought. *Think about helping him. Can't let my mind be distracted.* He reached for another rock and lowered himself slightly. *Must not let my fears jar my hand loose.* His feet kept struggling to find the rock holds. *Have to fight back panic. I will not yield or give in to this fear. Get away from me.*

"Damiaem!" Tony whispered as loud as he dared. "Damiaem! Please answer me."

Tony inched further down the slippery rock wall. A cloud moved over the moon, and the cave turned black. Swallowing hard, Tony knew he no longer had any idea of how close he was to the Dutchman, but he didn't dare jump. Besides landing on Damiaem, he might even fall further into the abyss.

"Please answer me!" Tony heard a slight groan just below him. "Damiaem, is that you?"

Tony's foot touched a hard surface and then the toe of his shoe nudged a soft form. "Damiaem, that's got to be you." Dropping down on his knees, he began searching with his hands, quickly touching a leg. The clouds moved away from the moon, and Van Doorninck's form became faintly visible.

Irving rolled his friend over slowly and carefully. Blood ran down the side of Van Doorninck's face. "Damiaem! Can you hear me?"

The Dutchman groaned and stirred slightly.

"Thank God! You're alive!"

"A-a-a-h," escaped from the Dutchman's mouth. "O-o-h."

"Praise the Lord! You're still with us!"

Damiaem's fingers began working in a sluggish, clawing motion in the soil. "Where . . . where . . . am I?" he asked without opening his eyes.

"You fell in a hole. We nearly walked off a cliff."

Van Doorninck's eyes fluttered. "My, my, head . . . it . . . hurts."

"You're lucky you are still wearing it. You must have landed on your feet and fallen forward."

The Dutchman's hand slowly rose to his forehead. "I . . . I . . . got . . . cut . . . I think."

"Yeah, I'm just glad you didn't lose your entire face on these rocks."

"It's dark." Damiaem raised his head slightly. "Very dark."

"Night's overtaken us. Remember?"

The moon's beams sent a shaft of light through the cave, covering Van Doorninck with a slight glow. "Must have taken a good bump. Oh, do I ever have a headache."

"I'm afraid you took quite a lick." Tony leaned back against a boulder. "We've got to be extremely careful. We're right on the edge of a cliff, and I have no idea how far the drop is."

"I see." Van Doorninck blinked his eyes several times. "I hope I haven't broken any bones."

"You and me both." Irving inched closer. "You ready for me to help you sit up?"

The Dutchman felt along the edge of the cut on the side of his head. "I don't think this wound is as deep as it looks. You always bleed like a stuck pig when you get hit on the head."

"I'm more concerned with getting you out of this hole, Damiaem. Do you think you can sit up?"

"I can try." Van Doorninck raised his hand. "Pull me up gently, mate."

Tony got a firm grasp on the large, bony hand and carefully pulled Damiaem forward. The captain slowly sat upright. "How does it feel?"

Van Doorninck shook his head. "Like I got the soup drained out of me." He rolled his neck to clear his mind. "But I don't feel like I broke anything."

"I don't see how you didn't. You dropped ten feet."

Van Doorninck inched his left leg forward and moved it from side to side. "Seems to be working okay."

"Damiaem, only the hand of God could have kept you from smashing your hip."

The Dutchman looked up into Tony's face and smiled. "That's a rather hard option for me to buy, but what can I say? I'm glad to be alive."

"You'd better be." Tony kept pulling on Damiaem's hand, trying to get the Dutchman on his feet. "Let's see if you can stand up."

With careful, deliberate movement, the captain's long, skinny legs held steady as he stood. He reached for the rock next to him and secured himself. "I seem to be functional. The legs feel like they might even get me out of this pit."

"Thank God! I was terrified I would have to carry you out over my shoulder."

"I'd be a bit of a hefty load for you, old boy." He stretched up on his toes, trying to get his body working again. "Afraid I'm on the tall side."

"Damiaem, I know you've not been a man of faith and I don't know what's ahead, but I have to give the Lord the credit for keeping us alive. We'd already made it through a long, dark night well before you even stepped into the hole."

"Mate, I can't argue with you." Van Doorninck smiled. "If the Almighty is out there and wants to walk with us, far be it from me to offer any resistance."

Tony grinned. "Hey, we're making progress. Let's see if you can get out of this place. I'll bring up the rear."

Van Doorninck looked up at the opening above his head. "Not a long climb, but I don't want to slip back into this little cell again."

"I'll grab you if you slide."

"Okay, cowboy. Here we go."

Van Doorninck got a firm hold on the rocks around him and pushed upward. He positioned his feet carefully to make sure his grip was certain. Damiaem crept up the wall at a snail's pace.

"You're doing okay?"

"Yes," the Dutchman said over his shoulder. "I feel a bit stiff and my head hurts, but I think I can make it out of the opening."

Tony followed behind him, ready to cushion the Dutchman if he slipped. He kept his eye on the opening at the top and positioned himself at every point to brace for the fall should Damiaem lose his grip.

"I'm almost out," Van Doorninck said. "I think I'll be able to roll over the edge in a moment."

Tony watched carefully, fearing that Damiaem's head wound might cause him to faint. He kept himself carefully propped against the rock.

"Hey, I'm through the opening," Van Doorninck whispered from the top. "I'm okay. I'm out of there."

Irving took a deep breath. "Excellent." He immediately started scampering toward the top. "We're in good shape." He reached for a rock to pull himself out of the precipice and abruptly stopped. Tony suddenly realized somewhere along the descent and the climb back out, he'd lost his fear of the narrow space. His heart wasn't beating wildly and the palms of his hands weren't sweating. He looked around. The cave was actually much larger than he'd remembered when he started down.

Tony's breath kept coming in a normal, easy pattern. He climbed out of the hole and for a moment lay on the ground, looking up at the moon. The cold night had become invigorating rather than terrifying, and he felt like a metal band around his chest had been broken. Invigoration poured into his soul. He took a deep breath, and revitalizing freshness filled his lungs.

"You saved my life," Damiaem said. "I'm not sure what would have become of me if you hadn't crawled down there to bring me around."

Tony smiled at his friend. "I think that little trip down *saved my own life*. No question about it. The hand of the Lord has been on both of us."

Damiaem nodded. "What can I say?" He grinned an unusual sly smile. "Except *thank God*."

FORTY-FOUR

Tony lay in the grass and stared at the stars beginning to appear from behind the clouds. He couldn't hear the sound of anyone chasing them, but he knew the clock was running and they needed to get back on their journey.

"Damiaem," Tony spoke softly. "I want to say something, but I don't want to offend you."

"Offend me?" Van Doorninck laughed. "You've just saved my life, and you are afraid you'll offend me? Come on. You can even speak ill of my mother and I'd not be offended. I owe you a big one."

"Some time back we got in a row because I tried to talk to you about a . . . spiritual problem. Obviously, it was none of my business, but . . ."

"You know, for a cowboy, you certainly wander off into strange territory. Don't you know soldiers aren't supposed to talk about God and holy things?"

Tony rubbed his chin thoughtfully. "Yeah, our business is supposed to be killing people, not inquiring about their souls."

"You got it, cowboy. War is the science of annihilation. The rest of the divine business we leave back at the church."

"I got that picture from observing you, Damiaem. I'm not trying to pry into your business, but I know you've seen many people killed, and that has to have ripped an important part of your soul to shreds." Tony took a deep breath. "I want you to know that I care."

For a long time the Dutchman didn't say anything. He sat with his head bowed, resting his chin on his knees. Finally, Damiaem straightened up. "Thank you," he said gently. "Thank you."

Tony had never heard such a vulnerable sound from Van Doorninck in all the time he had known him. The Dutchman's hard indifference seemed to have vanished. "This war has been worse than anything I could have thought possible," Tony confessed. "I had no idea human beings could treat each other so savagely. I heard terrible stories when the prisoners talked together in the castle. Of course, I don't know what you lived through when the Nazis came tearing through your country, but I'm sure the experiences were bitter."

Damiaem stiffened and then slumped. "*Bitter?*" he said quizzically. "Far more than bitter, the days were venomous. Maliciousness and rancor reigned supreme, reducing the goodness in men to violence and evil."

For a long time nothing was said. Tony stared into the darkness, feeling the emptiness and hollowness of the blackness surrounding them.

"I think . . . I became . . . angry," Damiaem said. "Yes. Angry. Like a disease eating goodness out of my heart, indignation and wrath devoured any conviction I had about goodness and hope. I set my face like a flint to avenge what the Nazis had done to me, my friends, my country. I shut off my finest emotions." He took a deep breath. "I lost myself as well as my faith because of my own bitterness. Tony, I was wrong."

Tony bit his lip but said nothing.

Finally the Dutchman spoke again. "I guess I didn't quit believing in God as much as I lost Him. Hate drove out His love. Well, it's time to put those feelings behind me, to let go of my anger and start thanking Him for His goodness and guidance."

"Oh, I think so too, Damiaem," Tony grinned broadly.

"I'll do my best to let go of the negative, cowboy. I promise."

"I know God will bless you, Damiaem. I believe that's a fact."

Van Doorninck nodded. "Okay. Look, we need to get going. No telling where we actually are." He reached down and picked up a handful of dirt, letting the dust run through his fingers. "On the other hand, we may have actually crossed the border." He stood up and took his home-made compass out of his pocket. "I hope this device is working." He swung the compass around several times. "In any case, we must still maintain silence. We don't want to take any chances this close to escaping Germany."

Irving stood up. "Absolutely. The clock is running and we need to keep moving."

"And at a good clip." Damiaem beckoned with his thumb and started walking. "Hang on, cowboy. I'm going to walk as fast as possible."

"Hey! You can run for all I'm concerned."

"You've got that old smell of freedom in your nose, boy." Van Doorninck stretched out his long legs in hefty strides. "Gives you a new burst of energy, doesn't it?"

"You bet. Just keep tracking."

"Hang on, mate. We're going to cut through these woods like it is our private pathway home."

The two escapees clopped through the forest at a backbreaking pace. Periodically, Van Doorninck stopped to look at his compass, examine the path, and make sure they hadn't strayed. The only sound they heard was the underbrush swishing against their bodies and the clomp of their feet in the gravel. Occasionally, the moon slipped out from behind the clouds and cast shimmering glimpses of light over their path.

One thought kept returning to Tony's mind. What was Rikki Beck doing at that very moment? Once he locked on to that track, his thoughts whirled back and forth in what had now become a familiar pattern. He always began by trying to see her face and remember her voice, but the sound of Rikki's words was long gone from his memory, and it only frustrated Tony to try to recall the sonorousness.

A loud sound broke through the trees and through Tony's reverie. Van Doorninck abruptly held up his hand and halted. Somewhere off in the distance a branch cracked. It sounded like a man accidentally stepping on a tree limb. The two men froze in place, not moving and barely breathing.

For fifteen minutes the Dutchman and the American stood in place, hardly breathing. Finally, Damiaem lowered his hand and turned around. "Could have been a German, but it could also have been a deer," he whispered. "A bear possibly."

"What do you think?" Tony asked.

"I think we should be in Switzerland, but I'm certainly far from sure."

Tony took a deep breath. "I don't hear anything out there, but we've only got two choices. Stay here until morning or walk slower."

The Dutchman chuckled. "Walk slower? Come on, mate. You're pulling my leg."

"Quit talking like a Brit!" Tony protested. "I say we move on more carefully. A tad more leisurely. That's all."

"I agree, but pay strict attention." Van Doorninck pointed forward and started walking at a more deliberate pace.

Tony fell into step again. For three miles he watched the path carefully but slowly began to relax. They had to have walked beyond where the noise originated. It was probably an animal. He began to think about Rikki again. Now that he was so close to the freedom to see her again, he could almost think of nothing else.

Was she still waiting for him? Two long, long years had dragged by. Probably none of his letters had gotten through because she had never written him. Maybe some other guy had come along and caught her eye. Maybe . . . maybe . . . maybe . . .

A surge of homesickness swept over Tony, and he nearly stumbled. Many times his stomach had rolled over from lack of food, but this pain was different. The loneliness of being left behind hurt as much as if the Germans had thrown him back into solitary confinement. Tony kept walking, but if Rikki wasn't waiting anymore, should he even think about coming home again?

FORTY-FIVE

The light of dawn began breaking through the trees, revealing a faint outline of rooftops and buildings on the horizon. Off in the distance the two escapees could see the contour of a village. The two men stopped and looked through the gray haze of early morning, studying the shapes in front of them.

"What do you think?" Tony asked.

"Hard to say." Damiaem took his handmade compass out of his pocket. "If this device didn't work right, could be the village of Hilzingen or Gottmadingen and we'd still be in Germany."

"Got any pleasant options?"

"The best news would be that we are looking at Frauenfeld and have stumbled into Switzerland."

Tony nodded his head. "I pray so."

"Well, cowboy, your praying and believing helped get us through a long hard night." Van Doorninck gently felt the bump and the cut on the side of his head where the blood had dried. "I'm not making anymore cracks about God, and I promise to be more than a bit more respectful, but praying won't answer our question about where we are. We've got to walk into town."

"Damiaem, you look pretty bad—like the Gestapo agent at the farm did a lot more than run," Tony said. "In the light of morning, it's obvious the fall into the cave not only bashed your head royally but it tore up your pants and scraped up your arms as well."

The Dutchman brushed himself off and looked around at his clothes. "I guess I look rather worn."

"'*Broken*' is a better word." Tony squinted at his friend. "Frankly, I don't see how you walked so fast last night."

"The pace helped push back some of the aches and pains." Damiaem rubbed the back of his neck. "To be honest, now that we've slowed down I don't feel so great. I'm not sure if I sat down that I could get up and start moving again. I'm afraid those are the cards I've been given. Got no choice but to play them."

"Yeah, I'm getting concerned too." Tony rubbed the side of his face.

Damiaem nodded. "One way or the other, we must eat fairly soon. I'm running below empty. I think you ought to start praying that we don't walk into a Nazi trap."

"I have been," Tony answered. "The people in that village will probably speak German regardless of their nationality because they are so close to the border, right?" Tony asked.

"I think that's safe to assume, and I'm the only one who speaks German around here." Van Doorninck raised his eyebrow solemnly. "You see, I have no choice but to keep on walking and talking."

Tony smiled. "Sorry, but that looks like those are the cards *we've* been dealt."

"Using my words on me, aren't you?" Damiaem looked toward the village. "I wonder what happened with Jacob, Stooge, and the other soldiers? Lord, I hope they made it out."

"Maybe they're down there in the village waiting for us." Tony grinned again. "Now, that would make a story to tell!"

Damiaem started walking again at a much slower pace. "I'm more concerned that our old friend Major Eggers or Corporal Schadlich and their Nazi buddies might be waiting in town to say a little hello." He kept swinging his leg stiffly around to the side.

Twenty minutes later the path out of the forest wound out on a dirt road. Straight ahead of the two men they could see the first houses of the village sparsely edged along the side of the road. A few cows stood penned behind the outbuildings. Chickens ran here and there, but the hour was early for the villagers. Most of the people were still asleep in bed. The two escapees approached the houses quietly and cautiously.

"What do you think?" Tony asked.

"I think the town looks like a rural village," Van Doorninck said. "That's a good sign because I'd expect a more urban feel from a place like Gottmadingen." He looked up and down the street carefully. "Of course, we're only on the edge of the town, and it may turn into a city."

"Nobody's up or around. At least we've not seen any German soldiers. I'd say we keep walking."

Damiaem nodded his head. "I suppose so." He started walking again, but his stride was more labored.

"You're not feeling so good, huh?" Tony said.

"I don't think I can get much farther than this town," Damiaem answered. "If this isn't Switzerland, you may have to go on without me."

"Not on your life!" Tony reached out to offer the Dutchman his hand. "We either escape together or we go back together, but I'm not letting you fall behind because we stepped into a hole last night."

Damiaem smiled one of his rare grins. "My, my, cowboy. How your attitude has changed. I believe you've made some progress since you first showed up at Colditz."

"Don't be funny." Irving slipped his shoulder under Van Doorninck's arm. "Let me give you some support."

The Dutchman sighed. "Never took help from anyone before, but I think it might make a difference this morning." He leaned on Tony. "Let's see how soon we can find a place for me to sit down."

The two men hobbled down the street at a slow, labored pace. The number of houses increased, but the street remained gravel. After walking six long blocks, a small square opened up with businesses situated around the open area. On the other side of the plaza, a sign hanging from a stucco wall indicated a pub was inside. Lights were already on in the restaurant's windows.

"I think we might buy breakfast in there," Tony said, shouldering the weight of his Dutch friend. "At least, we would find out where we are."

Van Doorninck tried to stand by himself. "I think I truly messed up my leg," he said resolutely. "I must sit down whether I like the result or not. I don't think we have much alternative but to try that pub. Let's go in and attempt to look normal."

"Normal?" Tony laughed. "You're kidding!"

Tony looked again at his friend. The sunlight had become much brighter, and Van Doorninck's appearance was obviously rugged. The left side of his pants leg was torn, and the cloth was stained with blood. The man had paid a high price to walk through the woods at night, particularly at the speed he had maintained. The soreness and strain of the excursion were setting in. Anyone in the restaurant who saw them would know the truth—that they looked liked escapees from either a jail or a pigpen.

Damiaem hobbled forward. "I'll go in and grab the first seat. I'm afraid my energy is about gone."

For the first time, Tony allowed himself to recognize how hungry he was and that his energy was exhausted as well. The two men stumbled into the pub like travelers on their last leg and slumped down at the first table.

A woman cleaning a table stopped and looked at them. Wearing a traditional German peasant's dress, she had a decidedly Austrian turn to her appearance. "*Wilkommen!*"

Tony nodded politely, but the woman frowned at them.

"*Hallo,*" the Dutchman answered and stretched his leg far out in front of him. "Please excuse our appearance," he said in German. "I fell in the woods last night."

"Oh no," the woman answered in German and immediately came over to the table. "Bless your hearts." Slightly on the heavy side, the waitress had a smiling face with attractive, dimpled cheeks. "You took quite a whack on your head now, didn't you!"

Van Doorninck forced a smile. "Afraid so. The journey has pushed us to our limits. We wondered if you served breakfast?"

"Of course!" The woman beamed. "We are a *gaststatte!* I will bring you a glass of milk to start. Maybe you would like some eggs? Toast? Coffee?"

Damiaem put his hand in front of his mouth and whispered in English, "She's got eggs."

Tony almost lurched forward. "*Eggs!*" he inadvertently said in English.

Damiaem grabbed his wrist. "My friend doesn't speak German," he explained.

"No problem," the woman said in English. "Everyvon in Switzerland speaks many languages."

"Switzerland!" Tony nearly shouted. "We're in Switzerland?"

"Of course!" the woman said in English. "You are in the town of Frauenfeld."

"Frauenfeld!" Tony stood up, waving his arms in the air. "Thank God! Praise God! We've escaped! We're free!"

The woman's mouth dropped. "Vhat? Escaped? Vhat are you saying?"

Tony beat on the table with the ends of his fist. "We've made it! We've gotten out of Germany. Hallelujah!"

Damiaem jerked Tony's arm down and looked up into the woman's face. "We are safe?" he asked with a tentative, questioning tone in his words. *"Safe with you?"*

"Aha!" The woman's eyes widened. "You are Allied soldiers running away from de Nazis!"

"Afraid so," the Dutchman said. "I hope we have found a friend."

"A friend?" Her face brightened and the woman kept speaking English. "Nazis? I hate Hitler and the Nazis! Crazy men. All of them! You are most velcome in dis house!"

"A-a-h-h!" The air rushed out of Damiaem's mouth and his entire body sagged. "Thank heavens!" Almost as if his last ounce of energy was spent, the Dutchman crumbled. "We have found *a friend.*"

"A friend?" The woman declared, "A comrade! Yes, I am glad you have come to my business. I fix you a true breakfast. Sausage! Fresh coffee! Everything!" She turned and hurried toward the kitchen. "We must help you in your escape."

"Wait!" Damiaem called out. "We don't have any Swiss money."

"Money?" The woman threw her hands up in the air. "Dis breakfast *is my gift.*" She twirled around and disappeared into the kitchen. "Especially for you brave men."

Tony tried to choke back his emotion, but the tears kept rolling down his cheeks. He couldn't speak. "Free," he barely muttered. "Free. Free . . . at last."

The Dutchman took a deep breath and his eyes watered. "Last night I wasn't sure I could make it," he said more faintly than he'd ever spoken before. "So many times I felt like my strength was completely gone." He tried to move his leg but had to use his hand to pull his knee up. "I don't know how we ever found our way out."

"I must tell you honestly," Tony said. "I can only attribute our endurance to the hand of God. I did pray and He has led us through a narrow door. It was the divine touch that kept us from falling and disappearing in the dark. My friend, we must thank God for our lives being sustained."

Damiaem nodded and looked at the floor solemnly. Finally, he lifted his head upward toward the ceiling. "All of my adult life I have wondered if there was really a God." Tears welled up in the corner of his eyes. "Never, never again. *Never again.*"

The hostess hustled out of the kitchen carrying two glasses of milk. "Start with dis," she said. "A nice cold milk vill help you."

"Thank you," Tony said and grabbed the glass. Almost in a single gulp, he downed the entire glass of milk.

"No! NO!" the woman cautioned. "You vill get sick. You must drink very slowly or up it all comes again."

"She's right, mate," Van Doorninck said. "Easy does it." He started sipping the milk but quickly gulped until the glass was empty. "Sorry," he muttered. "It's hard to drink slow."

"You must!" the waitress insisted and smiled. "Don't worry. I'll be back with more food." She smiled and hurried back to the kitchen.

"Damiaem," Tony said, "I can't believe we are out of that godforsaken castle."

Van Doorninck smiled weakly. "Neither can I. Only God could have led us to such a good place."

FORTY-SIX

After a day and a night in Frau Prawitt's *gaststatte*, both Tony Irving and Damiaem Van Doorninck felt and looked like new men. Following a ride on the back of a hay wagon to the larger town of Winterthur, the Swiss police provided a ride into Zurich. With unusual concern and hospitality, they were put up in Der Berg, an excellent hotel. The long imprisonment in Colditz Castle had finally come to an end.

Night had fallen again when the two men met in the lobby of the Der Berg hotel.

"How's it going, mate?" Damiaem asked Tony.

"I've been trying to get this phone call through to Dallas, Texas, for five and a half hours now. Nothing's happened."

"You'll be a lucky man if you can connect," Damiaem said. "We're in the midst of a terrible war that has disrupted everything. I'm surprised the telephone company paid any attention at all to your call."

"I told them that I escaped from more than two years in a Nazi concentration camp, and the woman on the other end of the line listened. I sensed she was pulling for me. I think they are trying hard to get my call through."

Van Doorninck grinned. "Ah, that old cowboy charm works every time. I hope you make it." He started to walk away and then turned around. "Hey, I bet you're trying to call that girlfriend. Her name was . . . Rosa . . . Robin . . ."

"Rikki." Tony grinned. "Rikki Beck. You got it, partner. I'm going to give her the chance of a lifetime to hear my voice."

"Aren't you generous," Damiaem said dryly. "A man of true magnanimity."

"I always try to give the ladies an even chance."

Van Doorninck smiled. "A true gentleman. Good luck. I'll be in the restaurant eating my fourth meal of the day."

"How much weight do you think we lost?" Tony asked.

"I'd guess I lost probably forty pounds," Damiaem said. "Hate to tell you, but your ribs are showing."

Tony nodded. "Yeah, I may not look so hot, but then, again, I'm alive. That's enough."

Damiaem's smile faded. "No small matter, lad. We *are* alive."

"What do you think happened to Bill Fowler and the rest of our crew?"

"I've made inquiries through the police, and no one's heard anything about them crossing the border. You know they settled down by the railway station to catch a ride, and I was concerned about that route. I hope they're still out there, trying to get across the frontier."

"Me, too." Tony took a deep breath. "It's sure not easy getting across the German border."

"Like I said, good luck on your phone call." Van Doorninck walked away with his usual sober look on his face.

Tony watched Damiaem's stiff, lame walk back across the hotel lobby. He had learned to watch what the Dutchman's eyes said. Behind the emotionless stare was a churning world of turbulent emotions. Damiaem cared passionately about Stooge Wardle, Bill Fowler, Lulu Lawton, and his friend Jacob Sas. Every man in Oflag 4C would always be Damiaem's intimate concern. Captain Van Doorninck remained a man with a blank face and a full heart.

"Sorry, sir." The clerk behind the hotel's front desk interrupted Tony's thoughts. "We are still attempting to connect with the United States, but nothing has gone through yet."

Tony looked at his watch. "It will be the early morning in Dallas. I'm sure my party will be at home. Please keep trying."

"Of course." The clerk smiled politely and went back to the switchboard. "We will continue. Should we make a connection, you can use the wall telephone to talk." He pointed to a stand lined with several telephones only feet from his desk.

"Thank you," Tony said and looked around the large, well-decorated lobby.

An overstuffed chair stood a short distance across the room from him. People kept walking back and forth, not seeming even to notice the American, but the anonymity felt pleasant. Knowing no one was watching him or had a machine gun pointed in his direction was like a lifelong dream come true. Tony strolled over to the comfortable chair and sat down.

The truth was that he was terrified that Rikki wouldn't be waiting for him. Possibly she had married someone else and left home. He would end up talking to one of her parents who would kindly give him the terrible news. For a moment, Tony contemplated running over and telling the clerk to cancel the phone call, but he didn't.

Several businessmen strolled past with attractive women on their arms. Down the hall, Tony could see the hotel bar and faintly hear raucous conversations going on inside. Damiaem would be to the left in the restaurant, eating like food was going out of style. Life in the hotel loped along like there was no war booming away just over the border. No men dying. No prisoners locked up in concentration camps. No problems. Life was little more than a fat piece of buttered toast.

The indifference of the patrons bothered Tony. At that very moment not three to four hundred miles away, a castle full of good, decent men were preparing to hunker down for the night, struggling and ill fed, looking for a way to get back to freedom. All of these fat cats floating around this affluent hotel lobby ought to sleep a night at Colditz Castle. An evening in the shadows of the ramparts would put them in touch with the hard realities of the twentieth century!

Tony's mind drifted back to Rikki. He trusted her. It wasn't that he carried any misgivings about Rikki, or did he? . . . Yes, he did. The struggles of the war had pushed him out of thinking like an idealistic adolescent into a hard-nosed realist. Tony had been missing a long time, and any normal person would have given up on him by now. Why wouldn't Rikki do the same? He couldn't hold it against her. Probably he would have done the identical thing he was now certain she had done.

Sure.

Tony could understand how Rikki had found some other man who hadn't been as crazy as he had to go flying off to the other side of the world and get captured. It all made sense. Rikki Beck was a normal girl with her own life to lead. She had done the sensible thing.

Tony took a long, deep breath. He would simply express his understanding and ask the Becks to call his family and tell them he was alive. Rikki Beck would eventually fade from his mind . . . maybe . . . maybe not ever . . . and he'd go back to fighting this appalling war.

"Sir!" the clerk called across the lobby. "Ah . . . Mister Irving. Please, I have your connection."

Tony leaped out of the chair and ran for the wall telephone. "I'm ready!" he yelled.

"Just a moment," the clerk shouted back. "Wait for my instruction." He paused several moments. "Yes, now, pick up the receiver."

Tony listened to a strange buzzing sound and then the line became clearer.

"Hello," a woman's voice said far off in the distance. "Hello."

"With whom am I speaking?" Tony said.

After a long delay, the woman answered. "Rikki. Rikki Beck."

"Rikki!" Tony sounded. "It's you."

A dead silence followed for several seconds. "Hello," the woman's voice said.

"Rikki?" Tony shouted.

"Yes." The line became clearer. "This is Rikki Beck. I can't hear you well. Who is this?"

"Rikki! It's me. Tony."

"Tony? Tony Irving?"

"Yes, I'm alive!"

"Tony!" Rikki's voice broke. "Oh, Tony. Thank God!" The sound of weeping filled the line. "You're alive! Alive!"

"I escaped! I escaped from the Germans."

"Thank God! Oh, thank God! You're alive!"

"I'm in Zurich, Switzerland! I wanted you to know I was out."

"I'm so happy!" Rikki sounded. "We've all been terrified for you. Worried sick. Every day we have all prayed for your well-being. Every day!"

"Rikki . . . Rikki." Tony cleared his voice. "Are you . . . are you . . . still waiting for me?"

"Waiting? I love you. Don't you know that I'll wait forever?"

Tony bit his lip and fought back the tears. "I'm so anxious to get home to see you. Don't worry, I'm still yours."

"I love you and . . . ," Rikki said and then the phone went dead. Nothing but silence filled the line.

"Rikki! Rikki!" Tony said so loudly that people in the lobby stopped and looked quizzically at him. He tapped the receiver several times but got nothing but silence.

"Sorry, sir," the clerk said, leaning over the counter. "The line went dead somewhere out there beyond our country."

Tony slowly put the receiver back on the hook. "Thank you," he said to the clerk. "No problem. I got the message I needed to receive. Yes, sir-ree! I got the word. I can go home. Rikki Beck is waiting for me!"

EPILOGUE

By nightfall of the day of the escape, Royal Air Force Captain Lulu Lawton and his party were captured at the train station. The next morning Lieutenant Bill Fowler's other group of escapees were seized by the Germans, and all the men returned to Colditz Castle to wait out the end of the war. However, Captain Damiaem Van Doorninck and Sergeant Tony Irving's escape inspired the prisoners in Colditz Castle, giving them new hope that freedom waited for them.

Corporal Otto Schadlich's report was filed with the *Oberkommando der Wehrmacht*, and a special investigation followed. Deeply disturbed by the brilliant escape, a group of six German soldiers was sent to enact every detail of the escape through the narrow door. Special photograph pictures of the German reenactment remain on file to this day.

It was clear to the upper echelons that Colonel Edgar Glaesche lacked the ability to maintain control of Oflag 4C. Less than six months after assuming control as the commandant, Glaesche was transferred to a position in a prison camp in the Ukraine, forever disappearing in the backwaters of history, swallowed by the Russians.